Mischief, *Mayhem,* and Marriage

Rebecca Connolly

Copyright © 2021 Rebecca Connolly

All rights reserved. This book or parts thereof may not be reproduced in any form, stored in any retrieval system, or transmitted in any form by any means; electronic, mechanical, photocopy, recording, or otherwise; without prior written permission of the publisher, except as provided by United States of America copyright law.

Any references to historical events, real people, or real places are used fictitiously. Names, characters, and places are products of the author's imagination.

Front cover design by Ashtyn Newbold

Printed by Rebecca Connolly, in the United States of America.

First printing edition 2021

www.rebeccaconnolly.com

To Heather, who has shown so much strength, grace, determination, faith, and courage in the darkest times. You are a warrior in the truest and most beautiful sense, battle scars and all. You are truly an inspiration, and I cannot wait to see the brilliance of a better life unfold for you. Love you, sweetie!

And for the Society for Obstinate, Headstrong Girls (Seriously Displeasing People Since 2019), who patiently endure my stories, stupidity, snippets, and general silliness without cutting me off and asking me out. Your support and friendship means so much!

Want to hear about future releases and upcoming events for Rebecca Connolly?
Sign up for the monthly Wit and Whimsy at:

www.rebeccaconnolly.com

CHAPTER 1

There was nothing that Taft Debenham, Earl of Harwood, loved so much as a good party.

And nothing he despised so much as a poor one.

This was, without a doubt, in the latter category.

It should have been an excellent evening, given the host and hostess and their connections with some of Taft's favorite associates, and yet it was quite the opposite. He would even venture to say that it was the dullest evening he had spent in several years.

Why it was turning out to be such a failure of an evening was beyond Taft's reckoning. The ball was well attended by Society in general without being a crush. The dinner had been delicious and well prepared without being overdone. There was plenty of dancing, all of the most sought-after young ladies and their favorite suitors were in attendance, and the Season was well underway, so it contained all of the necessary items for success in an event.

Yet it was entirely tepid. Boring. Spiritless. Mundane.

Monotonous.

Perhaps that was the problem, then. It was exactly like every other ball he had been to in the past two months, if not three years or so.

It was the same event. Over and over and over.

If there was anything destined to bore Taft, it was repetition.

Surely there had to be other events he could be using to fill his time and social calendar. He was in high demand, so he could obtain an invitation to anything he wished to, be it a house party, a private opera, or a scholarly debate evening. The latter might have raised a few eyebrows, but he could have surprised them.

Taft wasn't all fluff and no substance.

Just mostly.

He had sat for his exams at Cambridge, and managed very well, much to his own surprise. It had been as perfect a situation as he might have hoped, all things considered. If he was going to be a gentleman and maintain the reputation he wished to as a wealthy, high-ranking member of the peerage, it would be best if he accomplished everything generally expected of such without exception and without flaw.

The Earl of Harwood had always been a position that commanded great respect in previous generations, and the epitome of a fine gentleman.

Taft was not about to break that tradition.

He'd rather start a few traditions of his own, being the most sociable and popular bachelor this Season and last. And prior to that claim, he was in the top one percent of most popular bachelors.

His competition had all married off apart from one, who had lost his fortune on a wild gambling streak that had landed him in debtors' prison.

Now only Taft remained.

He rather enjoyed being so sought after and so well liked, and being able to be so without turning into a complete fop or perfect picture of propriety was truly a relief. He would lose some of that status if he were to marry, unless his wife were equally as popular, and while there were several candidates to such a position, Taft either had known them from his youth or considered *them* to be a youth. Despite being an earl and having a title and inheritance to pass on, he was not precisely worried about such a thing at the moment.

Nor was he particularly interested in it.

He preferred flirting and flippancy to adoration and attachment. He always flirted with sincerity, for what it was worth. And he had it on very good authority that he was quite accomplished at it.

"Why are you not dancing?"

Taft smirked in his usual sardonic way, turning to face one of his oldest and dearest friends. "Because, my dear Jane, I have run out of partners who are my equal."

Jane Appleby, formerly Richards, scoffed and looped her arm through his. "Nonsense. You haven't danced with me."

"You are in no condition to dance," he reminded her, his eyes flicking to the rounded surface of her stomach. "Appleby would not like it if I were to challenge that, and he is exactly the size, stature, and athleticism of a man that I distinctly avoid irritating. I've seen him in the ring, and I will not be made into a corpse over a jig."

"It might be worth it just to see the look on your face." Jane exhaled an almost wistful sigh, her smile rather fond. "He is a dear man. I adore him."

Taft had to smile at that. "I should hope so, my dear. You were not the match of the Season last year for nothing. Romance *and* connection? Masterfully done, truly."

Jane whacked his arm gently. "I did not marry him for your amusement, you know. Or the opinions and approval of Society."

"Of course not!" Taft protested in mock outrage. Then he

winked. "But when one can do as one chooses and manage to gain the envy of all in the process? Brilliance, my dear. Sheer brilliance."

She bobbed a very slight curtsey, her hold on him tightening as the action became a little unsteady. "I was once brilliant," she mumbled, shaking her head as she righted herself. "Now I am only awkward and ungainly. Swollen in places I did not know one could swell. Constantly fatigued and randomly irritable. Mark me, Taft, and take pity on your future wife when she should find herself in a similar situation."

Taft winced at the thought. "I haven't the faintest idea what you mean. My wife, when she is in existence, will be utterly radiant when in the aforementioned condition. Nothing like you at all."

A sharp elbow jabbed into his side. "Why do I ever confide in you, Taft?"

"Because you have no brothers and wish your parents had adopted me as one," he replied easily, dropping his facade to grin at her with real warmth. "Would you have come this evening at all if Maria had not insisted?"

"Of course not." Jane snorted softly. "Appleby and I much prefer quiet evenings at home. I've lost my taste for the fuss and bother of Society events, I believe."

Taft could see that, though he did not think he would ever feel the same. Even when he was at Battensay Park in Berkshire, he was always entertaining in some respect. House parties were in great demand, and it was unthinkable for him to not have at least two balls a year for all of his neighbors. Then there were the harvest suppers, the Boxing Day feast, the skating day on his lake for the local children, and the ever-popular fruit-picking outing in his extensive orchards.

He was the epitome of all hosts. And that was not his pride talking, it had been expressed to him by no less than four guests, none of whom he was related to.

But it might also have been his pride a little.

He was no saint, after all.

Really, it was astonishing he could even manage time away from his estate for the Season, given all he had to contend with there. But he always made a point of coming to London when the Season reached its fervor and had never once regretted doing so.

He'd be sure to have a house party in a few weeks or so, once the carefully subtle questions about it began to swirl. He never hosted in the same month from year to year, and thus far, had not even repeated in the same week. Those who wished to attend would either need to remain alert and available for his whims or make whatever arrangements they needed to at the time of invitation to ensure attendance.

More than one ill-prepared invitee had been left socially marooned by Taft's method of such things. He had no apologies for them. No person was worth moving heaven and earth to accommodate.

Which might have been why Taft had yet to marry.

Or why he had so few friends of genuine value.

Still, he was perfectly comfortable with his life and was not about to make any changes in it.

"So I take it you and Appleby will politely and regretfully decline the invitation to my house party?" Taft asked Jane as though with only passing interest.

She heaved a dramatic sigh. "Yes, and I am already feeling the loss keenly. I shall have to name this child Taft in recompense."

"Only if it is a boy, surely."

Jane glanced up at him with a playful smile. "Oh, no, regardless of gender. Miss Taft Appleby will be the envy of all. Wouldn't you like being so honored?"

Taft shuddered and shook his head. "Do not give my goddaughter such a curse, Janie. Not even I would enjoy that sort of attention."

"Well, you may not have a choice. How else might I show my

grief at missing such an illustrious occasion?"

He knew Jane was teasing him, was building up the significance of the event and her absence to ridicule his status, but she was also exactly the sort of person to do exactly as she teased just to prove a point.

Appleby would need to be warned.

"I've changed my mind," Taft said at once, sniffing as he raised his chin. "I am not inviting you. Given your condition, it would be tasteless and tactless to do so."

"What?" Jane retorted with a laugh. "Come now, you must invite me in spite of that."

"No." He shook his head again. "See to your confinement. You will not be invited. But I will bemoan your absence the entire time."

Jane sputtered a form of laughter and nudged him hard. "You are ridiculous."

"I am not the one requesting an invitation to a house party I cannot attend," he pointed out. "Ridiculous is as ridiculous does, Janie."

"Perhaps you are right." She patted his arm, looking around the room. "Hmm. Have you seen my cousin anywhere? I know she is here, but I do not see her."

Taft had also been scanning the room, more to plot his next course of action than anything else. "Which cousin? You have at least twelve."

"Alexandrina," she told him, ignoring the jab. "Lady Lawson."

He jerked and stared at her in horror. "Oh, heavens, is she here?"

Jane gave him a scolding look. "Be nice."

"What? I only asked if she was here!"

She rolled her eyes. "The pair of you are so dreadful in reference to each other, and yet I adore you both individually. Yes, she is here. Or I presume she still is, unless she has fled."

"She would flee from the gates of heaven, if the design did not suit," Taft mumbled, a shudder ricocheting up his spine. "Unpleasant, ill-tempered, prickly thundercloud of a woman."

"What did I say about adoring her?" Jane thumped him on the arm hard, her jaw tightening. "Apologize or compliment her."

Taft swallowed a rather bitter taste at the idea. "She has rather good teeth."

Jane groaned. "Weak, but I'll take it."

"I noted such when she bared them at me," he continued, keeping his tone conversational. "Not a fang among them."

"Taft . . ."

He glanced down at her with a slight smile. "I don't have to like everybody, you know. And Lord knows, she hasn't done anything to become likable in my eyes."

Jane sighed softly, but did not argue the point, which seemed significant. There was nothing Jane loved so much as a good argument fairly fought.

He thought the subject closed, then he heard her say, "You have no idea what she must contend with."

It was not like Jane to be melodramatic or mysterious, and Taft frowned at her a little. "What could she possibly have to contend with?"

"I cannot say." Jane shook her head, then patted his arm. "Try to think better of her. For my sake, at least." She moved away before he could reply, leaving him staring after her in confusion.

He'd never bothered to curb his tongue in her presence, even where Lady Lawson was concerned, and she'd always laughed it off, brushed him off, or jabbed him with excessively pointy elbows. She'd never given him reason to believe there was anything amiss with her cousin, or that her spiteful ways were anything less than her nature. She had never asked him to change his views or cease his commenting, though he certainly would have done so had he thought her truly offended in any way.

It did not necessarily alter his opinions about the lady in question, but it did give him pause.

His interactions with Lady Lawson had not been extensive, but they had been memorable. A house party at Rosennor Hall, home of his friend Larkin Roth and his now wife Sophia, had introduced them two years ago, and absolutely nothing about the event had given the woman pleasure. Everyone else had considered it a triumph, apart from its abrupt ending due to an unfortunate scene with Larkin's unwell mother, but Lady Lawson could not have been less pleased. She was not hostile in recollection of it; she simply did not care.

Why Jane had insisted on bringing her along was still a mystery.

Since then, he had crossed paths with the sour woman from time to time, usually at small events, and she had never been remotely pleased to see him. Or to be in attendance. Or to exist at all, it seemed. He had never in his life met a woman so incapable of smiling.

Oh, she managed to make her thin lips curve just enough upon greeting someone that politeness was maintained, but he would just as soon call a coyote a hound as to call that a smile.

And he was to believe she had cause to be thus?

Highly unlikely.

He would not call Jane's integrity into question, but her sympathetic nature for her relation had certainly clouded her judgment. Which was to be commended, however misplaced such sympathy might be.

Taft began to examine the room once more, his eyes darting from person to person as he looked for that unfortunate and unpleasant cousin. It should not be too difficult to discover her. He need only look for the only scowling face in the ballroom.

And her cousin was the hostess.

Unfathomable.

But as he searched each guest, he caught no sight of Lady Lawson, which did seem rather odd. Not disappointing by any stretch, only odd. While she might have been constantly unimpressed and unhappy in her surroundings, she was, he had to admit, never rude.

To the host or hostess, at any rate. She was quite impolite to Taft.

When he provoked her.

Which made her a worthy adversary, he supposed.

Still, she would not have intentionally disappeared from her cousin's party for long enough to draw comment. No one would likely miss her except her relations, but to cause them concern over her was certainly not something the lady would wish.

Someone ought to attempt to find her.

He counted the space of thirteen heartbeats before he pressed his tongue to his teeth, rolling his eyes and moving towards the doors to the garden.

It was such a shame he considered himself a gentleman, as the gentlemanly thing to do at the moment would be to go in search of the lady, given his connection with the family of the hostess.

Why could he not have been more of a villain?

Scowling for himself alone, leaving his facial expression blank for the company, Taft reached the doors and paused, turning back in the hopes that Jane or her sister had found the lost cousin so he would not have to.

Alas, neither was in the company of a desolate creature.

Nothing for it, then.

He pushed open the doors and moved out into the relative coolness of the night, taking a moment to let his eyes adjust. The gardens were not all that expansive, but they were rather full, and not in possession of the same brilliant lighting one might have wished for in such a place. Which made it a haven for those who did not wish to be found and a danger for those who did not know better.

Did he whistle for Lady Lawson? Call out to see if she was within?

If she were merely taking a moment for herself, he would irritate her by discovery. If her motives were something else entirely . . .

Gads. Was she intelligent enough or worldly enough to know the risks of being out in this with someone else?

Was that, perhaps, her plan?

Widows were admittedly freer than most about such assignations, but surely she would not have engaged in one at her own cousin's party.

Not of her own free will.

A jolt of icy awareness shot through him. What if her own free will was in danger here? He wouldn't stand for that, not even for her. Not for any woman. Any creature.

He peered into the gardens as much as he could, searching for any sign of her.

Something rustled to his northeast, and he heard a distinctly feminine voice hiss a curse.

Lady Lawson, he would presume.

His mouth curved into a slight smile, and he strode away from the house and into the dense growth of the gardens before him.

CHAPTER 2

Of all the ridiculous things, becoming entangled in rose bushes was chief.

Maria didn't even like roses—she had said so on a number of occasions throughout the years—and yet she had lined nearly a quarter of her garden paths with the thorned monstrosities. What's more, they were overgrown, so the branches could reach out and snag themselves on the skirts of any unsuspecting wanderer of the garden. And, as the roses were not white, they were not entirely obvious in the dim light of the evening, so one would never know they were wandering into danger when they walked the paths.

A bit of fresh air, that was all she had wanted. A bit of fresh, unstifled, quiet, cool air.

And now she was entangled and could not see nearly well enough to carefully disengage from the thing. Which meant she could not ensure her gown would remain intact. Which meant she would risk embarrassing her cousins by appearing in disarray upon her return to the ballroom.

Which meant she could not return.

And she had promised to actually remain at the ball until the end.

What a fine state for Lady Alexandrina Lawson to find herself in.

And this was exactly why Alexandrina shunned Society and avoided its folds.

Well, not getting her skirts trapped in a rosebush at her cousin's London party. That was a rather specific situation. But the focus on impressions and reputation, appearances and judgment, tailoring one's behavior and attitudes towards whatever would offend the hosts and guests the least, and impress their desired company the most.

It was utterly ludicrous.

She hadn't always felt that way, but one week into her marriage to Stephen, she had been shown the true way of things, leaving all impressions she had ever made in her life shattered upon the ground. Fit for nothing but to be tread upon and crushed further into the finest powder.

Nothing was as it appeared, she had learned. No person was as they appeared.

No life was as it appeared.

And certainly no marriage.

If she had any immediate family, she would have retreated to their homes and lives when Stephen had died. But she had no siblings and her parents had been dead for several years, leaving only cousins to take pity on her.

And in-laws.

But they had no pity.

She would not have wanted theirs anyway.

Nevertheless, she needed her cousins in her life, and needed their support, which was why she agreed to ludicrous things like balls and parties when she much preferred to enjoy no company at all but her own. There was nothing enjoyable about this fanfare and parade of finery, and nothing pleasant about showing her face to society. Everyone would only compliment her on her late husband and bemoan the loss of him among their ranks. They would praise his charm and his affable nature, his entertaining ways and engaging conversation, and all the while they would only be lowering themselves in her eyes.

Stephen had been none of the things they had thought him to be.

None of the things *she* had thought him to be.

She could not trust anyone or anything based on appearances and impressions, on anything they portrayed for the public. There were lies everywhere.

Lies in everyone.

She could not pretend, not anymore.

So she didn't.

Which was why she had taken herself outside for a breath, of all things, rather than endure the stuffy air for one more moment.

And why she was now stuck in a stupid bush that was only for appearances and brought her cousin no pleasure.

Lies everywhere.

It was fortunate that Alexandrina had no fondness for the gown she wore and had let Maria dictate her appearance for the evening, more to end the relentless pestering about frivolous things about which Alexandrina could not bring herself to care about. If there weren't a room filled with Society's most snobbish members just on the other side of the garden, she would free herself and return to the house without any further ado, tattered skirts and all.

But no, she had to attempt to salvage something here.

Alexandrina looked down at her skirts, frowning at the gauzy contraption fastened to the bulk of her skirts. If she could disconnect those pieces from the rest of the gown, and leave no shreds of fabric for evidence, she might be able to return to the ball without comment. She highly doubted anyone had paid enough attention to account for the exact details of her ensemble.

Turning herself a little, as much as the natural entrapment of her borrowed gown would permit, she focused on a careful and painstaking removal of thorns from her skirts.

It did not work well. At all.

Soon, it became apparent that gloved fingers were at a complete disadvantage under this situation, so Alexandrina quickly removed those, flinging them to the ground.

If she could not manage to do this perfectly, the state of her gloves would be the least of her concerns.

Bare fingers now at work, Alexandrina plucked thorn after thorn from the fabric, wincing slightly as an occasional thorn caught the pad of a finger a time or two.

"Stupid," she hissed to herself when it happened a third time. "Stupid, stupid. Stop catching on things . . ."

She twisted a bit further to reach for a particular thorn that was creating the most tension in the weak gauze of her skirts and laughed a soft sound of victory when she managed to snatch it loose.

Only to discover that she had managed to catch her bodice and sleeve on the overgrown shrubbery with spikes.

A snarl began to rise within her, and she shook her head, curling her fingers into fists as she stared down the offending thorns.

There was no salvaging something at those levels, which meant she would have to break free and figure out a new option for salvaging her evening. For her cousin's sake, at least.

Her own evening would be better spent in her bedchamber.

"Well, if tha's not a pretty prize of a fwower, I dunno wha is."

Alexandrina froze at the slurring male voice, its owner unrecognizable to her ears, but the sudden danger of the moment undeniable. She glanced over her shoulder, the fabric of her dress tearing already as she did so.

He was not a tall man, but neither did he bear the paunch of one she would have expected to overindulge at a party like this one. His complexion did bear all the hallmarks of intoxication, primarily being especially flushed and blotchy in areas, as well as being damp at his temples, plastering his pale hair to the skin there. He could not have been more than forty years old, and under other circumstances, might have been a decently attractive chap.

As it was, he was currently the most horrific of all creatures and she wished the earth would swallow him whole.

"I am quite well, sir," Alexandrina called out to him. "Please return to the party."

He laughed a little as he continued towards her, his steps wavering and unsteady. "Tha's not the party I'm here for now." His smile turned blearily crooked, though not quite villainous.

He would not remember any of this in the morning.

But she would.

"That is quite enough," Alexandrina snapped, shaking her head in irritation. Gritting her teeth, she wrenched herself free from the rose bushes, releasing the tension at her bodice, sleeve, and along her skirts, a chorus of tearing sounds accompanying the motion.

She glanced down at herself, sighing at the damage.

It was irreparable, and it was only by the grace of her stays and chemise that she was not truly scandalous, though it would certainly do enough if she was seen like this.

"Aw, you've torn your dress . . ."

Oh, hellfire, she'd forgotten about him for a moment.

She scowled at whoever he was and ground her teeth. "Go stumble into some brambles, you bumbling idiot."

He frowned rather impressively for someone so deep in drink. "You cannot speak to me like that! I'll show you!"

He charged at her, and she quickly moved to one side with a yelp, easily missing his swinging arms as they grabbed for her. But in his impressively drunken state, his maneuvering was not what it might have been sober, leaving him to stumble directly into the rose bushes that Alexandrina had just managed to extricate herself from.

He howled in protest, thrashing about and causing scratches to appear on his face from the thorns.

Alexandrina felt no sympathy for him. She scoffed a laugh. "Serves you right for such vile thoughts."

"Get me out of here!" he demanded, his words still jumbling together. "Now!"

"No." She looked towards the house, hissing, as the sounds of conversation could be heard. "And keep your voice down, do you want them to hear you?"

He either did not hear her or did not care, for he continued to make pained noises that were pitiful, pathetic, and painfully loud.

She had to run for it, or something far worse than a torn dress would come about.

Without a second look, Alexandrina turned towards the nearest path away from her now-trapped pursuer and started towards the house. She would use the smaller, less obvious way that would allow her to enter by the music room instead of returning to the ballroom. No one could come this way, she was sure of it.

She looked down at her hands, stopping suddenly.

Her gloves. They would still be on the ground near Mr. Foxed-Beyond-Sense, and it would not be difficult to discern which female guest was presently without gloves, even if she made no reappearance.

Even if they were not discovered until the morning, she would have to explain herself to her cousins, and if the so-called gentleman did not manage to free himself from his trouble, they would suspect . . .

She grumbled under her breath, glancing behind her at the

path, warring within herself. She could not fetch them, and she could not leave them. Could she come back down to the gardens before breakfast and take them away before they were discovered? But what of whoever would rescue her ardent drunk? They would find them, and she could not say for certain that the man was too intoxicated to recite her name, if he knew her identity.

And it was entirely possible that he did know it.

She was more trapped than he was at the moment.

Another wailing yell of dramatics came from the rose bushes, and the sound of conversation in the gardens increased.

There was no time.

Alexandrina moved again, hurrying towards the house.

"Lady Lawson!"

She jerked to a halt, the crossing of paths opening the way perfectly for three ladies headed in her direction to see her quite clearly.

In all her ragged finery.

Damn.

She exhaled and raised her chin, looking at each squarely. "Yes. Good evening."

Their horrified expressions confirmed her thoughts, and the buxom elderly woman fanned herself in shock. "Dear me, whatever have you been doing out here?"

The accusation in her tone was not hidden in the least, and it irked Alexandrina to no end.

"I was overheated in the ballroom," she explained, deciding to keep a civil tongue in her head. "I came into the gardens for fresh aid and became trapped in the roses. It damaged my gown quite effectively."

"I've never seen roses do that," the woman's vapid but nearly identical daughter said as she looked Alexandrina over from head to toe.

Alexandrina glared at her. "Clearly you have never met one

while wearing a gauze overlay."

"But who is making such noise?" the third lady asked, craning her neck as though she could see around and behind Alexandrina into the opening she had departed.

The ladies moved as one, rounding the path and effectively herding Alexandrina back the way she had come. She had the thought to barrel through them, knock them askew from their promenade of curiosity, but before she had a chance to charge towards them, a gasp sounded from within the section.

"Mr. Jenkins! However did you get yourself into such a state?"

Alexandrina hissed, shaking her head.

All three of the ladies in front of her suddenly looked at her with new suspicion, then moved with haste towards the groaning of Mr. Jenkins. There was no time to push them off, no protestations to make.

She had not been fast enough.

There were three other people in the opening now, two of whom were helping a bleary Jenkins from his thorny prison. All of them looked at Alexandrina as she entered, taking in the whole state of her with widening eyes.

"Lady Lawson . . ." an older gentleman murmured, his tone grave, his demeanor full of disappointment. "I would never have suspected."

"Suspected what, sir?" Alexandrina asked without shame. "That a lady going for a walk in the dark might encounter thorns? That, in her attempts to escape a drunken ambush, she might have sacrificed her appearance?"

He narrowed his eyes, looking at Jenkins. "Is that what happened, Jenkins?"

Jenkins looked at Alexandrina with a smile. "I missed you, my angel. So glad you returned."

Alexandrina glared at him. "I am *not* your angel."

"I think the state of your gown makes a statement enough," someone else said with enough airs to fill a ballroom. "Really, to allow Jenkins such liberties at your own cousin's ball . . ."

"Oh . . . erm . . . I did that."

Alexandrina had been preparing to lash quite a passionate vitriolic on the buffoon suspecting her of behavior unbecoming when the clear and decidedly sober voice from somewhere beyond the others made such an outrageous claim.

The makeshift tribunal turned to stare at the newcomer in shock.

The Earl of Harwood stood there, cravat decidedly askew, his hair rakishly disheveled, and two buttons on his weskit undone. She knew for a fact that he had been pristine in appearance when she had left the ballroom, as she had made it a point to avoid coming too close to him. The man was a ridiculous narcissist who existed for his own entertainment, and never appeared less than perfect at any given time, almost unnervingly so.

Which made his present state of disarray bewildering and shocking.

"My . . . my lord?" the man who had judged Alexandrina asked in a hushed voice.

Harwood smiled sheepishly, shrugging. "You will have to forgive me; my mad passion for my intended quite got away from me. She struck me for leaving her in such a state, as you can imagine, and I left to find my cloak to cover her. At which time, I recalled that I did not bring a cloak this evening and made a swift return." He laughed a little, as though he were a bit of an idiot, then suddenly stared at the drunken Jenkins. "But how dare Jenkins try to take advantage! I demand satisfaction, sir! A duel!"

He moved towards the man with determination, only to be stopped by the others easily.

He did not struggle much.

"I don't believe that is necessary, my lord," someone holding his arm said. "No harm was done to Lady Lawson. Erm, other than what you had already caused." His eyes flicked to Alexandrina in a hint of embarrassment. "But a quick resolution of your engagement will make amends for that."

"What?"

Every pair of eyes turned to Alexandrina at that moment, the outburst apparently unwelcome in the conversation.

"You must marry, of course," one of the ladies behind her said. "Whatever would people think otherwise?"

Alexandrina turned to them with a glower. "That would depend on who would say things, and what exactly they would say, would it not?"

To her mild satisfaction, all three women flushed, looking away.

One of the men cleared his throat. "You were already going to marry, so why not marry sooner?"

Alexandrina turned to face the men in the space, her lungs beginning to constrict and expand in very quick succession, heat building in her stomach and rising within her.

"Why not, indeed," Harwood broke in with a laugh. "May I speak with my intended, gentlemen? Under your watchful eyes, of course. I have no wish to embarrass either of us further."

"Yes, of course, my lord," a particular moron said, waving Harwood towards her.

Was nobody in this entire place going to ask Alexandrina what she thought or what her opinions were, what she wanted, if any of this was true? Was her presence even required when there were so many to make decisions for her?

Harwood came towards her with a placating, almost adoring look that made her queasy. "Come, my darling. We must discuss this." He took her arm, his hold on it clenching as he steered her pointedly away from the others.

"What do you think you are doing?" she hissed, trying to

wrench her arm out of his hold.

"Trying to save you," he returned in a cold tone, holding her arm more tightly. "God alone knows why."

Alexandrina scoffed in disgust. "I don't need saving by you!"

"Well, you need saving by someone or you wouldn't be in this mess." He moved his hand up and down her arm in an attempt at a soothing manner, though it was quite painful to be so gripped and have the motion then move up her arm. "I am sorry I was not faster in finding you and preventing all of this."

"There is nothing to prevent!" Alexandrina insisted, though a slight catch in her voice betrayed her anxiety of the sudden helplessness of the situation. "Nothing happened!"

Harwood snorted softly. "Of course, it didn't. Anybody with a modicum of intellect would know that Jenkins is so soused, he couldn't walk half a dozen steps without toppling. And considering the pattern of tearing in your skirts . . . There is no question as to your complete innocence."

"Well, then," Alexandrina replied with a nod, her heart lurching towards her throat in hope.

"No one in this garden besides you and I have that intellect," Harwood went on, shaking his head to contradict her. "And the trio of badly dressed songbirds will squawk the moment they are returned to the ballroom. I assure you, I did not promise myself to you on a whim." He smiled very slightly. "You'd better come closer; they think we are mad for each other."

Alexandrina shuddered. "What did you call it? Your mad . . . passion?"

"Indeed." Harwood chuckled to himself. "If I ever had passion, it would surely be mad. All about the extremes, am I." He turned his head over his shoulder towards the others. "And I have not ruled out a duel for my beloved's honor!"

She smacked him in the stomach with the back of her hand.

"A duel? Over my torn dress?"

He looked down at her in surprise. "Someone should be punished for justice, don't you agree?"

She could not have agreed less to any of this. She only wanted to forget the lot of it and go to bed. And she certainly did not want to be discussing matrimony with a buffoon to save her from a drunken idiot.

What made Harwood think he was a better prospect than Jenkins?

She would not marry again. No one could make her. She would not do it.

Alexandrina could only shake her head repeatedly. "We're not even friends! I don't even like you!"

"Well, I'm defending your honor at the expense of my life," Harwood pointed out through the gritted teeth of his smile. "And my beloved bachelorhood, so you'd better start liking me."

"I will not marry you," she vowed on a harsh whisper, not caring in the least that he would hear her distress.

"We can discuss that," came the impossible reply.

"No!"

"Yes."

"No!"

"Do you want a reputation as a lightskirt?" he inquired without sympathy. "A widow taking advantage of her status in the most worldly way?

Alexandrina huffed against a sob, glaring up at him. "You're the one who said you tore the dress."

Harwood uttered a low laugh. "Yes, but you let me."

She coughed in shock. "I did not!"

His expression became superior, pitying, and all too knowing. "In this hypothetical, I can assure you, if I were lost in a mad passion for you, you would have let me."

A flicker of something unsettling lit the back of her stomach, an unpleasant flame that made her squirm and wish for something to drink. And along with it, a fear that was born from a memory, calling up the endless nights of agony that had been her first marriage.

A second one would be the end of her.

Harwood saw something in her face, but could not have known its cause, and at once, he had returned to the boyish man she could safely contend with. "I did say you struck me."

She rolled her eyes as the wave of emotions subsided. "Oh, what a gesture. I hypothetically struck you."

"It was kindly meant."

"Hold my arm any longer, and I'll show you how kind that gesture would be from me." She pointedly tugged her arm and he released her, stealing her victory by then kissing her head.

She was going to kill him.

"Please, ladies, gentlemen," Harwood said to their companions, spreading his arms out in a dramatic plea, "allow me to take Lady Lawson inside. Sir David, would you be so good as to ask our host and Mr. Richards if they would meet me in the study? I believe we have things to arrange."

Alexandrina folded her arms, fighting the urge to cry in earnest as she stared at him.

He gave her a warning look as he approached, gesturing for her to lead the way.

She did so, marching like a moody child towards her punishment.

"Go get changed," Harwood whispered, placing his hand at her back, thankfully not in a suggestive place. "I'll try to salvage something with your uncle, and I'm sure Corbett will help."

"Corbett is an idiot," Alexandrina replied harshly. "He'll think the marriage a good idea!"

Harwood grunted once. "Not if your uncle disagrees. Leave this to me, all right? Come down if you can without being seen by the guests. Lord knows, we need your say."

They did? She glanced back at him in surprise, though her anger still roared within her. "You think I should be in there with you?"

He seemed surprised she would ask. "Yes, of course. I may have said what I did for the gaggle of gossips without consulting you, but only because I know my reputation and I know yours. I hold the cards there, and I took advantage of it. But in this? There is no way I am deciding anything for you."

Well, there was that, at least. But it would all be fruitless, and she knew it well.

"You did make that decision," she retorted without her usual venom. "You said we were to be married."

"But I never said that we actually would." He shrugged lightly. "Technicality. They inferred it, certainly, but we never said. It is a tight spot, but I think we can use it to our advantage. It is not as though you are a young miss in her first Season, so perhaps a little creativity will work."

Alexandrina gave him a thoughtful look, not quite hating the sight of him at the moment. "You think so?"

"I hope so," he corrected, his smile reappearing. "I'd rather live to see my next birthday, and you'd smother me in my sleep on our wedding night."

She hummed a faint note of acknowledgement, as though she might give the idea some thought, and turned her attention back to her path, her mind spinning at the possibilities and options that lay before her.

If any.

CHAPTER 3

Taft was a moron.

Surely there had to be a better word, but that was the only one coming to mind at the moment.

Pacing the study of the Corbetts' home, he could only think that a temporary madness had come over him as he'd rearranged his appearance to claim he had been the one to make Lady Lawson look so disheveled and beyond repair. To claim she was his intended and that his passion for her could not be contained. To even imagine . . .

Her horror at his admission had matched his own, but no one had been looking at her. Who could blame them? He'd never been seen to speak more than a dozen words to the lady, and now he was claiming to be mad for her?

Did no one notice that her lips were exactly the same shape and size they had ever been? That her color was not high? That her hair was intact even if her dress was not?

He should never have been able to convince them so easily. But perhaps their desperation for a comfortable resolution blinded their common sense and observation skills.

If they had any.

He could only say that he'd had to step in. Once he'd heard the tone and the accusation, knowing where it would end, he'd acted. Lady Lawson, for all her evils, did not deserve to be trapped in marriage to Jenkins. He was a bumbling bore at best and a lout at worst, and her wit would have been wasted on such a pin cushion.

Besides, no woman deserved to be trapped in a marriage because of the perception of others.

He hated how they all ignored her protestations, even if he'd played on them for the moment.

He'd created a mess to get her out of a mess, and he'd get her out of this one if he could.

Widows could do as they liked, all things considered. If she hated Society as much as he thought she did, and as much as she seemed to, she could jilt him and remove to Scotland. He'd fund it himself if he had to. His reputation would reach untold heights out of such a perceived injury to his honor, she would be free of having to endure Society, and neither of them would be trapped.

It was a perfect plan.

"What is this I hear about you compromising my niece?"

Taft turned towards the bemused question that ought to have been an angry accusation, grinning freely. "You know me better than that, Gerald. I'd never compromise any woman, let alone get caught doing so."

Gerald Richards, one of Taft's oldest family friends, laughed heartily and came to him, hand outstretched. "True enough, and for you to have been caught, in a word, with Alexandrina . . . My word, it is an impossibility."

"The claws, yes?" Taft chuckled to show his teasing, though he truly did suspect Lady Lawson of being in possession of such. "No, there was no compromising, though it will not be easily believed. Your niece got into a spot of trouble with Maria's overgrown rose bushes, and the tearing was extensive. A drunken Jenkins happened upon her, and assumptions were made. To spare her any attachment to him, I claimed the indignity as my own. Which now leaves us with my apparent attachment to her."

Gerald frowned, his brow creasing with the action. "No flesh was seen? No attentions witnessed?"

"None," Taft assured him. "Her bodice and sleeve were certainly destroyed, but her modesty is preserved. The skirts were far worse than the rest, not that anyone cared to notice."

Corbett, a rather fussy man, made a sound of discontent. "Who were the witnesses?"

"Sir David, Mr. Kent, Mr. Bracken, Lady Betancourt, Miss Briggs, and Mrs. Herrin." Taft winced and shook his head. "Busybodies, the lot of them. And then there is Jenkins, who won't remember a thing. I did challenge him to a duel, for what it's worth."

Gerald gave him a look. "Was that strictly necessary?"

Taft shrugged. "Who can say? If he had taken advantage of a woman to whom I was engaged, I would certainly have thrown down the challenge. Under the circumstances, I judged overreaction to be better than the reverse."

"Probably correct in that." Gerald pursed his lips, glancing at Corbett. "What do you think, Corbett? It is your ball, and rumors are bound to fly."

Corbett looked uneasy about being asked anything. "Erm . . . Maria would not like rumors . . ." His mouth worked soundlessly after that statement, which proved he was as empty headed as Lady Lawson had suggested.

One point for the lady.

Gerald did not seem at all surprised by his son-in-law's bland and unhelpful statement and gave Taft a tight smile. "I'll have Appleby take a quick inventory of gossip and opinions around the room. Has Alexandrina gone to bed?"

"No, I suggested she change and meet us here." Taft tried for a smile in return. "I did not think she would appreciate being told what to do without having a say herself."

"Indeed," Gerald murmured, his skin seeming to blanch slightly. "Well, you had best remain here, given you are an involved party. Corbett, have a servant send for Appleby. I'll meet him in the corridor. And then I will fetch my wife. She will need to calm Alexandrina if this all goes sideways. Which, I fear, it very much could."

The two men left the study before Taft could offer his thoughts or apologies for choosing this particular vein of resolution for the garden situation, nor express his own concerns about what Gerald had said.

Why should it go sideways? He had thought the whole thing out, come up with a perfect situation for everyone, and it was truly the best version of circumstances anyone could wish for. Lady Lawson, for all her poison, should not be punished for an ill step into a thorn plant and a drunken fool seeing an opportunity. If she truly had been caught in a passionate situation, that would be different, as there would be moderate feelings involved that could be improved upon. But for something that was not in the least scandalous except for appearances, and even that being a stretch, the drastic conjoining of lives together to save face was wholly unnecessary.

It was the one thing about Society that Taft truly could not abide. He knew how to work it, could arrange a great deal to avoid such things, and had done in the past, but he hated that such tactics had to be employed at all. Two years ago, he had helped his friend Larkin Roth with a bizarre inheritance he'd had to share with Sophia Anson, and what could have been a truly scandalous arrangement had been instead turned into an odd quirk of fate that had made both parties more admirable candidates for marriage and connection rather than shocking pariahs to be shunned by polite society.

Of course, the fools had gone on to marry each other, which Taft had predicted from the beginning, but there was nothing to be done about that. He could claim, and had claimed, that his efforts on their behalf had endeared them to each other and spurred on their feelings for each other, which both Sophia and Larkin argued vehemently. But it was the truth.

Taft could manage the impossible and will it into being. He had done so before and he could do it again.

But not while he was alone in the study of the Corbett home.

This was the most useless of all places to be in.

The door to the study opened and Taft straightened, ready to hear the news, good or bad.

Lady Lawson walked in, her hair nearly identical to how it had been a few minutes earlier, her gown completely different. She had opted for a simple evening dress of pale blue, and it made her complexion seem like that of porcelain and rose.

It was rather lovely, actually.

Her eyes glossed right over him as she sought for her uncle in the room. She frowned when she did not find him, and only then looked at Taft. "Have I missed it?"

Taft shook his head, swallowing against his suddenly strangling cravat. "Not at all. Corbett has gone to recruit Appleby to sniff out the gossip around the ballroom, and Gerald is waiting to hear about it in the corridor. And also to fetch his wife."

Lady Lawson had moved further into the room, and now gave Taft a bewildered look. "Aunt Mary? Why?"

"Apparently, she can settle you." Taft held up his hands in defense, shaking his head. "I had nothing to do with it."

The scowl from the woman did remarkable things to the canvas of her beauty. "I believe it. Do I need settling?"

Taft gave her a quick looking over. "Not particularly, but I have no notion what sort of information your uncle and cousin will bring back to us. It could be heartily distressing for you."

Lady Lawson rested her forearms against the top of a wingback chair, raising a brow at him as she laced her fingers together. "For me? Not for you?"

"Well, if worse comes to worst, you'd be forced into marrying me." He made a face at that. "I don't envy you that prospect."

"As long as you are aware of the travesty that would be." She nodded her agreement, and then, without smiling, added, "But you would be marrying me. So fair is fair."

Taft grimaced even more dramatically. "Is it though? Is it?"

The rolling of her eyes was magnificent. "You are no gentleman, Harwood. You pretend it, but you are not."

"And you consider yourself the pinnacle of a demure and genteel lady?" he retorted, folding his arms. "Please."

Her expression did not alter a jot. "I do not pretend. I will not apologize for that. What you see is what you receive."

He tilted his head at that, considering the idea. She was not wrong about that, but it was an interesting tenet to live by. In a world where appearances were everything, she was opting to defy all and avoid any pretense or affectation. She refused to conform to the ideals of manner and being, which, in all honesty, was an admirable mode of integrity.

He could not do the same himself, not with how he enjoyed Society and its extravagance, but he would give Lady Lawson a bit more respect for living such a forthright life.

"I suppose I should thank you," the lady said with blatant reluctance.

"Undoubtedly," Taft quipped without hesitation. "What for?"

She ignored him. "For ridding me of the problem of Jenkins. Your supposed duel aside. It is far better to be conspiring with you than enduring him."

"You're welcome." Taft managed a smile, though she was

looking at something on the floor in front of him rather than directly at him. "Let us hope your uncle brings us good news so that we both might escape unscathed."

Lady Lawson shook her head a little. "It is so unfair," she whispered, and Taft was not certain he was meant to hear it.

But hear it he did, and he could not let it go unanswered.

"I know."

Her eyes did rise to his now, an air of almost vulnerability seeming to circle about her features. "What could you possibly know about it?"

The bitterness in her tone did not strike him as so much attacking as debating, and he was fine with that.

He could debate.

He maintained his smile, slight as it was, his arms still loosely folded. "I know that I could take any of the young misses in that ballroom out to that garden and actually be seen without a stitch of clothing on either of us, and the world would be scandalized that she could lower herself to such a thing, leaving me as I ever was. I know full well that I could gamble away my entire inheritance and still hold my head up in Almack's, while a young woman without fortune would have to scrape for favors for assembly rooms in Richmond. I know that anything I say in any given room will be heard and respected, while you could recite Shakespeare and have your words refuted. I know there is a discrepancy, a divide that neither you nor I can change, that will forever favor me and belittle you."

Her shoulders lowered with every example he stated, her jaw softening, and she began to slowly nod.

Taft would count that as a victory.

"I know," he told her once more. "And that is why I stepped in. I've no fondness for you, nor you for me, but I was not about to let you be trapped into a farce like that while I could have influence. And if you ask those who know me, they would assure you that I am, in fact, rather gentlemanly in that regard. If gentlemen did such things." He allowed his smile to spread slightly with the irony of the statement.

Her mouth twitched but did not spread.

But it had twitched.

"You surprise me," she said in a low voice, no discernible emotion in it for good or for ill. "Not quite the huff and fluff I took you for."

The admission made his ears heat, but no other reaction took place within him. "I have not your honesty of character, at least where the public eye is concerned. Perhaps if I were more comfortable in my own nature, I might be so free."

"There is nothing comfortable about being unlikable," Lady Lawson told him simply.

"You could be less unlikable."

"And still be myself?"

He considered that. "Would it be so dreadful to smile more?"

She made a face, which immediately had him laughing. "What?" she demanded.

"Never mind," he chuckled. "Forget I asked."

"I usually forget everything you say." She shrugged lightly, looking more human than he had ever seen her.

He bowed a little in acknowledgement. "Fair enough."

They waited in silence then, Taft beginning to pace again while Lady Lawson seemed to be playing some complicated Mozart piece on the top of the chair she stood behind. He'd have gone out to discover for himself what was being said and by whom, but as he was one of the parties involved in the new scandal, it would not do to be witnessed sniffing out gossip about it.

Not even for one as popular and frequently discussed as Taft.

He still felt right in his actions. He had no doubt that Lady Lawson would have managed well enough on her own, giving

Jenkins a jab to the face or a swift kick to his shins that would drop him to the ground, but even that would not have saved her from speculation. And in this day and age, speculation could do plenty of damage, regardless of what the truth was.

It would do just enough.

At long last, the door to the study opened, and Gerald, Corbett, and Appleby entered, each looking fairly blank in expression. Behind them came Gerald's wife, Mary Richards.

She looked rather less blank.

She looked almost sick.

This could not be good.

"Well, niece," Gerald said as he looked at Lady Lawson, heaving a great sigh.

Lady Lawson swallowed. "Well, Uncle?"

He smiled a little, the most sympathetic one Taft had ever seen on any face. "I think we must begin to plan a hasty wedding to your intended here."

Taft blinked, his ears surely waging a war against the rest of him. "Come again?"

Appleby looked at Taft, wincing a little. "It's not good, Harwood. The whole room is buzzing with speculation about the two of you."

Lady Lawson huffed loudly, her outrage anything but discreet. "I may be his intended, but he is certainly not mine!"

"The carriage runs both ways, my lady," Taft snapped, refolding his arms, this time rather tightly. "Look, I only intended to spare her humiliation. Now you are telling me I have to marry her?"

"That would not spare me anything!" Lady Lawson agreed vehemently.

Taft gestured at her, as the sign of their agreement must be miraculous to a biblical extreme.

"Then perhaps you ought to have created a better story,

Harwood," Gerald suggested sympathetically, but there was a firmness to his voice that was unsettling.

At least he was not coming after Taft with a rifle.

"Gerald," Taft tried, moderating his tone to something far more placating. "Marriage is not the only solution here. Lady Lawson, you have no great desire to be in Society, do you?"

"Not in the least," she told him with great feeling, shaking her head. "I'd avoid it at all costs if I could."

Taft repeated his gesture at her. "You see there? Why abide by what Society dictates when she has no desire to participate in it? We could set up a comfortable, lovely situation for her in Scotland. Or Wales, if that would suit better. Even Ireland. Away from this place, she might have her own life and liberty without judgment." He glanced at her again. "You wouldn't mind being considered a jilt, would you?"

Her angry expression had vanished and been replaced by one of resignation, something of a defeated air in her eyes. "No, but . . ."

"We could ensure it will not adversely affect your family, of course," he assured her, overriding her concerns with a nod. "I can see to that. People will expect a reaction from me, and through that, I can maintain respectability for you. It will not be as dreadful as it sounds, believe me. Nothing like exile or banishment, simply a life away from London for as long as you like. Just until the gossip fades for good, which shouldn't take long, in this day and age." He laughed at his own jab, knowing all too well how quickly scandal, or perceived scandal, could capture the interest of Society.

It took him a moment to realize that he was the only one laughing. Being in the company of some rather good-humored people, that was disconcerting.

His humor faded and he looked around at all of the relatively drawn faces. "What?"

Gerald looked at Lady Lawson, who was now focusing her

attention on the floor. "Niece?"

She nodded once, her throat tightening. "Tell him."

"Tell me what?" Taft demanded, wondering if he had fallen headfirst into some deep well of disaster unwittingly.

"Alexandrina has a child," Gerald told him in a low voice, though there was no hope of anyone outside of the room hearing them. "A son. He is in the care of his grandmother, the dowager Lady Lawson, at Stonehall Abbey in Gloucestershire. She will not give him over to Alexandrina to raise, as Lord Lawson's will names his brother as guardian. The brother is out of the country, has been for years, so the mother has the boy."

Taft exhaled a harsh burst of air, his lungs squeezing painfully tight at the thought of a child being so parted from his mother. Even if he received the best upbringing, education, and affection from his father's relations, it could not replace the love and care of his mother.

He looked at Lady Lawson, his entire perspective on her shifting, though the direction of that shifting was difficult to determine. She was still the most unpleasant woman he had ever met, but he had never considered her to be villainous or the like. She was proper in every way, apart from the lack of artifice that was expected from all in Society. She had a tongue of knives, but at least she was not truly evil.

She would never have taken a child away from its mother for her own ends.

"How old is the boy?" he ventured to ask, wondering if she would even confide in him that far.

"Five," she replied, her fingers drumming on the back of the chair absently, still not looking at him. "I've not seen him in eight months, three weeks, and two days."

Taft nodded, sympathy rising in waves he did not anticipate. There were so many questions he wanted to ask, so much that needed more information to truly understand, and yet . . .

"We have been trying," Gerald said, breaking into Taft's thoughts, "to get another person named as guardian of the boy. Unfortunately, the Lawsons hold a great deal of power and influence, and there is no easy way to overturn the will of an established peer."

"And I imagine that living with the Lawsons in their home is . . .?" Taft ventured with a glance around the room.

"Unthinkable," Lady Lawson replied without any hesitation. "Firstly, they do not want me there, and secondly, I do not want to be in their power. I would have to relinquish all rights to my son and become their creature. Some widowed aunt with no influence over his life, forced to do as they pleased and marry again at their bidding. Believe me, they made my role quite clear."

Taft found himself grinding his teeth at that. "And there is no way to fight them?"

"Not unless we find a more creative solicitor, or someone more powerful can take over guardianship. Which, thus far, has not worked." She closed her eyes, then raised her chin and opened them again, staring directly at Taft. "I cannot leave England. And while I do not like Society, I must move about in it to keep up my efforts for my son."

He nodded in understanding, a sinking feeling taking hold of his stomach. He looked at Lady Lawson's family, each of them wearing the same expression of hesitant resignation.

Which meant only one thing.

Taft heaved an almost silent sigh. "When is the wedding?"

CHAPTER 4

The comparison between her feelings surrounding her first wedding and her second was one of extremes for Alexandrina. When she had prepared to marry Stephen, she had been beside herself with joy and exhilaration. In love to such a degree that she could think of nothing but the wedding and her intended for weeks on end. A handsome husband who bore both a title and a fortune, who found her to be charming, lovely, and worthy of his affection, and the prospect of a blissful future before them . . . She had overseen every single detail of the wedding to ensure she would not miss a thing.

For this second wedding . . . she hadn't done a single thing.

And all she felt was dread.

She would have gotten out of it had there been any option, and she felt certain that Lord Harwood felt the same, for all his attempts to find solutions for them. There were no solutions, however, which was why she was resigned to the marriage.

He called daily with a new suggestion, and a new apology, to the point where she was tempted to forbid him from doing either ever again, if not to cease showing his face until they were actually wed.

But she wouldn't forbid him, no matter how he might irritate her. After all, she was going to marry him.

However ridiculous that was.

This could not have been more different than her first wedding. She did not care about the details. Was not excited about any part of it. Wanted it to be over.

And she wanted the marriage to be very, very different.

The Earl of Harwood was a peacock, there was no question. From the moment she had met him, she'd written him off as just another one of the fools that paraded everywhere in London. He was just as puffed up, just as elaborately dressed, just as obsessed with nonsense, and for some reason, her cousins had adopted him as practically a member of the family.

She had yet to see why.

She *was* grateful to him for stepping in when the situation got out of hand with Jenkins in the roses. He had certainly been thinking quickly and saving her from far worse by stepping in, and perhaps he truly had been gauging the situation correctly. Perhaps she had been doomed from the moment she had become ensnared in the rose bushes, and the only way to save her had been to claim his own involvement in the suspected situation.

He was better than Jenkins, there was no question. Jenkins would have taken advantage of Alexandrina without hesitation had she not freed herself from the bushes. Given the rapidity of the appearance of party guests in the garden, there was no doubt that Alexandrina would have been discovered and immediately forced to marry him. It would have been a complete scandal because of what had been witnessed and the perception of it. She was not a popular individual in Society, no matter how her cousins were respected and valued, or her husband's memory treasured, so her involvement with whatever disgrace was supposedly occurring would have been accepted and believed regardless.

Having Harwood match his appearance to hers, to play on their suspicions, and then make light of it, knowing he was Society's pet . . .

It changed the situation from scandalous to sensational, and while the interest around it would not change, the tone of it would.

She would not be castigated for the supposed incident; she would be smiled at for it, given Harwood was charming and adored and particularly handsome.

But would that be enough to change the mind of her mother-in-law? Dowager Lady Lawson, who would only be called Lady Lawson and never by her Christian name, had taken Adam under her control from the day of Stephen's funeral, even before the will and testament had been read. She had no power to send Alexandrina away until the official documents came to light, but it had not stopped her from shutting her out. She had been kind enough to Alexandrina leading up to the wedding and in the year or so after, but when the truth of her husband's nature began to reveal itself, when she heard about the first mistress, her mother-in-law told her to stop whining and do her duty.

When the mistress began living in Stonehall Abbey with them, Alexandrina went to her husband to complain.

That was when the whole truth came out.

Her mother-in-law had held no sympathy for Alexandrina or her shattered illusions of matrimony and men. She could not understand the fuss Alexandrina was making and went so far as to say that if she had known this was how Alexandrina would handle such things, she would never have agreed to the match.

Which was when Alexandrina had learned about the process of Stephen's courtship of her, and that it had very little to do with her nature or person and everything to do with her family and favorable status.

Everything she had known, thought, or believed had been a lie.

At least she would not have that with Harwood.

She knew herself better now, did not accept face value, expected nothing from anyone, and understood all too well that the future could hold as much despair as anything else. She had no illusions about Harwood or his feelings for her, had no intention of hoping for happiness, and saw all of this as only an opportunity for protection.

And perhaps, in time, he might be willing to help her fight for her son.

He had seemed rather genuine in his response about Adam, but she had failed to go into much detail there. She never spoke of her son in company, and until the bonds were forged there in all legal aspects, she would not relate the specifics to Harwood. He seemed decent enough, despite his very evident flaws, and she would be willing to offer a very great sacrifice to persuade him to take up the cause.

She had been up all night the night before considering it and had settled it in her mind. They were not going to be a marriage of affection, and hardly one of convenience, as it could not be less convenient, but she would bear him a child if he wished it.

Surely he would want an heir, and she would give that to him. Even if they had a daughter first, she would keep trying for a son. It might have been the expected thing of a wife, but he had to understand what it meant for her to offer such a thing. After what she had endured for her son in her first marriage, and its aftereffects, the idea of ever risking her heart in such a way when she had no rights to the child was terrifying.

No matter what she thought of Harwood, what she knew of him, she knew he was not a cruel man. He would never fling mistresses in her face or bring them under their roof.

She could cope with anything else, particularly when her heart was so protected from such things now. No attachment to Harwood, and therefore, no disappointment to bear. No pain to be felt at his hand. No dreams to diminish.

In that sense, this marriage could be rather successful.

Alexandrina might not have wished for another marriage ever again, but a simple one made for straightforward reasons that would offend no one . . .

She might be able to make this work.

"Lord Harwood, my lady."

Alexandrina stilled, blinking herself out of her torrent of thoughts, and set down her pen, though she hadn't written a single word in her new letter to Adam. She nodded quickly, rising from the desk and moving to the sofa in the room. "Would you let my uncle know, please?"

"Certainly," the butler replied. "Lord Harwood did ask for a private word with you, if you did not object. I told him I would inquire . . ." He trailed off, clearly waiting for her to answer one way or the other.

A private word? About what? They were going to wed as soon as he could manage a license, that was already decided. A simple affair, no frills or finery, minimal guests, and that was that.

They had never had a private conversation without insults or clipped words. Could they manage better than that now they were to wed?

"Fine," she managed to say, nodding absently.

The butler left, and Alexandrina exhaled a long, slow breath. Private conversations with men without the company of others had yet to turn out well for her, all things considered.

Stephen asking for a private conversation had been how she had become pregnant with Adam. The experience had been lacking, but at least it had paid off with her sweet boy.

If he was still sweet. His grandmother was more than capable of poisoning him into a spoiled and selfish re-creation of her own boys.

Harwood was not Stephen, she reminded herself. He had

stepped in to keep her from being entrapped in another farce of a marriage to someone who might have treated her the same. He respected her uncle and aunt, as well as her cousins, and meeting with him privately in their house was as safe as safe could be.

It would all be fine.

She might still snap at him, but it would be fine.

He entered the parlor then, looking more relaxed than she had ever seen him, though his appearance was perfectly neat and in keeping with his standard finery. His dark golden hair seemed a trifle less set, his deep blue eyes less stifling, his smile less forced. He seemed . . . remarkably approachable like this.

What could that mean?

She could not presently recall how she had affixed her hair or what exactly she was wearing, and in lieu of blatantly examining herself, she tossed her head, despite the fact that not a single hair was loose enough to bounce with the motion.

If he noticed the delay in her action, he did not show it. He bowed without fanfare. "Lady Lawson."

She rose from the couch and inclined her head. "Lord Harwood."

His smile did not change. He gestured to a chair opposite her. "May I?"

Alexandrina glanced at it, then nodded as she looked back at him. "Of course."

"Thank you." He moved to the chair and sat, keeping his posture almost formal, despite the relative ease of all else about him.

And then he simply stared at her. Smiling, but staring.

She waited as long as she could possibly tolerate, pressing her tongue into her upper lip and widening her eyes. When even that failed to prompt a response or any kind of conversation, she exhaled roughly and gave him a look. "Was there a point to your asking to speak privately? Or did you simply want to blatantly stare without judgment?"

"I did have a point," he assured her without spite. "I am trying to find the best words for it. I thought I had them until I got here in front of you, and now I have doubts."

"About me?" she asked sharply, her vision of the carefully constructed plan around the scandal beginning to crumble.

He shook his head. "About the words, my lady. It helps if you listen to all that I say rather than what only grabs your attention."

It was said so simply, so patiently, that she almost missed the barb in it. She scowled when she did catch it, but she had to appreciate the tidy placement of it.

"I've run out of plausible alternatives for getting us out of this wedding," he eventually said, sighing with the defeat of it.

"Plausible went by the wayside two days ago," Alexandrina told him with a soft snort of derision. "We've been humoring you."

He smiled at that, though avoided laughing, which surprised her. "I truly thought I could find a way to spare you this."

Alexandrina reared back a little. "To spare me? What about you?"

Harwood offered a shrug of his broad shoulders. "What about me? I've nothing against marriage, and I've never done the thing. I could just as easily get married tomorrow as I could in fifteen years. I'm wealthy and I have a title, so there will always be options. I've no romantic notions of marriage, but my parents were a fair example of a good one. I'm hoping to find something similar in my own."

There was nothing to do but hiss softly in regret. "And you are marrying me. Rather a dismal thing, that."

He tilted his head a little, giving her a curious look. "I don't know that I'd extend that far. Surprising, perhaps. Unlikely, certainly. Combative, undoubtedly, but hardly dismal. You've no intention of murdering me, have you?"

"Of course not," Alexandrina scoffed. "That would be far too much work, and the aftermath would be nearly as troublesome."

"My thoughts exactly." His smile seemed more natural and filled with amusement, though it did not quite reach his eyes. "I wanted to spare you, my lady, because of your distaste for your first marriage and all the suffering it brought you. I may be a cad, but I am not heartless. I am sorry that there is no way out of this but another marriage."

The sincerity in his tone was something she was entirely unprepared for, and it caught her off guard. Tears began to form, and she looked away quickly to keep them from falling. Despite having been rather resigned about the whole affair, once she'd got over the shock of it, she could not deny that there was a measure of fear and trepidation about it. Dreams that were haunted by memories of her pain and humiliation. A silence about her thoughts that was unsettling. The growing knot of dread that began to reside in her stomach. Breath that, for a moment or two, would not come.

She did not want this marriage. She did not want any marriage. She hated marriage. Hated being trapped. Hated being powerless. Hated . . .

"I'll do my best by you," Harwood said in a low voice, barely audible amid her inner turmoil. "I won't pretend I can promise you love, and I don't believe you want me to. What I can promise you is respect and honor, and I do mean that, despite what you may think of me."

Alexandrina swallowed a potential wash of tears, glancing over at him against her better judgment. "I've never thought ill of you. You may annoy me, act ridiculous, and parade like a peacock, but I've never considered you a villain."

"Thank God for that." He leaned forward, resting his elbows on his knees and folding his hands, his eyes locking on hers with a surprising strength. "You will have all the independence I can offer you. All the authority. I've no interest in owning a person or exercising dominion. I'd rather we make this a partnership. My estate will also be your estate. You can be as involved as you like in the running and day-to-day dealings. Plan out the gardens. Renovate every corridor. Advise the estate agent as to the needs of the tenants, fire the estate agent for being a dunce, open a village school . . ."

His earnest offer had her laughing in spite of her still-lingering tears. "Be careful, my lord. You'll be handing me the fatted calf and the bulk of your fortune, if you continue to scrape for offerings to placate me."

Harwood's brows shot up. "I'm not placating you. I truly wish to offer you any part of Battensay Park and its running that you've an interest in. If you don't want any part of it, I'll not force it on you. What I want . . ." He paused, exhaling and wetting his lips. "What I would like is for you to feel at home at Battensay. That it is not simply the place where you reside, but a place where you can build a life. With me, yes, but by yourself as well. I hope to one day find a friendship between us, if we can manage not to irk one another to early graves, and that our marriage will be the one you recall more often than not, rather than the one you had before."

Who was this man and what had he done with the Harwood she had thought she'd known? Which was his true version? Who would he be when she was finally invested in Battensay and making the changes he had just offered?

When would he first inquire as to siring an heir?

She could not brush aside what he had said, not when she struggled to find any falsehood or airs in it, when he seemed so very genuine, so different from every version of him she had ever seen. She had to proceed as though he were in earnest, though she would not offer more of herself than she had to.

She could not.

"Thank you," she managed a bit awkwardly, finding speaking a trifle difficult after fighting tears for so long. "I may not know what I would like until we are at Battensay, and I have learned its ways."

"Perfectly understandable," Harwood replied with a firm nod. "Nothing is restricted there. No his and hers, apart from bedchambers, parlors, and the odd closet. No secret caches, no mysterious dealings, no meeting I am ever in that you are forbidden from."

It was an interesting point he was making, and she would have to ask him about that when they knew each other better. In his attempts to improve her perception of this marriage, he was taking away a good deal of his own power and privacy. She might be able to use some of that to her advantage.

Should she need to, of course.

"For my part," Alexandrina began, folding her hands in her lap, "I will say that I perfectly understand if you wish to keep a mistress, as this marriage is not exactly a love match, or even a companionable one."

Harwood appeared rather thunderstruck, and a scant moment later, rather thunderous. "I beg your pardon?"

"I would prefer one at a time, however," she went on, averting her eyes to keep from embarrassing herself when it became clear this was not as open as he wished them to be. "I've been rather too embarrassed by a harem in my home before. To face it again would be agony, even if there's no affection between us."

"You think that I am planning on marrying you while also preparing to install another woman somewhere in my life to tend to my baser needs?"

He sounded rather upset by the idea, but it could just be at her. She lifted a shoulder in a light shrug. "I know how men are."

Harwood grunted a dark sound. "You know how one man is, or was. You know very little about men in general, and even less about me, it seems."

Alexandrina flicked her eyes back to him, something sharp lancing through her chest. "Are you telling me my husband was an aberration to the male sex? I find that difficult to believe."

"No, I am not saying that," he assured her, completely unruffled by her suggestion. "I am, however, saying that I am not cut from that same cloth, stained and cheap quality that it is. I have no intention of keeping a mistress, finding the idea of one rather distasteful and degrading to one's own wife, if not a man's honor."

She had never heard anything like that in her entire life, not that she'd asked anyone apart from her husband about the subject. Her eyes widened in surprise, and suddenly words were difficult. "You can't be serious. You must know I have no intention of . . . That I'm not . . ."

Harwood simply raised a brow. "As fascinated as I am to hear how you would like to finish that statement, I'd much rather end this conversation. I do not have a mistress, I will not have a mistress, and if I make the acquaintance of someone who makes me forget myself and think of potentially having a mistress, I will come directly to you, confess all, and beg you to strike me dead. Fair enough?"

The imagery was enough to make her smile in spite of her startlement, and she found herself nodding. "Yes. But now you know where I stand."

"And you know where I stand." He inclined his chin in a half-nod of acknowledgement. "It will not be all roses and delight being married to me, but it should not be mortifying. Will that do?"

"Very well, if you mean it."

"Why would I not mean it?" he asked, his brow furrowing at the question.

She laughed very softly without humor. "I have learned that honesty is relative, my lord, and integrity subjective. I believe you mean these things now, but it does not follow that you will mean them later. I am not accusing you of inconsistency, only mortality."

"I see." His eyes narrowed, the side of one cheek pulling a little as though he bit the inside. "Lawson did a great deal of damage, I think."

"I am not damaged, Harwood," Alexandrina snapped, defenses roaring into place.

He shook his head slowly. "No, you're not. But I think you were. I think you were hurt a very great deal, and that is why you have become this version of yourself. Why you see the world so darkly. It is not a flaw, only a fact. Lawson should have to account for that."

Alexandrina gave him a wry look, fighting the sudden sense of being exposed and rather unsettled. "He has been dead for three years, and I am hardly clinging to my vengeance for the afterlife."

"Then there is hope for me yet." His smile was slight, but this time it reached his eyes, which, oddly enough, settled her, as it rendered him the more familiar version of the man she had known. "I hope that one day, you will trust me enough to confide more about what you endured, but I will never press you for that information. And I further hope that, with time, you will find me a more constant man than what you have known or suspected. Time will be our ally here. Only time can give you that assurance, and I promise not to throw it in your face when you do finally see it."

Her jaw dropped at the jab when they had been speaking so seriously, but she had to laugh at the audacity. "Am I supposed to find that a magnanimous offer?"

"Probably," he quipped, rubbing his hands together a little. "I am rather competitive and rather enjoy being proven right. Let that be the first of my faults on the list you start."

"Harwood, I've had that list for years now, and it will indeed be added to the rest. On the third page. Near the bottom. If there is still space." She smiled rather mockingly, batting her lashes at him.

His laughter was rich and deep, effectively turning her false smile into a true one, and he made a show of bowing to her, despite his seated position. "Never let it be said that I am a perfect man."

"I don't," she replied at once. "I feel it my duty to correct that presumption."

Harwood nodded, grinning, then shook his head. "With a wife like you, my lady, I will have no need for humility."

"I was not aware you knew that word, my lord."

He snickered softly and pushed to his feet. "Oh gads, Lady Lawson, what are we going to do with each other?"

She pretended to think on the subject. "Avoid manslaughter, I think. I doubt either of us would fare well in the gallows."

"I shall do my best." He set his hands at his hips, something rather athletic in the way he did so. "I've managed the special license, and I will go speak to your uncle about it. Have you a wish to be involved in the conversation as to the where and when?"

"Not even a little," Alexandrina told him firmly. "Only inform me as to the where and when, and I will appear. I do not care at all about the rest of it."

"I thought as much." He reached out a hand rather politely, and she warily obliged the gesture by placing her hand in his. "Then I will see you at our wedding."

Alexandrina would be lying if she said her heart did not jump to her throat at his words, and at the cradling sensation of her hand in his. "Let us hope you still accept the vows when you do," she said, trying for another smile that wobbled on her lips.

His mouth curved a little, appearing slightly crooked in a rather charming way. "I'll be at the altar waiting. Waiting to begin this life with you. Waiting to take your hand in mine. Waiting for you."

Harwood bowed, bringing her hand to his lips and kissing softly, not quite perfunctory, but hardly anything more. Still, it seemed to seal something between them, and brought Alexandrina's heart slowly down from her throat in a river of warmth.

"Don't flatter me," she whispered against the sensation.

"I won't," he whispered back, still smiling, still holding her hand. "That's just where I'll be. Waiting."

His fingers gripped hers for a moment, then released them, and he stepped back to incline his head again before turning and leaving the room.

Alone once more, Alexandrina exhaled very slowly. She refused to hope that Harwood would be as good as his word, that he would allow her freedom and independence, demand nothing of her, and respect her in the ways he described. But she would give him some credit for saying so.

She desperately needed a word with her cousin, though. If anyone would know Harwood's way and if his professed sense of honor was genuine, it was her.

CHAPTER 5

"Have I mentioned that I dislike weddings?"

"Only every five minutes since you arrived. I'm not sure I've grasped the notion yet."

Larkin Roth grumbled incoherently beside Taft, remarkably cantankerous for being the groomsman for Taft's wedding. "I don't know why I made the effort to get here. Lord knows, Sophia could have used the rest, and Adrian does not travel well."

"I did not particularly invite you," Taft reminded him. "No matter how I adore my godson, he is barely eighteen months of age, so I don't know why you thought he would appreciate the rapid carriage ride. And your wife is with child, so really, you're rather insensitive."

"Do you think I had any say in the matter?" Larkin hissed. "She insisted!"

"Which is why I adore her, but you cannot very well whine about it when you have both made these choices." Taft shrugged, craning his neck in his elaborate cravat. "There is no one here besides family and yourselves, so no one would have commented on my lack of guests. They all know what happened."

Larkin heaved a sigh that was in keeping with his surly nature. "Are you going to argue with me about my attendance at your wedding moments before you make the vows? You wrote to me about what had happened, and what could be the result, and I came down to London to help. And now I'm helping."

"Yes, you make an excellent accessory. As to your particular usefulness, do you have the ring?"

"Was that supposed to come with me? Oh, damn it."

Taft exhaled with a great deal of would-be patience for his closest friend, his sarcastic tone entirely uncalled for at the moment. It was Taft's wedding, for pity's sake, and his only one at that. Though he was not especially anxious, there was a strange pulling at one's nerves standing in the front of a church before an altar, trying not to stare at the clergyman, waiting for the bride to arrive.

Did such clergymen judge those persons who came to be married by special license? There was no missing the rumors and gossip that swirled around particular pairings, and Taft collected gossip the way others collected shoes. He did not intend to; it rather followed him like puppies after a butcher.

If he could recollect the clergyman's name, he might ask him if he knew why they were there.

But perhaps he was of a holier mindset and never judged those who came before God and man in this way.

How many people had insisted that they were marrying for convenience because of a misunderstanding and not for the actual sins that were suspected of them? How many parties insisted that what they said was the truth and the gossip was all scurrilous? How many of them were *actually* being falsely accused and not to blame at all?

How many were just idiots like Taft who could not think of a better story?

"I know that face. What are you plotting?"

Taft glanced at his friend with the most superior expression he could manage. "How dare you. Me, plotting in a church on my wedding day. The very idea."

Larkin's face remained impassive. "You've done worse. Well?"

"I am not plotting, as it happens. Only thinking." He returned his attention to the clergyman, who was looking rather pious and clearly anticipating the bride. "How many couples has he married on special license who did not actually do something amiss?"

"Honestly?"

Taft shrugged. "There is a stigma around the special license, and it washes away no sins, despite having to be given out by a man of the church. Look at us. I'll be shortly married to a woman I do not actually like very much, who likes me even less, because people think we've a mad passion for each other based purely on speculation."

"You offered that idea, Taft," Larkin pointed out. "She could have been forced to marry Jenkins, and the idiot would have no idea why."

"I don't despise her enough to leave her to that fate." Taft shook his head, grimacing. "Though part of me wishes I did."

Larkin tsked softly. "I can't say I blame you. Not regarding her, of course, but the forced marriage part. I'd say you did something noble, but as she was not actually in that danger, having been more than capable of getting herself out . . ."

There was nothing to do but chuckle at that, and Taft found himself smiling rather wryly. "Yes, my intended is more than capable, and I aim to use that to my advantage."

"Explain, please."

Taft smiled rather proudly as he thought back on his brilliance. "I've offered her whatever role she pleases at Battensay. However involved she wishes to be. A partnership, if you will. I see no reason why we should be forced to look at this marriage as a prison just because we did not enter it of our own accord. If she wants to be left alone, I'll leave her alone. If she wants to manage the running of the farms, I'll make sure she learns every possible aspect of it. Marriage to me will be freedom, Larkin. And who doesn't want that?"

"I'll draw up a list for you," Larkin replied without missing a beat. "In your delusion, I think you're forgetting something."

"I doubt it, but go ahead."

"An heir, Taft. You're going to need one at some point, unless you want your title to pass to a cousin."

No, Taft did not want his title to pass to a cousin. Every single one of his cousins, no matter their separation from his direct line, was an idiot. There was no hope for the reputation of the Earl of Harwood or of Battensay Park if the title went to them. Taft might be a Society pet, but at least he was respected and never mocked.

Still, his friend was mistaken if he thought that Taft had neglected this detail.

"Give it time, Larkin, give it time," he soothed, as though his friend had expressed some air of distress about the problem. "One must not rush these things."

"You think Lady Lawson will let you anywhere near her bed at any time?" Larkin snorted a laugh entirely inappropriate for a church. "Be certain your affairs are in order before you attempt it."

Taft only smiled, finding no need to reply.

The truth of it was that he did not know if Lady Lawson would have any interest in bearing a child with him. Initially, he felt quite certain she would not. She was so skittish about marriage and men in general, though she went to great lengths to appear otherwise. What he had learned of the situation with Lawson and his family thus far was enough to understand why, but there was certainly more to the story, and he hoped to be told at some point. Not to satiate his curiosity, but to be able to fully comprehend what his wife had endured.

He had no power to act on her behalf until these vows were done and the documents signed, but the moment he was able, he would hire any of the best solicitors in London to assist his usual man in protecting his wife and her son, and in overpowering whatever Lawson had set up.

He would not presume to do much else for his wife without her permission or involvement, but he could see, in those scant moments she allowed it, how much she loved her son and how she missed him. The child might not have been conceived in love or affection, if her attitudes towards her late husband now were any indication, but it was clear she adored him. He could not imagine a mother feeling such tender feelings being separated from her child and wondered at the Lawson relations elevating their own interests above that of the child himself, or his mother.

They would both be Taft's responsibility now, and he would not fail them.

But how might he configure his own will and testament, his matter of inheritance and progeny, to such a degree that there was no power to interfere from the Lawsons if he did not know the details of the existing edicts?

"Your solicitor in London," Taft murmured to Larkin, his brow furrowing in thought. "The one tied up in the Rosennor business. What's his name?"

"Tuttle-Kirk. Why?"

"Capable man, is he?"

"Very. Why?"

"Understand the specifics and more complicated avenues of the law?"

"He does. Why?"

"Would he be able to assist in the creative negotiation of a will and legacy in order to ensure their completeness and render them impenetrable?"

"Of all the . . . Yes, Taft. Why?"

Taft nodded once to himself. "No reason. Only asking."

Larkin's irritated grumbling beside him brought a smile to his face, and he felt absolutely no shame about it.

The lady who would shortly be his wife, whom he probably ought to think of in other terms than Lady Lawson, given she would soon bear an entirely different surname, had a great many secrets, some of them rather private, and he was not about to spout them off before someone who had not also been brought into her confidence. He was fairly certain more people would know a few of the details sooner rather than later, as a child would be coming to live at Battensay who Taft was most certainly not the father of, but no one need anticipate such a thing prematurely.

There was no telling what sort of legal war would soon be waging, and Taft would need as much of the element of surprise as he could arrange.

It was far and away better to attack one's foes when they had little chance to raise their defenses. Surely Wellington would agree there.

The church organ began to play a soft but regal tune, and Taft felt himself straightening where he stood. The creaking of pews and benches behind him spoke to the arrival of his bride, and he wondered if a new gown had been purchased for the occasion, or if his bride-to-be had rummaged in her bureau for a gown to wear. He did not care one way or the other; it was simply a question that could speak to the mindset of the woman.

Her name, he reminded himself, was Alexandrina. Beautiful name. Bit of a mouthful, but certainly elegant. He'd never called her so, and would not start from the 'I wills,' but calling her Lady Harwood did not suit either. Formality was tiresome, and he'd rather not stand on ceremony in his own home.

Deuced awkward, this. What did one call one's wife when addressing her if there was no affection in the arrangement and one did not wish to exude pretension over breakfast or the like?

"Not sure I ever realized that she was so lovely in appearance," Larkin murmured thoughtfully. "She's really quite pretty. I think you'll make quite the stirring pair."

"She's beautiful," Taft assured him without looking at his approaching bride. "Particularly when she does not scowl. Is she scowling?"

Larkin snorted a laugh. "No. Not smiling, but she does not look murderous. Composed, elegant, graceful, and striking."

"I see you've been working on your vocabulary," Taft said with a smile, despite his interest piquing at the descriptors.

His friend ignored him. "I never thought I'd see the day when Lady Harwood would come into existence, but I believe she will do."

"What a relief." Holding his breath just a touch, Taft turned a little to his left, sensing Alexandrina's approach.

She was remarkably pretty, which was no surprise, but he did not expect his chest to catch fire. Her gown was cream colored and sprigged with blue flowers, matching the folds of blue in her bodice and sleeves. Such a shade brought out a hint of blue in her eyes, which he had always thought to be more green than anything else. Her hair was curled, coiled, and pinned, glinting with a deep tone of red that he hadn't anticipated. She'd always seemed fairly dull in her coloring before, brown hair and greenish eyes in a pale complexion. Yet now he was seeing auburn hints and sparks of blue, porcelain in her cheeks and sunrise in her blush.

Gads, he was a poet.

Not a very good one, but it would have to do.

Alexandrina did not smile, just as Larkin had said, but Taft did not mind that much. Knowing a hint of her reservations about this whole thing, in spite of the helplessness of the situation, she did not have to smile today.

Even if he did a little.

"Good morning," Taft greeted softly, in lieu of paying her a compliment she might hate.

"It's two in the afternoon," she replied without sharpness as she came to stand beside him.

"Well, that is morning somewhere." He nodded at Gerald, who was giving the bride away, then turned his attention to the nameless clergyman before them.

"Dearly beloved," the man began, his tone shockingly formal in tone and timbre, as though he had been plucked from the garden of the Archbishop of Canterbury himself and planted here in his image. "We are gathered together here in the sight of God, and in the face of this congregation, to join together this man and this woman in holy matrimony; which is an honourable estate, instituted of God in the time of man's innocency . . ."

"Is it only me," Taft whispered, unsure if he was asking Larkin or Alexandrina, "or does he sound like some foreigner pretending to be a member of the British clergy rather than someone actually in it?"

"It sounds as though he swallowed one of the princes and now speaks with their tones," Alexandrina suggested, keeping her voice low. "Or perhaps their grandfather."

Taft snickered softly. "The Hanoverian? I doubt that very much. The accent is all wrong."

"You're a fine pair, the both of you," Gerald hissed. "Let the man speak."

Alexandrina glanced at her uncle, though Taft could not see her expression. "Who is stopping him? Indeed, he is still droning. I know the causes for matrimony, I hardly need a primer on the subject."

Taft was silently shaking with laughter now, praying he might manage to endure the ceremony without losing his composure entirely.

One must at least appear to respect religious things.

"I require and charge you both," the clergyman went on, now

looking directly at Taft and Alexandrina, ending their whispered conversation for the moment, "as ye will answer at the dreadful day of judgement when the secrets of all hearts shall be disclosed, that if either of you know any impediment, why ye may not be lawfully joined together in Matrimony, ye do now confess it."

It was all Taft could do not to watch Alexandrina's face throughout this bit. Would she object? Would she claim an impediment? Would she decide that one of Taft's more ludicrous ideas was actually less ludicrous than she'd thought and ask to try that instead of marrying him?

If she had any of those thoughts, or any doubts, she kept them rather decidedly to herself.

Nothing was said from either party, from the witnesses, or from the very few people in the church, all of whom the clergyman looked at directly and in turn as though to make sure they had opportunity.

Perhaps he was less pious and more judgmental than Taft had thought.

What a delightful idea.

His attention moved to Taft, then, his expression severe. "Taft Anthony Edward John, wilt thou have this Woman to thy wedded Wife, to live together after God's ordinance in the holy estate of Matrimony? Wilt thou love her, comfort her, honour, and keep her in sickness and in health; and, forsaking all other, keep thee only unto her, so long as ye both shall live?"

Heavens, that seemed like a lot to ask, but he could certainly promise to honor and keep her, as well as forsake others. The love and comfort parts were entirely up to her to decide.

Still, one could not answer the vows before God with, "Depends on the day."

"I will," he said clearly, nodding once as though that was needed, too.

The clergyman did not look impressed and turned to

Alexandrina. "Alexandrina Catherine, wilt thou have this Man to thy wedded Husband, to live together after God's ordinance in the holy estate of Matrimony? Wilt thou obey him, and serve him, love, honour, and keep him in sickness and in health; and, forsaking all other, keep thee only unto him, so long as ye both shall live?"

Obey? Serve? Not bloody likely. There was no way she would agree to this.

"I will," she answered briskly, her words clipped.

"Really?" Taft whispered. "Did you listen to the whole thing?"

"Did *you*?" she shot back. "You're supposed to love and comfort. Ready when you are, Harwood."

She had an excellent point there, and he would not refute it.

"Who giveth this Woman to be married to this Man?" the clergyman asked, which seemed a rather stupid question, considering Gerald was standing just beside her and held her hand.

Still, Gerald reached her hand out to the clergyman, who then placed it in Taft's waiting one.

Waiting.

He had told her he would be waiting for her at the altar and waiting to take her hand. He'd meant every word of it, being taken over by some rare serious air for that conversation. It had been his hope that she would take comfort from his words, find some ease with her resignation, though he realized now that it could have all been taken in some romantic sense, which, of course, he had not meant at all. She had even said not to flatter her.

He hadn't been flattering her, in that sense. It was simply his affirmation to her that he would be a man of his word, and better than. He would be at the church, he would take her hand, he would make the vows, and he would do right by her.

Nothing more and nothing less.

"Repeat after me," the clergyman instructed Taft. "I, Taft

Anthony Edward John, take thee, Alexandrina Catherine . . ."

Taft repeated after him throughout the entire troth portion, wondering what cherishing Alexandrina would look like. He had never taken any interest in holy orders, nor would he begin now, but what did these men placing husbands and wives under such troths expect when they used that word?

Cherish. He would need to think about that one.

At the clergyman's direction, they adjusted their hands so that this time, it was Alexandrina who held Taft's hand, which was an interesting sensation.

If she noticed, she gave no hint.

"I, Alexandrina Catherine, take thee, Taft Anthony Edward John, to my wedded Husband, to have and to hold from this day forward . . ."

She said the words almost absently, although her diction was perfection and every syllable perfectly clear. She had been through this before, he reminded himself, and it was entirely possible that she remembered that day with painful clarity. Had she married Lawson for love? For connection? After a promising courtship that gave her hope for a marriage of the same? How did the vows that one man made hold any value when another had made the same vows and trampled them in due course?

Taft watched her in fascination, noticing the smallest details as he did so. The faint freckle that sat exactly where a dimple might have done. The pert turning up of the tip of her nose. The tightening of her throat at certain words in her troth. The white and blue flowers and pearl pins dotted throughout her hair that seemed almost too whimsical for her.

That had to be the work of her cousins or her aunt. The pearls, she might have done on her own, but in his experience, she was not a woman of excesses and favored simplicity over extravagance.

He did not mind the flowers in her hair, certainly. They were beautiful and delicate, and were well matched with her ensemble.

But surely every woman should come entirely as herself and in her own tastes on her wedding day, even if it was her second.

"Harwood."

Taft looked up at the clergyman with wide eyes, realizing he had completely drifted away from the ceremony while considering the woman beside him.

That was uncalled for.

"The ring," Alexandrina hissed beside him.

Larkin nudged him, and Taft turned to take the ring from him, placing it on the proffered book from the clergyman. He blessed the ring, then indicated Taft pick it up.

He turned towards Alexandrina, taking her hand once more, holding the ring just beyond her fingers.

At the instruction of the clergyman, Taft repeated, "With this Ring I thee wed, with my Body I thee worship, and with all my worldly Goods I thee endow: In the Name of the Father, and of the Son, and of the Holy Ghost. Amen."

Something about that vow stirred him, and Taft found himself struggling to swallow as he pressed the gold band onto Alexandrina's finger. Her hand splayed ever so slightly in his hold, and he felt the motion down to his toes.

He met her eyes, curious as to the moment around them, and in her not-quite-green eyes, he saw shadows of the same. A beautiful vulnerability and hesitancy that bound him far more than anything he had just vowed.

She would never fear him. Never feel pain from him. Never feel dismissed, rejected, or abandoned by him.

She would never regret marrying him.

As much as any of it was in his power.

"Let us pray," the clergyman intoned.

Taft nodded, his throat constricting. "Yes. Let's."

CHAPTER 6

The first words of her husband after the wedding was over and done were, "Shall we dine?"

What exactly she ought to take from that had been unclear, but it had made her laugh.

Now she was Lady Harwood, officially and with the blessing of God and her family. It was a right sight better than being Lady Lawson, or all that had brought her, but it was a strange alteration to her identity.

Having a special license, they had not been bound by marrying in the morning or having a large wedding breakfast, which also meant there was no need for them to be on display. She supposed that Harwood, being the fixture among Society that he was, might have done a grand luncheon of sorts, but it had never once been suggested in her presence. And it had not taken place, which seemed to say a great deal as well.

She would not have wanted a party, and there was not one. No one had asked her; they had simply known.

Had he wanted one and been told it was not to her liking? Given his influence over the whole situation, his rather successful navigation of Society in general, he could have insisted on one to rid the taint of speculation from them. But he had not.

They were enjoying a quiet meal with their family and his friends, the Roths, and that was all.

The only true pain she had from the day was that Adam was not here to celebrate with her. He would have found the ceremony dull, but the food would have excited him, particularly the cake. He would have adored the cake and would have been certain it was the finest cake he had ever seen. And she, who had been to far too many weddings and their celebrations, would not have the heart to tell him that it was the simplest wedding cake she had seen of people of their status.

"You are quiet," her cousin Jane said from beside her at the table. "Are you well?"

Jane had been her near-constant companion in the days following the incident, coming to her parents' home daily, despite her own engagements and responsibilities, not to mention her condition. It had been a comfort to have her there, and while they had always been close as cousins, the last several days had meant even more to Alexandrina than the years of friendship prior.

"I think so," she replied, trying for a smile. "I am relieved it is over, but now I am married again. I had hoped that the difference between the two weddings would help me to have less trepidation about this one, and yet . . ." Looking about them to see if they were observed, Alexandrina held her hand above her lap so her cousin might observe its trembling.

"Oh, Alexandrina . . ." Jane soothed, taking her hand tightly. "Truly, it will not be so bad."

Alexandrina smiled a little. "That is what Aunt Mary said about marriage when I married Stephen, Janie. Look how that turned out."

Jane wrinkled up her nose, then sighed a little, her free hand going to the rise of her stomach. "Darling, I've known Taft for ages.

He is like a brother to me. Believe me, I know he is not a paragon of a man, but I can promise you that there will be no repeat of your previous marriage here. He is a good man, and shockingly, rather more human than he portrays to the world. You have seen the Society pet, but there is so much more to him."

"That is all well and good," Alexandrina murmured, her eyes flicking down the table to her new husband, happily chatting away with Jane's younger sister Clara. "But is he patient enough to endure marriage to me? I am not the woman I used to be, Jane. There is no sunshine in my countenance."

"Sunshine is highly overrated," Jane replied with a sniff, squeezing her hand before returning to the meal before them. "What is wrong with a little rain? I think the two of you have entered this arrangement with your eyes wide open, unlike most other couples, and I further believe that you can make this marriage whatever you like. Talk to him. He's not unfeeling, and he is not an idiot."

Alexandrina made a soft sound of indecision. "Not sure I can agree with you there, but there is no accounting for taste."

Jane coughed a delicate laugh into her napkin before reaching for her water, giving Alexandrina a scolding look. "Not fair."

"Not untrue either," Alexandrina told her. She took a bite of potato from her plate, wishing her heart and stomach could feel in any way settled about any of this. Her mind was perfectly clear, had adjusted to the idea of the wedding and marriage, and had even found the merit in it. But the rest of her . . .

Time, Harwood had said, would be their ally. He had been speaking with regards to himself and his apparent constancy, but time would be important for her as well. Time to see if she could settle into being a wife. Time to see if she could find any hint of the happier, brighter woman she had once been. Time to see if she could be the mother to her son that she wanted to be rather than what she had been designated to.

Time to see if her son would even want to live with her after the life his grandmother had been giving him.

Provided they could get him back.

Provided Harwood wished to.

They had not yet had that conversation, but she would need it to happen soon. She would not underestimate the ability of the Lawsons to poison her son against her, if not remove him from England altogether as part of his supposed education. She needed to be free of them in every possible way if she ever wished to be truly independent, or to feel fully content in her life. She and her son.

Adam would never be entirely free, given he was Lord Lawson now, or would be when he reached fifteen. One could only hope he would find being so caught in familiar snares just as confining and unpleasant as Alexandrina did so that he might then cut whatever ties that bound him. That he would wish to be his own man rather than a creature of someone's creation.

Perhaps Harwood could teach him something of the sort.

If there was anything he excelled at, it was being his own man. No one else would have created him as he was, there was no mistaking it.

"Do the pair of you stay in London now?" Jane asked, prodding Alexandrina's hand with her smallest finger as she held the handle of her fork.

"I haven't the faintest idea," Alexandrina admitted. She smiled, laughing at how ridiculous that sounded. "I don't know what we're doing, or if we're doing something, or when we're doing it. I haven't asked any questions of the sort. I told him I did not care about the wedding details, and that was where we left it. Considering Harwood is who he is, I imagine he'd want to stay in London as long as possible."

Jane chewed her food while adopting a thoughtful expression. "Perhaps, though he does have the house party at

Battensay in a few weeks, though the date has not been announced. He may not stay in London long at all to return there and begin arrangements."

Alexandrina groaned, barely avoiding slumping back in her chair at the thought. "I forgot about that. Such a stupid thing. Why have a surprise house party every summer? That does not make any sense or hold any logic."

"Because it works," Jane insisted with a laugh. "It has given him such popularity over the years, and his estate has prospered all the more for it."

"How can a party for members of Society help his estate prosper?" Alexandrina asked dubiously. "Are his guests buying up the farms and moving in?"

Jane snorted a little. "No, though there are a few that I would love to see try. No, they become more aware of the village and its shops, and they make purchases. They tell others about the purchases they've made there, and in an attempt to be liked by Taft, the others, too, make such purchases from the shops. When the village prospers, so do its people. And when the people prosper, so does the land, if the weather and circumstances have held. It is a miraculous thing, truly."

Alexandrina had no idea how one man could have such power in a community without actually doing anything, and she was not certain she wanted to understand. "Personally, I will save the designation of miracles for more biblical occasions." She looked at Harwood again, frowning a little. "How did he get to be so influential?"

"Oh, his parents were much the same," Jane explained with a quick wave of her hand. "Always attending everything and being well liked. There were no other families of equal status in the neighborhood, and when they were in London, one was simply drawn to them. They were decent people, good to their tenants and servants, seen to be charitable, and the like . . ."

"But?" Alexandrina prodded, sensing something lay beneath.

Jane grimaced ever so slightly. "Taft was an only child, and often lacked playmates or friends. His parents were always darting off to this event or that, and until he was old enough to accompany them, he rarely saw them. It is astounding that he does not have worse manners or behavior, that he has any warmth or friendliness in his nature, but he does. The outcry over their deaths was monumental—there was no seat to be had for the funeral service. I think Taft rather inherited much of his popularity at first, and then adopted it as his own."

"That sounds dreadful." Alexandrina shuddered at the very idea, grateful that she had never had to endure such a thing as Societal expectations of entertainment. She'd have failed at the first turn and only made a name for herself in the most contradictory ways.

She was already close to doing so.

But if she had her way, she and Adam would be away from London, Society, and anything remotely resembling the public. Some quiet house or cottage in Yorkshire or Durham or Somerset. She'd take him to Cornwall or Lancashire, if he'd rather, and live a rustic version of a life until he was old enough to inherit Stonehall Abbey. Once his grandmother was dead, his uncle would certainly remain on the Continent, and Adam could do whatever he pleased with his title and estate. The house itself was a beautiful relic of a place, modernized only for safety, convenience, and fashion, and one had to secure a great many permissions for doing so, given its history. She distinctly remembered Stephen bemoaning such a thing in the early days of their marriage.

When he was still speaking with her of his own volition.

But nothing could happen until the dowager Lady Lawson was deceased. Her hold was too great.

An errant thought crossed Alexandrina's mind then, and she

found herself laughing quietly.

"What?" Jane asked with wide eyes.

Alexandrina beamed at her. "I've only just realized that I now outrank my mother-in-law. Is it dreadful that I want to go to Stonehall now and present myself to her?"

Jane burst out laughing, bringing her clasped hands to her mouth. "Oh heavens, you must. I know we did not fit you for a wedding trousseau, but surely we must create an exquisite gown for you. Something regal and astounding."

"I would dearly love to see her gape at my appearance," Alexandrina admitted on a fond sigh. "She spent so much time criticizing me for every possible aspect."

"Indeed," Jane agreed with firmness. "So we must arrange a victory gown for you."

"If you consider marrying Harwood a victory," Alexandrina muttered as she flicked her eyes back to him.

"Forget Taft," Jane snapped, rapping her knuckles on the table beside her. "You are a countess now. That is the material point. You outrank her. She has no power over you anymore."

Alexandrina nodded, clinging to that fact. "But will it be enough to get Adam back from her?"

"I don't see why not." Jane's brow furrowed as she looked over at Harwood now. "We should ask him."

"No!" Alexandrina gripped her arm tightly. "No, Janie, please."

Her cousin looked at her with wide eyes. "Why ever not?"

Alexandrina smiled in apology, her heart still racing within her chest. "I cannot speak to him about Adam in front of everyone. I cannot ask favors of him in such a way when we have been married all of two hours. And his friends are here."

Jane looked almost bewildered by that. "The Roths? Alexandrina, those are my friends, too. And yours, if you recall."

"Acquaintances is all I can claim," Alexandrina corrected,

shaking her head. "The house party at Rosennor was tolerable, and I did feel for them in that whole business with Mr. Roth's mother and her illness, but I could not call us friends. It is my own fault, not theirs, and I am well aware of it. I did not take any pains to get to know anyone at that party, and purely went to satisfy you. I was fresh out of mourning, you recall."

"The appearance of mourning, at any rate." Jane scoffed a little, rolling her eyes. "If only the world knew."

"But they cannot." Alexandrina smiled sadly, rubbing her cousin's arm. "I have made my peace with it, so to speak. Stephen will always be adored in his death, just as he was in his life, and only I will bear witness to the falsehoods."

"Alexandrina," Maria called from further down the table. "What are your plans now? Will you all remove to Battensay?"

Alexandrina looked at her quickly, then over at Harwood with wide eyes. "Well, I think . . . I believe . . ."

Harwood dipped his chin very briefly before smiling and turning to the whole of the table at once. "We will stay in London for a few weeks more, just to maintain appearances. There was such a fuss about the whole thing, it would do us both good to be seen from time to time at select events. There is nothing the gossips love more than speculation, and now that the marriage is official, they must run their course on us. Showing ourselves together will settle the wagging tongues, and they will soon find other topics to discuss. Then, I think, we might go to Battensay." His eyes returned to hers, a question in them.

Just as he had done, she ducked her chin just enough to acknowledge it.

She hated that they would have to remain, but at least she would not be rushed off into a new life that she was not entirely prepared for. She would, of course, have to remove from this house and into his, but her trunks had been packed since this morning, so there was hardly any trouble there.

Oh heavens, tonight was her wedding night.

Again.

Would he actually wish for such a thing? Perhaps she could create a headache and retire early with it. And stay in bed. For several days.

How many days and nights could one claim a headache before a doctor must be sent for? She could probably create symptoms vague enough to avoid certain diagnoses, and she was hardy enough to endure a few sessions of bleeding, if the physician ascribed to that method. But she could not claim an eternal headache.

And if Harwood went along with her plans for securing Adam, she would offer to give him a child.

But what if he demanded one as his husbandly rights and she held no power there? Harwood did not seem like the dictator Stephen had been, nor as one who would demand such intimate things from an unwilling wife, but she had been mistaken before.

She would assume nothing of her new husband, just as she would expect nothing. She had gained some status and influence in marrying him, and certainly some measure of protection by having him as her husband, but beyond that . . .

"You will likely be anxious to be on your way, my lord," Aunt Mary was suddenly saying, rising from her seat. "Allow me to help Alexandrina change and then she will be ready to go."

What? Why was she being shuttled out of the house just as the meal had ended? They could have spent the entire day here without any difficulty, and they had not even sampled the cake. Not that Alexandrina was eager to delve into the confection, but surely the appearance of tradition must be upheld.

Had Harwood said something about wishing to leave that Alexandrina had somehow missed? Had he yawned at a lull in the conversation? Looked utterly bored by those surrounding him?

She looked at him, only to find his expression as surprised as she felt.

She doubted even he was that skilled of an actor.

"If you like," he answered almost uncertainly, his eyes flicking from Alexandrina to her aunt as he awkwardly rose. "I am not in haste."

"Very good of you," Aunt Mary said with a placating smile, giving Alexandrina a pointed look and nudging her head towards the rest of the house.

"What is she doing?" Alexandrina hissed to Jane through a false smile, pushing to her feet.

Jane shook her head. "No idea."

If no one was actually in haste to have them away but her aunt, why was she being shepherded away as though by some edict?

She rounded the table, giving her aunt a curious look. "Why the rush, Aunt?" Alexandrina whispered when she reached her. "I believe we are all at our leisure."

Aunt Mary took her arm as though they were merely taking a turn and escorted her from the room. "The Carters are having a dinner party this evening, and a great many of their guests are watching our house. It would be prudent for the pair of you to make your exit sooner rather than later. End the speculation, if you will."

Alexandrina heaved a sigh. "And scandal must have its resolution."

"Just so." Her aunt gave her an apologetic smile and rubbed her arm. "Harwood will be a kind husband, darling, I am sure of it."

"Rather a better statement than being a good husband," Alexandrina mused sourly, "which is what everyone told me about Stephen."

Her aunt wisely said nothing in response to that. She had thankfully never been one to say so, but none of them had anticipated the sort of husband Stephen would really have been. And the shocking part of it was that the sort of husband he was would not have raised many eyebrows in Society.

That was the worst of it. Even if the truth were known, it would not have changed much at all. It was simply the way things were, and she had been a fool for believing in the idea of devotion.

Which was why she had told Harwood she would not expect that of him.

Which had apparently offended him.

There was no understanding the way of things, or the standard by which gentlemen were measured. It was a fluctuating thing, and no one could give her the same answer as another. She could not trust the judgment of anyone but herself, which was why she had vowed not to marry again.

But now she was married, and there was nothing she feared more than getting to know her husband.

"Have you selected something for me to wear for my grand exit?" Alexandrina asked as they reached her bedchambers.

"I have, actually," her aunt admitted. "One of Clara's new gowns. She doesn't mind. If you are going to be exiting the house with your new husband to settle rumors, you must do so with the most modern fashions. The lemon and white silk has been laid out for you."

"Silk?" Alexandrina repeated, laughing in disbelief. "Who wears silk for travelling?"

Her aunt did not laugh. "Lady Harwood does. On her wedding day." She gestured for Alexandrina to go into the room, her expression set as one of the lady's maids joined them.

There was nothing for it, then.

Once she had changed from her wedding gown into her overdone travelling gown, the blue flowers switched for yellow, and a new cloak to match the ensemble fastened about her, Alexandrina was paraded down the stairs to the others. Her trunks were being carried down, no doubt going directly to the coach that had already been brought around. In her absence, Harwood and the rest had vacated the dining room and waited for them in the front drawing room.

The only person looking even remotely uprooted by the sudden shift in the schedule of their day was Harwood, and there was something comforting about seeing his confusion as he saw her enter.

His eyes ran down the length of her, then blinked, and then he started towards her, a smile appearing. "My lady." He plucked up her hand and kissed the back of her glove. "What the devil is going on?" he whispered for her alone. "Why the push and shove?"

Alexandrina grinned at him, not entirely for effect. "We have gawkers across the square at a party. We must give the scandal a resolution."

Harwood's face was a priceless mask of disbelief and incredulity. "Did they think we paid off a clergyman to pretend to marry us? Good heavens." He shook his head and tucked her hand in his arm. "Very well, then let us give them a show and be on our way home."

She blanched a little, fighting hard to swallow.

He caught it and squeezed her hand. "Not to worry. There will be no demands or discussion of rights or the like tonight. Or this week. Or . . . well, I am sure you get the idea."

"Surely you aren't suggesting forever," Alexandrina replied with a faint scoffing sound.

"No, but far be it from me to put a date on such a thing." He cast a quick wink at her, which seemed to shake something in her left knee. "It will be up for negotiation at some point, but not yet."

Before she could make a response to that exquisite remark, he turned to the rest of the room. "Well, we must be off. I trust we may return for dinner in a few days. Would Tuesday suit?"

"Of course, we shall look forward to it," Gerald conceded with a combination of a bow and a nod.

Harwood turned to Mr. Roth, who seemed to be on the verge of laughing about something. "Larkin, Sophia, will we see you at the opera this week?"

The opera? When had that been discussed?

"I would love it," Mrs. Roth replied with a laugh. "Larkin will endure it."

Alexandrina smiled at that, wondering if she and Harwood would match them there, or if Mr. Roth would be alone in his misery.

"We'll send a note," Harwood assured them. He glanced down at Alexandrina. "Do you need to make farewells?"

"Not really," she told him. "We'll be back on Tuesday."

Jane coughed a faint laugh, and she caught the twitch of Harwood's smile. "Very well, then. Good day, all."

He bowed, she curtseyed, and they turned for the doors, which the butler opened as though for royalty.

"Should we wave for the gawkers?" Harwood asked through his smile as they started down the stairs.

"I don't think so," Alexandrina laughed. "That would be so obvious."

"True. But they must have something. Hmm." He paused on a stair, pulling her to a stop as well, and looked at her with some speculation. "Will you trust me implicitly for a brief moment? Just one, and it won't mean anything."

Alexandrina squinted up at him, more curious than wary. "If I must."

He nodded once. "Thank you." Without warning, he cupped her cheek in one hand and brought his lips to hers.

She stiffened at the contact, marveling at the audacity, and suddenly alight with the feeling of his mouth against her now-tingling lips.

The kiss was slow and soft, his thumb brushing her cheek as though to soothe a rising temper. If there was heat rising in her cheek, it was not from anger.

Yet.

He broke off, pointedly stroking her cheek once more, a little firmly. "Don't strike me," he whispered, his eyes darker than she recalled. "It will stop the gossip. I apologize for being forward."

Alexandrina swallowed hard, nodding at the explanation. "That makes sense. I suppose it would help matters if I smile."

"Probably," he replied, grinning at her. "But I won't ask you to."

She returned his smile, imagining the gasps that would sound from their observers on all sides of the square. "I am perfectly capable of acting in my own interest."

Harwood chuckled, nodding in approval. "I never doubted it. Come on, let's go. I'd rather fancy a quiet evening without any sort of pretension. You are welcome to join me if you like, but you may do whatever you please."

"If this is any indication of the husband you are going to be, Harwood," Alexandrina said as they moved down to the coach, "I'll consider my prospects rather promising."

"Yes, I've been trying to explain that to you."

CHAPTER 7

It had been three days, and his wife had not yet struck him for kissing her on the front steps of her uncle's home. Nor had she threatened him with a knife, shoved him down a flight of stairs, or smashed him over the head with one of the porcelain urns.

It seemed a bit early to hope the pattern would continue, but Taft was beginning to breathe a little easier.

Unless he thought of the kiss itself.

He hadn't expected a reaction to kissing her, aside from her stiffening at the contact, and he had fully intended on pulling back when she did so. But she hadn't resisted him, despite her surprise, and that had startled him into continuing the kiss. Almost as though to test her, though it sounded utterly shameful to admit that. He hadn't intended anything of the sort, had simply thought that kissing her after their wedding in view of gawkers would end speculation as to the veracity of the rumors.

How could he have known that her lips were the softest he had ever kissed? That there was a natural lushness to their depths that removed the ground from beneath his feet. That her slightest motion of tilting her chin up, likely without even noticing, had brought her closer to him and drew him in. That the tightening of her hand on his arm as he'd kissed her might as well have been her fingers in his hair. That the fact she had not pulled away, bit his lip, stomped on his foot, or struck him when it was done gave him an odd sense of hope. Though he had no idea what exactly he was hoping for.

It was a kiss Taft had been entirely unprepared for, and it had taken him quite some time to hear his own words over the pounding of his heart.

He had never been so grateful to have a marriage without affection in his entire life. For all of the few hours he'd had a marriage at all.

He'd never wanted a marriage without affection, but he hadn't exactly thought of making a love match for himself. He'd never really thought of the type of marriage he wanted at all, only that he ought to have a marriage at some point.

Now he had one.

They had dined with her family again the night before, this time without any gawkers across the square, and Alexandrina had seemed more at ease then she had at the wedding luncheon. More at ease than she had been at Harwood House, perhaps.

She was an interesting woman. For all their past bickering and sharpness, she had been almost resolutely quiet, even at their meals together. He'd asked the housekeeper, Mrs. Cole, and Alexandrina had taken tea with her the day after the wedding, asked a couple of questions, and then simply requested the housekeeper tell her about the house, the family, and herself. Nothing about the running of the place, no hint of her interests, not even particular personal details about herself.

No answers to his questions about her, and he had promised not to press.

Well, he had promised himself not to press her on such things. He had promised her not to press the issue of husbandly rights, demanding she permit him in her chambers, or bearing children. Not explicitly so, but she had certainly ascertained his meaning. And he would hold to that. He had no intention of treating her as the vessel for his own pleasure or his legacy.

She was his wife. And that meant more than what sort of relations they were or were not having.

His wife.

Whom he had practically abandoned for their first few days of marriage.

Not entirely. He had seen her a few times, and they ate together every evening, but he had been occupied throughout the day as he worked with his solicitor to arrange a will and testament. And then there was reaching out to the solicitor Mr. Tuttle-Kirk to ask for a meeting and see what they might arrange to help the young Lord Lawson to escape the clutches of his grandmother and return to life with his mother. The first meeting was to take place shortly, and he frowned now as he thought of it.

Was this something he ought to discuss with Alexandrina before he moved forward?

He pushed off from his chair and strode out into the corridor, glancing up and down for the nearest servant, none of whom were immediately visible. He started towards the drawing rooms, unsure what sort of routine his wife had settled into and where she might be at this time of day.

Mrs. Cole suddenly appeared from the servants' stair, and he turned to meet her. "Mrs. Cole! Have you seen my wife, by chance?"

The housekeeper smiled and gestured in the exact path he'd been walking. "East drawing room, my lord. I believe she is going through invitations."

Taft's eyes widened. "Those shouldn't go to her; she'll refuse them all."

"She said they should not go to you, as you'd accept them

all." Mrs. Cole clamped down on her lips, clearly holding back laughter.

"Of course, she did," Taft grumbled. "Thank you, Mrs. Cole, I will address it." He turned to continue on and headed for the east drawing room, which was, ironically, the finest of the drawing rooms in the house. If Alexandrina were to select any particular room to situate herself during the day, he would have thought the Blue Room to be more to her taste.

There was practically nothing in it.

He rounded into the drawing room, finding her sitting at a writing desk beside a stack of invitations that made him grin.

She, however, was not grinning.

"Alexandrina," he greeted, leaning against the doorjamb and folding his arms.

She paused in her writing, then glanced over at him. "Yes, Taft?"

She had never called him by his given name before, and he barked a laugh at hearing it now. "That's not going to make me stop calling you by your given name. I like informality."

"Perhaps I feel the same way," she replied, turning in her chair and facing him more fully. "Have you come to object to my examination of the invitations? I am not refusing all of them, only the ridiculous ones."

"But your definition of ridiculous and mine surely vary," Taft pointed out. "And that is not fair." He shook his head quickly, raising a hand. "That is not actually what I sought you out for. I'm due to a meeting with a solicitor."

Alexandrina frowned. "Yes, you've been doing so since the wedding. I hope you're not making things as complicated as possible for me in the end—that would be quite beastly of you."

He laughed once, her words truer than she knew. "Not intentionally, and this is a new solicitor. One I know to be acquainted with complicated issues of legacy, entailment, and guardianship."

His wife's eyes widened, and she was silent for a moment. "You mean . . .?"

Taft nodded once. "By any chance, do you have something in writing about the details of Lawson's will?"

"I have the exact letter I received from the solicitor and executor of the will," Alexandrina told him as she shot to her feet. "Will that do?"

"Does it explain it in detail?" Taft asked, grinning at her excitement.

"Word for word," she said firmly. "I checked when I was at Stonehall for the funeral."

Taft nodded eagerly. "Get it. Do you want to come with me?"

"Yes!" She bolted from the room in a rush, the invitations on the desk forgotten and blown about as though by a dervish.

He stepped to the desk to look them over, taking quick stock of them and understanding in short order which pile was accepting and which was rejecting. He shuffled through them, only pulling aside two or three that she had rejected, leaving the rest for her judgment.

She could not win every argument, and it was best that she learned that lesson now.

It could not have been more than five minutes before she was back, her gown the same, her hair repinned, and her eyes as bright as he'd ever seen them.

More than that, she was smiling.

It baffled him into smiling back.

"What's this for?" he asked, gesturing to his own mouth.

Alexandrina merely raised a brow. "Simple. We are plotting against my mother-in-law. I've been wanting to do this for years."

"A cry uttered by many women everywhere, I am sure," Taft said with a nod, gesturing for her to lead the way.

She did so, snatching her bonnet and pelisse from the maid

who offered them. "What is your plan, then?"

Taft chuckled as he took his own hat from the maid, nodding his thanks. "Outmaneuver the Lawsons, however we can make that happen. I've been chatting with my solicitor about it as we arrange my current will to account for your presence, which, by the way, is coming along splendidly. My apologies for losing your dower rights."

She flicked her hand in a swishing motion as she got into the coach. "It was the smallest possible portion he could legally give me, and I don't mind the loss of it. I presume my dowry is much diminished?"

"Why would you think so?" Taft settled himself across from her in the coach, jostling just a little as it started off.

"Stephen was pleased to inform me, towards the end of our marriage, that it was the best thing I brought to the union," Alexandrina replied with a bland smile. "And that it had given him great pleasure to buy gems for his Friday mistress with a great deal of it."

Taft gaped at the statement, splotches of red beginning to appear in his vision as the words began to process in his mind. "His Friday mistress?"

Alexandrina nodded once. "He had several by the end, you see. Friday was his favorite. She was also his mistress on Saturday and Tuesday, but Friday was their card night, which was always a great success. Her rooms overlooked the groves and orchards, which were lovely. The Sunday mistress was also Wednesday, and her rooms provided a view of the pond. Monday was also Thursday, and she lived on the other side of the gallery. Never did understand why, but it was conveniently located by the stairs that led to the stables." She shrugged her shoulders, her jaw hard, her eyes cold. "My rooms saw the church, of all things. A lovely church, and the path to it was strewn with wildflowers . . ."

"You don't have to do this," Taft told her roughly, fire

streaking up and down his neck the more she described life with her first husband.

"This is easy enough to discuss," she assured him, her smile spreading, though it did not gain any warmth. "You see, I have never known a day of marriage with Stephen without a mistress overshadowing it. He was not with a mistress every day, but when I discovered he had one, about a year into the marriage, I also discovered that my husband had left our marriage bed and rode to that of his mistress. As though he needed to scrub the memory of me from his mind and body as soon as possible. At least he was considerate enough not to move any mistress into Stonehall officially until after I was carrying Adam, and he kept them in a separate wing from me when he did. They had their own dining room, so I never dined with them. I suppose that was a kindness, of sorts."

Taft shook his head as his chest tightened in sympathetic agony. "I am so sorry."

She did not seem to hear him. "The only blessing I ever had from him was that of my child. The only happiness I ever had from him, too. My son was always good-natured, always curious, always eager in everything he did, not that Stephen cared. He did not see a use for infants, and claimed he would take an interest when there was something to take an interest in."

If the man were not already deceased, Taft would have ridden to Stonehall himself and done the world that favor.

"And nobody cared," Alexandrina said softly. "No one could find fault with my husband, even when I tried to express my pain. After all, men are men, as they say. He was providing for his mistresses, and not casting them aside, so was that not admirable? And he was, in all other aspects, perfectly respectable. A good match, they said. A perfect couple and their perfect heir." She shook her head, her eyes staring blankly at nothing at all. "I have never understood what is meant by wedded bliss, when the phrase is used. I spent the first year of marriage wondering where the man who courted me disappeared to, and the rest of it realizing I knew nothing of marriage at all. Wedded bliss died the day it was born, and what heart I had died as well, but at a much slower pace."

He could not stay silent, could not stand by and let the forlorn, empty tone of her voice continue a moment longer. He scooted to the end of the seat and took his wife's hands, noting too late that she did not wear gloves, and feeling oddly grateful for it when he felt the iciness of her skin.

"Alexandrina."

She did not move, nor respond, completely lost to her thoughts and memories.

Taft squeezed her hands, bringing them lightly to his lips. "Alexandrina."

Her throat worked and her once-brilliant eyes turned to his. "What?"

"I promise you," he vowed in a low voice, praying she could hear him over the sounds of the carriage wheels, "that we will get your son back. I will not rest until I am named his guardian and he spends every hour of every day under your watchful eye. Until he is barreling down the halls of Battensay and making you want to tear your hair out."

Her lips curved at that, making his heart lurch. "He is too well behaved for that."

"That won't last," Taft assured her with a quick grin. "Not with me as his stepfather." He sobered, rubbing her hands more for warmth than for comfort. "Do you remember what I told you about a mistress?"

She nodded, her fingers shifting a little in his hold. "Yes."

"I meant it with all my heart." He kissed her knuckles. "You will never suffer that indignity again. Ever. There will be no woman superior to you in my esteem or my respect, and no woman at all in our home but those hired to serve us. Unless you decide to adopt a village girl to be your companion when you've decided I'm quite a waste of your considerable intellect."

Alexandrina chortled a surprised laugh, then smiled with real sincerity. Her fingers gripped at his hands now, the pressure almost more encouraging than the smile. "You'd never look twice at a pretty maid?"

"I don't hire pretty maids," Taft said at once. "Only exceptionally plain ones. Much better workers, and the footmen are less distracted."

She laughed again, shaking her head. "Do you have an answer for everything?"

"Pretty much. I also make up a very great deal." He winked at her, then sighed. "I don't know what else I can say, Alexandrina, but that I am not Stephen, and I won't become him. And together, I think we can see to it that your son does not as well."

He watched her swallow, caught the suspicious sheen in her eyes, and felt the sudden clenching in her hold. "You'll really help me fight for him? You'll welcome him into your home and care for him with me?"

"I'll give the boy my name, if you despise the one he has," Taft told her with a nod. "I'll fight for your right to raise him without interference until Stonehall and Battensay are both burned to the ground. And you should know, I am frightfully competitive, and a particularly poor loser."

"That might be the least surprising thing you have ever said," Alexandrina managed, her words slightly clogged. She cleared her throat, tossed her head, and straightened, giving him a much clearer look. "Thank you, Taft. Truly."

He squeezed her hands once more, acknowledging her thanks with a nod and sliding back against the seat, releasing his hold on her. "Thank me when we've won. I have every intention of watching as you march triumphantly into that place of your nightmares and vanquish the Lawson bat."

"I thought I was the Lawson bat."

"Please," he scoffed loudly. "You are a Harwood now. I would never call you any such thing."

"Of course not." She smiled a little, all trace of tears gone. "I presume you agree with your cousin, that I need a victory gown for that day when we go to fetch Adam."

"Oh, yes!" he exclaimed. "Absolutely." He laughed, looking up at the ceiling. "Yes, indeed. We'll spare no expense. Whatever you want, and then a gold-lined sash or ribbon across a shoulder, clasped with a Harwood crest. Would you like a diadem? I'll get you a diadem."

He continued to rattle off any number of ridiculous things they could adorn her with, to the point where she stopped listening and looked out of the window instead.

It was far better than seeing her look so drawn and lost as he had seen her before.

If he never saw that again, he would still not be able to forget it.

And he had thought this woman without feelings? She was *all* feeling, and she hated herself for it. Someday, he would tell her how extraordinary this discovery was for him, and how the glimpses of such had earned her a begrudging admiration and respect from him that would not have come in any other avenue, he was sure. There was a natural respect for her, even when he twitched at the sight of her, but that had been in a general sense, just as he might have respected any woman in Society.

Not particular to her.

But now . . .

Well, it was a little early in their marriage for sweeping declarations of any kind, but he was certainly beginning to respect her in a more particular and personal manner.

Worthy marriages had been built on less.

The carriage pulled to a stop, and Taft was quick to alight, offering a hand to Alexandrina to help her down. She took it but released her hold the moment her feet touched the ground.

Of course, she did.

He offered his arm, which she belatedly flung her hand into, shaking her head a little without saying a word.

"Not quite the patience for display this time, eh?" he asked as they moved towards the building. "Have I pushed you too far?"

"I dislike acting and pretense," she hissed. "The very idea of putting on a show is one of engaging in a lie, and I have had far too many lies in my life to wish for anything more."

"What is acting and pretense about a husband offering his wife his arm as they walk together?" Taft pulled open the door and gestured for her to precede him. "That is common politeness and decency."

"It means I must pretend that we like each other," Alexandrina replied in a much lower voice. "Which we do not."

Taft could hear the defiance in her voice and smiled at it, knowing she did not quite mean what she said, even if she thought she did. "Don't we? How interesting. You will have to tell me more about us on the journey back. I rather thought we were getting on well."

"Do you ever stop talking?"

"Only when someone else says something more interesting."

"Try conversing with a pigeon, my lord. They are far more interesting than you."

"I shall bow to your knowledge on the subject." He cleared his throat, leaning just a little closer. "Mr. Tuttle-Kirk is renowned for his skill in matters of inheritance and legality, but he is a little eccentric. Try not to let that cloud your judgment of him."

She nodded, seemingly also willing to let their spat lie in the face of their task. "If he can work the miracle that will get my Adam back, I do not care if he stands on his desk dressed as a cook and sings an aria for the king."

"I don't think we'll have to endure anything that outlandish, but I applaud your fortitude if we do."

He showed his card to the approaching clerk, a lad no older than twenty-three, who nodded. "Very good, my lord. Mr. Tuttle-Kirk is expecting you in his office. This way, please." He started down the corridor ahead of them, the walls a little cramped and dark, and through the open doorway, a balding man with erratic white hair at the sides and back sat, his bushy mustache of equally snowy white instantly drawing one's eye.

Were the spectacles sitting upon his nose or upon those dense whiskers? They sat so precariously, it was impossible to tell.

The man with the mustache turned at their approach and hastily got to his feet, the motion awkward and stuttering, the shift in his position revealing a light sheen of perspiration on his brow.

And this was before the discussion had started?

"My lord Harwood," he greeted, bowing rather well. "And Lady Harwood, I presume?"

Alexandrina dipped her chin as regally as any monarch could hope to. "Good day."

"John Tuttle-Kirk," he continued, extending a hand to Taft, which he shook firmly. He then extended a hand to Alexandrina, which she shook with some confusion. "Oh, apologies, my lady, how uncouth. Thank you for indulging my nonsense. Come, come, let us talk." He turned back to his desk, moving a pile of books and papers to one side, three sheets of paper falling out of it as he did so.

"Oh my lord," Alexandrina breathed in horror.

"Dressed as a cook, did you say?" Taft mused, putting a hand at her back as though to press her into the room.

She went, heading to a pair of chairs before the desk and sitting in one, Taft taking the seat beside her.

"Did you bring the details of the will in question, my lord?" Mr. Tuttle-Kirk asked without preamble. "It is best we get straight to business, given the amount of work to be done."

"My lady has it," Taft replied with a nod to Alexandrina.

She fished the letter out of her reticule and handed it over. "This is the letter I received on the occasion of my late husband's death."

Mr. Tuttle-Kirk nodded, his mustache twitching to one side and then another as he took the letter, unfolding it. The light in the room glinted off his spectacles, as though to indicate the exact motion of his eyes as he read. "Ah, yes . . . Yes, yes, this will indeed be difficult. Not impossible, certainly, but they were most thorough. Yes . . . I believe I can find a way through this."

"Indeed, sir?" Taft asked, more to force the man to engage with them rather than the letter.

The spectacles and mustache lifted a little to meet his eyes, then Alexandrina's. "Indeed, my lord. My lady. I am quite certain I can."

CHAPTER 8

Alexandrina had never particularly cared for the opera, but tonight, there was no place she would rather be.

The last few days had been a flurry of activity, and it had been wonderful to take an active part in it rather than hear the details from her husband. It would have been so easy for him to do all of the managing and arranging on her behalf, or so he might claim, and then give her the basic points over their evening lamb. But Taft had never once suggested she remain at home when he was off to visit Tuttle-Kirk. Indeed, he sought her out and discussed their strategy and plan for the meeting ahead.

He was always reviewing their goals and aims, engaging in a debriefing of what had happened in the previous meeting so they might be reminded of the situation at hand and what had yet to be done. He was constantly asking her opinion and her thoughts, giving her ample time to think and to reply without ever once making her feel patronized. She had no experience with matters of law, estate, or inheritance, and certainly had no great understanding of primogeniture, as she was constantly reminding him, but that did not seem to hinder his determination to involve her.

As though he needed to prove that he would not make decisions for her.

There was something undeniably sweet in that.

If she had to admit anything her husband did was sweet.

He was certainly proving himself to be different from what she had anticipated in the man, let alone as a husband. What she had considered to be all stuff and nonsense, all silliness and frippery, was actually rather intelligent, determined, and even serious at times. Not constantly, as he was still provoking her in the most childish ways, but he had a quick mind and a sound understanding of a great many things.

Perhaps most curious of all, he seemed to always attempt to console her if she were ever even slightly overcome with her own emotions. Why she continued to have the tendency to confide in him when she least expected it, or when the timing could not be worse, she had yet to fully grasp, but he had yet to dismiss those emotions or treat her in any way different for indulging in them, however briefly. It was far different from Stephen, who would ask her not to cry, but with a tone of disgust rather than sympathy. She inconvenienced him with her tears, rather than moved him by them.

Which was why she had stopped shedding tears.

Even with Taft, her tears had yet to fall. So long as they stayed contained in her eyes, she could not fully consider herself as crying. Would not.

Once they secured Adam from the clutches of the Lawsons, once they were removed to Battensay, she would feel safer to be herself, to not always be composed, to settle into a routine that would fulfill her.

That would fulfill them all.

Would Taft still wish to be such partners in their aims when he was Adam's guardian? She had no suspicions of his molding the boy for his own interests—she was well aware how he felt about the boy being with his mother. But could he be wishing for Adam to join them in order to give Alexandrina an occupation? Something to get her out of his way, so to speak, and let them both lead lives independent of each other.

She wouldn't mind, if that were the case, truly. An independent marriage would be better than the painful one she had known before. Taft was a decent man, even with his fluff, and she would be better treated by him than she was by Stephen.

And she had not even made him the offer of children to help her secure Adam. She had not needed to. The subject had not even been brought up, not in any regard.

She could not hope for a stay from it for eternity.

But she would not necessarily keep Taft at arm's length on principle any longer. She would not be inviting him to her bed, but she was here with him at the opera.

And she had let him kiss her.

That had been a little less out of her control. She had understood the need for it while in the midst of the attention, and despite what he had said in the gardens of the Corbett house, she had yet to strike him in any condition. And she understood that appearances in London had to be kept up, and, thankfully, the tastes of Society still swayed towards the particularly polite and restrained, so her husband would not be kissing her in public on the regular.

She grew quite flushed at the merest thought of it.

The kiss had been pleasurable, but the only other kisses she had known had been Stephen's, and even when she had loved him, those had been strange and awkward.

Still, being seen on Taft's arm was not a hardship, despite her distaste for Society. The opera this evening was rumored to be quite good, and if the meetings with Mr. Tuttle-Kirk were any indication, they would soon be in a position to fetch Adam, which meant leaving London.

For a very great while, if Alexandrina had anything to say about it. Taft could do as he pleased, flitting in and out of Town on a whim, but she would be quite content to remain in Berkshire for several years without once making a return to London.

If Battensay was as lovely as she had heard, she would like it a very great deal. With the promise of her son at her side, she could be content nearly everywhere, but at a great estate where no one would interfere with her or her child? It would be heaven on earth.

Stonehall was an excellent building, filled with history and beauty, wealth and status, but it had been a prison for her. A perfectly gilded prison.

No more, she thought to herself as Taft guided her towards their box. No more prisons, no more interference.

Only life and only light. Independence and joy.

If Taft brought nothing else to this marriage than that, she would consider this all worth it.

"Do you like opera, Alexandrina?" Taft asked in a soft tone as he nodded to a passerby. "I don't even know."

"I enjoy well-performed opera," she admitted through her forced smile, which was, admittedly, very small. "And a good story in one. I see no reason for these talented individuals to sing so extraordinarily about nothing at all."

Taft chuckled a low laugh. "You prefer a point to everything, don't you?"

She looked up at him, hating how the fabric of her overdone gown rustled loudly when she did so. "A purpose is preferable in a great many things. Else why are we here?"

"At the opera?" He shrugged a shoulder. "Because the music is grand, and people must have something to do that renders them a little more cultured."

"Is there culture here? How bizarre." Alexandrina looked around as though to search for it, trying to ignore the whispers she could hear as they passed groups. "They still talk of us," she hissed in a much lower whisper. "I thought we had settled that."

Taft covered her hand with his. "We have, but Jenkins, unfortunately, continues to claim he knows nothing of the gardens and is wholly innocent of his apparent attempt to take advantage."

"He was wholly foxed, of course he does not recollect it." Alexandrina shook her head, huffing a little.

"Nevertheless, his noise about the thing is bringing it up. And there may have been my claim of challenging him to a duel . . ."

Alexandrina groaned and dug her fingers into his sleeve, the action a little less painful than she would have liked due to her gloves. "You idiot."

"You're welcome," he shot back. "At any rate, he has not come to me himself to argue the point, or ask me to refute the claims, so perhaps leaving London sooner than later would be prudent. Else he might actually do so."

Something in her chest squeezed impossibly tight just then. "Surely, you would not actually go through with it. The duel, I mean. It is ridiculous."

"Perhaps so, but the power of rumor and gossip is undeniable, Alexandrina. And a gentleman cannot afford slander, particularly when he has a wife and a stepson to look after and provide for. His reputation reflects on them, too."

The almost absent manner in which he mentioned Adam took her by surprise, and that he would consider them both where his own reputation was concerned . . .

It meant more to her than she could have expressed.

"Duels are so stupid," Alexandrina managed around her emotions. "And pointless."

"And we are back to all things requiring a purpose," Taft replied on a heavy sigh, making no attempt to disguise his moving away from the topic. "My word, you are relentless, Alexandrina." He stopped, gesturing into a box beside them. "Here we are."

She gave him a dark look before entering. "I am not relentless, I am practical. How can men firing pistols at one another resolve any kind of insult?"

"Alexandrina," Taft said again, less as a correction, as she expected, and more as a thought. "Hmm."

"What?" she asked, sitting in a chair and looking back at him.

He shook his head, coming around to sit beside her. "Your name is exceptionally long, that is all. Beautiful, certainly, but long. Can I not shorten it?"

She gaped at him, wondering where in the world this ridiculous line of conversation had come from. "Just because your given name takes no effort to spit out does not mean it is in any way better than mine."

"I didn't say it was, I'm just exhausted by the time I finish your name." He yawned as though to prove his point.

She rolled her eyes, opening her fan and beginning to use it gently. "Yes, thinking that much must be a dreadful exercise for you."

Taft grunted an almost laugh and crossed one leg over the other, looking out over the other guests at the opera currently situating themselves in their seats. "I am going to shorten it, and if you want a say in what I call you, speak now."

"I have no idea what you could call me," she told him with a sniff. "I have always only been Alexandrina." She left out the detail of Jane having a particular name for her, wanting to keep that portion of her past for herself alone.

"Let me think of some alternatives for you," her husband offered, as though she might need the assistance. "I can call you Alex, Drina, Andri, Exan, Ina, Allie, Lexa, Exxie, Drinie . . ."

She laughed once, reluctantly finding humor in the game, as well as absurdity. "This is the most ridiculous thing I have ever heard."

Taft raised a brow, grinning. "But it is not pointless."

Snapping her fan shut, she rapped his knee with it. "Rude."

"I could call you Al."

She gaped in horror. "Don't you dare."

"Then pick something, for heaven's sake." He laughed and settled into his seat more comfortably. "When I want to call for you, I do not want to have the syllables of your name slurring together on the echo. No one will make out anything there. And it feels so formal to call you Alexandrina in private conversation. Think of this as the first step in us becoming friends."

Friends, was it? Spouses, partners, and now friends? It was an interesting order of relationships accomplished, there was no mistaking it.

"Likely the second step," she corrected gently. "The first being your help in getting Adam back from the Lawsons."

He seemed surprised by that. "Did you think I wouldn't do so? I'd like to think that what we're doing isn't extraordinary, but rather what any sensible gentleman of morals would do for his wife. And for his stepson, too. This isn't a step towards any particular aims for me. It is simply what is right."

"Nevertheless," Alexandrina went on, nodding a little, "it is all I have ever wanted, and I cannot thank you enough for doing so. I was preparing to ask you if we might make efforts towards such a thing, and had even been willing to offer . . ." She bit her lip, her cheeks heating.

Taft tilted his head, his brow creasing as he listened. "Offer . . .?"

"To bear you a child in exchange," she whispered, feeling almost ashamed of the thing now. "I would have tried for an heir for you, since my son cannot inherit your title and estate."

"Did you really think I would barter one child against another in such a way?" he asked her, his tone lacking any and all accusation, despite the words themselves. "That I would expect you to offer yourself to me in order to act in your interest?"

Her lips parted as though she would speak, but there were no words. She could only lift a shoulder in the slightest of shrugs.

Taft mirrored her by shaking his own head far more slowly. "I would never have accepted that offer, Alix. Never. I would have agreed without anything in return, just as I do now. Not because I am such a good and honorable man, but because I am decent. There does not need to be an exchange in this, and there will not be. Your son belongs with you, and I will tell anyone the same. And as for an heir for me . . ." He exhaled and looked out over the guests again.

"What?" Alexandrina whispered.

He made a face of unconcerned consideration. "We'll get around to the discussion eventually, I have no doubt, but I'm not about to demand one, nice as it might be for any child at all to bear my name. I have no doubt we can get just as creative with the rules of my inheritance as we are about your son's guardianship. And that will suffice for me."

That could not be all, could not be the end. Could not be the resolution. Yet he made no move to make a joke, to laugh, to give any indication that he was less than sincere.

Who was this man she had married?

"Thank you," she murmured, feeling the words a trifle light for the moment, but not knowing what else to say.

"You are quite welcome, Alix." He slid his gaze to her, a smile curving crookedly. "I've called you Alix twice now, and you have not twitched. Does that mean you consent?"

With a helpless laugh, and a hint of a snort, Alexandrina put a hand to her brow. "Oh, heavens, why not? It is not too simple or common and does not grate the nerves. Call me that, if you must."

"I think I must, Alix. It is quite charming." He continued to smile at her, something almost childlike in the curve of it.

Almost. But not entirely.

And heaven help her, she had to smile back.

Apparently, that was all the indication he needed. His eyes still on her, he reached out and took her hand, not lacing their fingers, but simply holding it. "Don't strike me," he warned softly.

Alexandrina looked at their hands, then up at him, daring him to continue holding on.

Which he did.

She tried to draw her smile back as she turned to look at the stage, but it utterly refused to subside into nothingness. And as the opera began, her husband still holding tight to her hand, she fought the smile less and less.

CHAPTER 9

Alexandrina was a mess.

She looked perfect, there was no question, and Taft was quite certain he had never seen anything so beautiful, let alone any woman. But this was the day she had been waiting several years for.

This was the day they were going to fetch her son and place him squarely back into her care alone.

And if the present wringing of her fingers was any indication, she was a mess. Beyond a mess. Utterly scattered to the wind and barely conscious that she was sitting there in the carriage.

Taft had divested her of her gloves all of six minutes into the ride from the coaching inn, though she really hadn't noticed. He'd thought it was best for the condition of her gloves, and knowing how much they had spent on them for this day in particular . . .

Now he was more concerned that she would wring the very skin from her fingers.

It had been a flurry, leaving London, but a pleasant one. Alexandrina had been the most delightful, excited version of herself he had ever seen the closer they neared to completion of the legal details. She had nearly skipped about the house, smiled at everyone and everything, and chatted away in her meals with Taft as though they were old friends.

He was still recovering from the repeated shock of it.

Once the terms and stipulation of the will had been settled, approved by both Taft's usual solicitor as well as Mr. Tuttle-Kirk, and all were in agreement that it would overpower anything the Lawsons could claim on the boy, Alexandrina had not wanted to wait a single moment more to be gone.

Of course, leaving quickly would have been impossible had they not already been planning on doing so. Before they had finalized the will, she had allowed Jane to take her to an extremely popular modiste and let Taft pay an exorbitant amount of money to take priority over whatever other gowns the woman was due to make in order to arrange something splendid for this particular day.

She was wearing the extraordinary garment now. It was a rich, deep ruby-red satin with an even deeper gauze overlay embroidered with gold that became more apparent the further down the skirts it went, fashioned into a cutaway at the waistline to reveal the rich depth of her skirts beneath. The red and gold wove together in folds at her sleeves, then disappeared into the sheer red gauze from the elbow down to her wrists. The bodice was rather simple, due to the blue riband crossing her left shoulder, clasped with the Harwood crest, just as Taft wore now.

He had to match her, naturally, though the only extraordinary garment he wore was the ruby and gold weskit.

But this day was not about him. It was about her.

Perhaps his favorite part of her ensemble was her hair. It really was the most extraordinary auburn and brown blend, sometimes one shade more than another, some pieces one color more than another. The beauty of it was on full display in twisting, coiled elegance, pulling back into an arranged crown of sorts that somehow also included several curls that descended from it, the tips of which rested at the base of her neck. He did not get her a diadem, despite his vow to, but the simple gold florets and ruby pins dotted throughout were utter perfection.

She was stunning and would have stolen the breath of any man who looked upon her.

Had she appeared thus in the gardens at the Corbett home, Jenkins would not have been the only one Taft would have needed to challenge.

And she was his wife.

The woman was a queen among women. An empress. A goddess, if they would deign to look more regal than ethereal.

If any Lawson in the house, male or female, managed to say a word coherently in her presence, he would be most surprised.

Alexandrina seemed to tremble as she stared out of the window, sitting stiffly upright, looking more like a girl in costume waiting for a governess to judge her posture. He had no idea how far it was to Stonehall from their inn, but she likely knew every inch of this road.

Hated every inch of it.

"Are we nearly there?" he asked softly.

Her chin dipped in a nod, her slender throat bobbing twice. "I do not know if I can do this."

Taft was immediately before her, kneeling awkwardly between the carriage seats and taking her hands. "You can, Alix. We have the law on our side. You are the boy's mother, and as the Countess of Harwood, you outrank everyone in that house. I am declaring myself guardian of my wife's son, as is my legal right, and have provided the family with as many stipulations as I can to satisfy them without being indulgent. You approved each one. Remember?"

She nodded shakily. "It is the idea of facing *her*. She will stand in the Great Hall, surrounded by those dreadful family portraits and suits of armor, glaring at me as though I am nothing more than the scullery maid, despite the fact that I bore the heir to the estate. She ignored my pains and my fears, belittled me for them, stole my son . . ."

"Alix." Taft reached a hand up to cup her cheek, brushing his thumb gently across her skin. "This is the day of your victory. Your triumph. All of that is over. She holds no power over you anymore."

"She won't know that," Alexandrina whispered, hiccupping on a sob that came without tears. "She is the lord and master of Stonehall, and all will bow to her."

"They will bow to Lady Harwood," Taft insisted firmly, pressing his palm against her cheek. "Any argument may be referred to her solicitor, who is receiving every legal instruction on the matter. Adam will come with us if I have to storm the nursery myself. If you like, I can call the local magistrate to accompany us in this. I've already got his name, as well as the nearest duke. Happens to be an old family friend of mine, owes me a favor for getting his daughter married off from an introduction at my last house party."

Alexandrina uttered a startled laugh at that, turning her hands to grip Taft's tightly. "I'm not nearly as brave as you think I am, or as thunderous as I appear. Most of the time, I do not care about my surroundings or the people there, so I may behave as I like. I care so much about this, I am quite paralyzed by my emotions." She bit down on her bottom lip, shaking her head. "Perhaps you should be the one to go in and speak to her. It will be more effective coming from a man."

"It will be more poetic coming from *you*." He dropped his hand from her face to rest on top of hers. "You care about your son, about bringing him home with us, about freeing him from their influence."

"Yes."

"You don't need to care about her," he went on, rubbing her hands soothingly. "Not at all. This is one of those rare moments where the distinction of rank will prevail, and you may march into the Great Hall and stare down each portrait and suit of armor with the superiority of every duchess you've ever despised for such airs. You may look down on this woman, who did not sympathize with your pains nor intervene on your behalf, perhaps even down the length of your rather perfect nose, and demand her acquiescence."

A new light entered her eyes, the brilliant green with blue hints now tinged with steel as they searched his eyes intently.

Taft smiled at her, delighted by the show of strength. "You will prevail, Alix. There is no other alternative. We've seen to that. If you wish to show kindness as you do so, you certainly may. If you wish to be imperious, I fully support that. If you wish to do all of this in silence and send me up to fetch the boy while you glare ominously at your foe, I am at your service. This is *your* triumph. I only want to watch with pride."

Alexandrina's throat worked again, and she exhaled slowly. "I could have married before, you know. I knew it was a simple solution to my problem. I could have made myself more agreeable, more desirable, sought out powerful suitors to bring all of this about sooner."

Of course, that was true, and he had thought of that himself, but he had simply presumed she had no desire for a husband, and so she had not. What was the point of bringing it up now?

"I could not marry again," she whispered harshly. "It nearly killed me the first time. I could not do it, not even for my son. I have hated myself for that for years. That I could not sacrifice myself to do what was best for him, could not overcome my own shame and torment to give him the life of joy and light he deserved. That I have had to leave him there, in that dark and loveless place, because I was not strong enough to overcome it."

A deep and resounding crack sounded within Taft's chest, he

was certain, and spread into both lungs and several ribs, pain and helplessness rapidly filling him. "No, Alix. No, don't say that, love." He brought her hands to his lips, not so much kissing them as trying to breathe life into them, to breathe hope, to connect himself to her as though something within him could rid her of such thoughts.

Her fingers brushed against his mouth ever so slightly. "I tried every alternative available to me as I was, applied to every family member of station, influence, or note, and each of them were exerting all their influence on my behalf. It was all coming to naught. I was at Maria's ball as part of those efforts, if not to improve my reputation for our cause. And then the gardens happened."

"And you had to marry anyway," he murmured, now kissing her hands in earnest, a tender apology for a pain he did not know he had been inflicting when he suggested impending matrimony that night. "I am so sorry."

"I did not realize that I could have a marriage that would not traumatize me and would actually be the resolution I so desperately needed." Swallowing again, she pulled one hand from beneath his and laid it gently alongside his cheek, the fingertips all he could feel upon his suddenly burning skin. "And for that, I can only thank you with every fiber of my being." She wet her lips and leaned close, pressing her lips softly at his other cheek, her fingertips curling just a little against his face.

Robbed of thought, sense, and breath, Taft exhaled roughly, closing his eyes and giving himself up to the sweetness, the tenderness, the utter magnitude of this moment. This woman he had so snidely riled against, so naively been irritated by, so blindly trapped into marriage in an attempt to be helpful, had just completely unmanned him and left him feeling encased in exquisite flame and crushed by a very great, very delightful weight that might never leave.

However was he going to get himself off of this carriage floor after that?

He opened his eyes as the touch of her lips left his skin, seeing the welling tears in her own, catching every motion of her mouth as it formed a gentle smile that dropped his stomach through the floor beneath him and saw it trampled under horse hooves.

There was nothing to do but return it, no matter how breathless and stupid it would look.

Her smile spread further, crinkling her eyes, and she sat fully back, settling her now perfectly calm hands in her lap.

Taft made a show of exhaling slowly and shaking his head. "I was afraid for a moment that you might finally strike me for all of the trouble I've caused thus far." He groaned, pushing himself up from the carriage floor and returning to his seat.

"I am saving up for a pummeling," Alexandrina told him with a calmness that made him laugh out loud.

He grinned at her and dipped his chin in a grand nod. "I look forward to it, my lady Harwood." He looked out of the window, sobering just a little at the change in scenery. "Are we arriving?"

She also looked out and nodded once. "We are. That is the dower house. I wanted to move there when the mistresses moved in, but Stephen refused."

"His mother didn't live there?" Taft asked in surprise. "The actual dowager Lady Lawson?"

Alexandrina shook her head, her smile rather flat. "She did not. Would not. So it has sat empty for quite some time."

"When Adam is older, we might ask if he'll allow us to make that our summer cottage of sorts. Heaven knows he won't need it."

"And Lady Lawson?" Alexandrina asked with a slight laugh. "Where will you have her deposited?"

Taft made a face of consideration. "I've heard Australia has its beauties."

She snorted a startled bout of laughter that had him grinning, and he felt that, now, his wife was ready to take on the one-time gorgon in her life, now stripped of all power.

And that was all he had wanted.

The coach pulled into the drive, then stopped before a door more fitted to a castle than to a country estate.

Taft looked at it, scoffing. "What, no moat?"

"That is on the other side," Alexandrina assured him, batting her lashes. "Shall we?"

He returned her look. "We? I meant what I said, Lady Harwood. This is your victory and your day. I will wait right here for you to return triumphant after slaying the dragon."

His wife speared him with a dark look. "I intend to. But surely you want to see the battle with your own eyes rather than hear the account after the fact?"

He pretended to think about it, then nodded quickly. "Yes, I do." He gestured for her to go first, then stepped out behind her, straightening his jacket as he did so. He looked at her as she adjusted her own appearance.

"Well?" she asked as she brushed at her skirts, looking up at him.

He gave her an appreciative smile. "Majestic, my dear. Utterly majestic."

The most superior smile she had ever worn in his presence crossed her lips. "I should hope so. When I am arrayed thusly, how could I be anything less?" She turned to face the house, tossing her hair just enough to bounce the curls, and strode ahead of him for it.

Taft watched her go for a moment, bemused and beaming with pride. He did not have the heart to tell her that her majesty had nothing at all to do with the gown she wore or the manner in which she was dressed.

Lifting his chin and removing himself of his smile in an attempt to match her regality, Taft followed her, his pulse pounding in anticipation of his wife's impending and long overdue battle.

The Great Hall was just as imposing and intimidating as Alexandrina had intimated, complete with suits of armor and massive portraits hung on the walls high above them, intricate windows stretching high between each one. It was impossible for one's eye to not be drawn ever upward, the cavernous space complete with murals in the ceiling and marble detailing that was a blatant display of finery more than any testament to mastery.

"And I thought Battensay was grand," Taft murmured.

"Having not seen it yet," Alexandrina told him tightly, "I will let you know how it compares later."

A middle-aged man with a rather impressive patch of balding on the very top of his head appeared from a corridor, straightening his jacket in anticipation of greeting guests, then stopped when he saw that they were already in the hall.

Perhaps a great house ought to keep the door locked if unexpected guests who had no intention of waiting for entrance were unwelcome.

No one was going to stop Alexandrina when she was on her mettle.

"Lady Lawson?" the butler asked, wide eyed and gaping, and if Taft was any judge, not entirely upset by the sight of her.

Interesting.

Alexandrina raised her chin a touch. "It's Lady Harwood now, and I am here to see Lady Lawson. No need to have us wait in the drawing room, this will not take long."

The butler's expression morphed entirely as he smiled at her. "Have you done it, then?" he queried softly. "Are you going to take the young master away? Please say yes, my lady, that child needs to be away from here."

Taft took a step forward. "Has something happened?"

"No, sir," the butler said quickly, acknowledging him for the first time. "Not one thing, certainly, but her ladyship . . . If I might speak freely, sir, her ladyship has stolen the boy's light and spirit. We've all been talking below stairs, and we've been hoping you would find a way, madam."

What Taft wouldn't give to see his wife's expression at that moment, but he stayed resolutely behind her, determined to let her shine alone in this.

"Now I have," she said simply, her tone cautious, but polite. "Will you ask Lady Lawson to come down?"

The butler bowed respectfully. "At once, madam. And my felicitations on your wedding. With your permission, I'll relay that to the others."

Taft heard Alexandrina laugh very softly before replying, "Please do."

He stepped forward. "And if anyone decides they want to be free of here as well, apply to the housekeeper at Battensay Park in Berkshire."

"Yes, sir. Thank you, sir." The butler turned to move back into the depths of the house, his bald patch glinting in the light streaming through the windows.

When he was gone, Taft leaned forward. "I hope you don't mind that. He seemed decent enough."

Alexandrina nodded once. "He is. The only absolute refusals I have on staff are Stephen's valet, Lady Lawson's maid, and a certain housemaid that waited on the mistresses. She was angling for her own day of the week and made it her daily aim to find the line of insubordination foul enough to earn reprimand."

"Does the butler know that?"

"Oh, yes. He'll know."

Taft nodded in approval. "Perfect." He put a hand on her arm, squeezing gently, reminding her that he would be there, and then stepped back several feet.

He'd have hidden himself in an alcove to give her full

independence if she had not asked him to be there. But he would give her enough separation to prove the point.

This was *her* battle. He was only present for it.

Alexandrina gave no indication that she was in any way nervous now, no wringing of fingers, no sign of trembling. The only thing he noticed at all was a slight inhale followed by a slow exhale that moved her shoulders into a lowered position. But it only served to make her more regal, more towering, and he had to hide a smile of pride as he watched her.

Clipped footsteps sounded from somewhere in the house, and Taft sobered further, clasping his hands behind him in anticipation. A woman of small stature but superior bearing came into the Great Hall then, following the same path the butler had just done, her expression clear. Her face was very faintly lined with age, though he had the sneaking suspicion that she would have resented any such implication. Golden hair streaked with silver was pulled tightly back into elaborate coils at the back of her head, and her slender form was wreathed in brocade silks seeming more suited to the previous generation of Society than the present one.

The moment she caught sight of Alexandrina, the woman's expression altered, becoming almost contorted with arrogance and loathing. "What are you doing here?"

"I am here for my son, Hester," Alexandrina announced without greeting.

Lady Lawson smiled smugly. "We have had this discussion before, Alexandrina. You know the conditions, and I do not appreciate you barging into Stonehall unannounced."

"The conditions have changed," Alexandrina snapped. "And I do not appreciate the disrespect. I am the Countess of Harwood now, and you would do well to treat me as such."

The older woman's eyes widened, and she looked Alexandrina up and down in shock. "Countess? Surely you have not married again. You had such a dreadful time coping with the first."

"Yes, my choice in husband was flawed for the first, but thankfully, not the second." She flicked two fingers towards Taft. "The Earl of Harwood, Hester. Do greet him appropriately, won't you?"

Lady Lawson followed the gesture, catching sight of Taft. "Are you truly the Earl of Harwood?"

Employing every ounce of imperiousness he possessed, Taft raised a brow. "You question it?"

She swallowed once and curtseyed the bare minimum depth for politeness. "My lord."

Taft bowed with roughly the same respect. "I believe you neglected to give that same courtesy to my wife."

Lady Lawson looked at Alexandrina with utter contempt. "I pray you will excuse me, but my knees are not what they used to be."

Alexandrina was unflappable. "A pity, as you will be going up to the nursery now and procuring my son. The earl is his guardian now. Your solicitor will have all the necessary documents."

"You cannot be serious," Lady Lawson said with a laugh. "He is the next Lord Lawson, and Stephen's heir. Thomas is his guardian, as you well know."

"Then we will discuss the matter with him," Alexandrina replied with seemingly great patience. "Will you send for him?"

Taft could have kissed his wife for the utter dignity of such a question, knowing full well that the man was not in England.

"Thomas is at his estate in Italy, Alexandrina," Lady Lawson sneered, her lip all but curling in a snarl.

Taft cleared his throat for effect.

Lady Lawson speared him with a dark look. "What?"

"I believe the correct address of a countess who has not given you express permission to be familiar is 'my lady,' madam." He indicated that she continue. "As you were."

The side of one of Lady Lawson's cheeks tucked in against her teeth, and she coolly surveyed Alexandrina again. "Thomas prefers Italy, which is why I raise the boy. You know all of this, why are you fighting against it?"

"Because legally, you were never named guardian of my son," Alexandrina informed her, straightening where she stood. "Only Mr. Thomas Drake. As he is not in the country, and has not been for some time, our application to the Court of Chancery has found that it is most preferable for Adam to have the Earl of Harwood named as his guardian instead. Given he is, in fact, Adam's stepfather. Being married to me, Adam's mother."

"Lord Lawson," the older woman ground out, "will remain here. This is the boy's estate and his inheritance. His home. He must stay and see to it."

Alexandrina laughed very softly. "And you mean to tell me that you have given him authority over Stonehall? At all of five years old? Surely you mean when he reaches his majority. Believe me, I have no intention of declaring him anything but Lord Lawson when the time comes. He is entitled to his full inheritance, and in all matters pertaining to Stonehall, we are perfectly content for Mr. Drake to continue overseeing Adam's interests. If, however, we find that either of you has gone to the extremes of misusing, squandering, or in any way diminishing what Adam has a right to, we will be encouraging him to sue you both for every penny."

"He is Lord Lawson," Lady Lawson insisted again. "He is my grandson. The boy remains here."

"Adam," Alexandrina said again, taking an ominous step forward, "comes with me. There is no battle for you to win, Hester. It is done. I suggest you write to your solicitor and ask for an explanation. And should you choose to argue the point, Lord Harwood and I will make very, very sure that Adam's entire inheritance is transferred into our care until he reaches his majority, leaving you with nothing. You will be removed from this house and dismissed from his life with only the dowry you brought to this estate, and I cannot imagine there is much of that left."

The pure ice in his wife's voice was enough to make Taft shiver, though he was entirely on her side. It was simply the air about it, the effect her power and influence had, and he was surprised that his breath did not come in clouds before him.

Lady Lawson appeared uneasy for the first time throughout the exchange, blinking owlishly at her former daughter-in-law. "Surely you would not take him from me. You would not have the boy leave his grandmother. He would miss it here." She sniffled, though Taft could see no sign of tears.

"If you had even once, in this entire exchange, called Adam by his name, I might now feel something in what you say," Alexandrina murmured, shaking her head. "But you have not. I will not allow Adam to be raised in a place where he is not loved for who he is rather than the blood that flows through him. I will not allow him to become even a shadow of his father. I will not allow you to change him from the sweet, funny, loving boy he is to some emotionless, snobbish, cruel creature better suited to your opinions. I did not have the power or authority to fight this before, but I certainly do now." She lowered her chin just a touch, now daring the woman before her to contradict her one more time. "Get my son," she demanded, emphasizing each word in turn. "Now."

The word echoed through the cavernous Great Hall, carried by each suit of armor, brushing by each and every stiff portrait looking down on them. There was no other sound, no breath of noise, rustle of skirts, or creak of floors above or around them.

Lady Lawson stared at her coldly, unmoving for a moment. Then, with a sudden flicker of her lashes, she turned on her heel and marched back into the depths of the house. "Howard! Fetch the boy and have his things packed immediately!"

Alexandrina released a shuddering breath that seemed somehow combined with a laugh and a sob. Taft was to her in a moment, hands on her arms in case she should crumple. She shook in his hold and leaned back against him. "Did that really happen?"

"Yes," he laughed softly, kissing her hair. "Masterfully done, Alix. Every inch a queen."

She took in another breath, exhaling very slowly. "That was terrifying. I'm not sure I'll believe it until I hold Adam in my arms."

"Soon enough." He rubbed her arms gently. "You heard her bellow. You've won."

"Have I?" She rested her head back against his shoulder. "Is it really over?"

It took all of Taft's strength and restraint not to wrap his arms around her and hold her close, give her the comfort he sought to, risk the chance of her having yet another reason to strike him.

The day had held too many surprises and miracles already.

"I think so, Alix," he murmured. "Breathe."

She nodded against him, and they waited, hearing faint sounds of bustling somewhere else in the house. But none of those sounds belonged to a child. No raucous cheers, no demanding questions, no tears or giggles.

A nanny started down the stairs near them, her hand clasping a dark-haired lad who kept his eyes lowered. He was dressed like a miniature gentleman rather than a boy, complete with cravat and weskit, both perfectly stiff. His shoes were shined to a reflective nature, his stockings whiter than snow, and he bore a distinct resemblance to his mother, although only in her more unpleasant moods.

Alexandrina took in a startled breath, and Taft squeezed her arms before releasing her, smiling a little as she moved to the stairs almost haltingly.

"Good day, Adam," she murmured, stooping to his level. "Do you remember me?"

He nodded without looking, releasing his nanny's hand.

"Would you like to come to a new home with me?" Alexandrina asked him, her voice hitching emotionally.

Again, the boy nodded, though this time his mouth twitched as though he would smile.

"Well, come on, then." Alexandrina held out her hand, leaving the choice and action up to him.

Without hesitation, Adam placed his hand in his mother's and started walking from the stairs towards the door. Alexandrina looked at Taft as they passed him, her smile tender, her eyes moist.

Taft nodded in approval, then followed the pair out without another word.

CHAPTER 10

"Is that it?"

The innocent question was the first that had been asked all day, the first real words that had been spoken since they had left the coaching inn, outside of instructions to the driver and the like. Alexandrina tried not to show her excitement that Adam had said anything and looked out of the window at the sight that had captured his attention.

A stirring, sprawling, stately estate with countless windows, each of which glistened in the daylight, sat nestled in the hills of green about them, dotted with groves of trees and a great lake to one side. Columns, balconies, and stairs greeted them on the face they could presently see, but she could spot more windows and bays on the face extending away from them. It was a stunning piece of architecture, and she could suddenly understand well enough why it was host to a popular house party every summer.

Who would not want to spend time in such a place?

"I believe so," Alexandrina murmured. She glanced over at Taft, who was watching the pair of them in some amusement, just as he had been from the moment they had left Stonehall. "Is that

Battensay?"

He took a quick look out of the window, then nodded, sitting back. "Yes, it is. Welcome home to you both."

She smiled at him, wishing she did not find the statement so sweet, knowing he understood just how much it would mean to her. Sitting across from them, he was more relaxed in appearance than she had seen him in a time, and there was something impossibly attractive about his manner. In his looks, too, certainly, but he was always handsome in looks. This was something a little different, and she was not immune to it.

That was a terrifying thought.

She needed to be immune to him. Her heart had been broken before, and the only way to protect it was to be impervious to such things. She could not, would not, deny that Taft had been generous and instrumental in all things where securing Adam had been concerned, and had been very good to make no demands of her in their marriage. He had taken no liberties but what she had allowed, and his insistence on her confronting Lady Lawson on her own had been empowering. Despite her fierceness in thought about the woman, about the family, about Stonehall itself, she would never have had the courage to actually present herself before the woman and be so fierce in reality.

Not only had Taft given her the power and position to do so, but he had also handed her the opportunity and bolstered her enough to face the woman who had failed her in so many ways. To reclaim her dignity. To reclaim her son.

She would be indebted to him forever for that alone, but for the rest . . .

They had the rest of their lives before them, and so much had changed already from the day they had wed. Now they were away from London, from all of his favorite parties and events, and it would just be the three of them in this great estate.

For the first time in a very great while, Alexandrina felt like she could breathe freely, and that breath felt light and easy.

She hadn't known air like this existed anymore, let alone that she was capable of breathing it.

All of that from looking at Battensay and looking at Taft.

She would need to be very, very careful, indeed.

She looked out of the window again, wrapping an arm around her son and hugging him close. The sun seemed to shine upon Battensay as well as from within it, beckoning her with the promise of hope, of light, of comfort, of safety . . .

Of home.

She'd not had a home in so long, and now . . .

"It's beautiful," she whispered, smiling at the sight of it.

Taft made some sort of soft laugh, and she slid her eyes to him, catching a smile she had never seen him wear before. Something amused and tender, gentle and affectionate, and it was not for her alone. He was taking in her embrace of Adam as well, and that kept Alexandrina's smile right where it was, directed solely at him.

He held her gaze for a long moment, then dropped his down to her son. "Do you like to fish, Adam?"

Adam looked over at him, not quite settled against Alexandrina, but not pushing her off. "I've never done it, sir."

Taft gaped playfully. "Never fished? How old are you? Twelve?"

"Five," Adam replied without laughing, though he did smile a little.

"Surely not," Taft said with a scoffing sound. "You are far too tall to be five."

Adam's smile grew by several degrees. "I *am* five. But I will be six when this month is over."

Alexandrina bit down on her lip to hear him speak so much at once when he had said almost nothing since they'd had him.

"Ah," Taft replied with a thoughtful nod. "That must be it.

Well, would you like to learn to fish?"

Adam frowned a little, his sweet brow creasing deeply, just as Stephen's had done. "Is it something that gentlemen do?"

It would have been an adorable question had it not held so many answers to the life he had led before they had secured him. What sort of childhood he'd had so far. How changed her boy was from the one she had left.

How much she would have to help him recover.

"Certainly," Taft told him without hesitation. "Many of them. I am a gentleman, and I fish."

"I am a baron," Adam said in a matter-of-fact manner. "Grandmother says I will be a great man when I am grown. What are you?"

Alexandrina winced, looking away and fighting to control her irritation. A boy of five, nearly six, should not know much of status or titles, let alone ask a man about his. He meant nothing by it, could not with his youth and ignorance, but he had been trained up to know such things, to see the world as a hierarchy that he belonged to.

"A gentleman," Taft answered, his tone matching her son's. "Same as you will be. I am not a great man myself, but I hope someday to be."

She looked at Taft curiously, wondering why he would not mention his title just as Adam had. She appreciated the distinction in their both being gentlemen, but she did not wish to have anything less than honesty with her son.

He kept his attention on Adam, who was frowning again. "I thought your name was Lord Harwood."

Taft nodded once. "It is. I am the Earl of Harwood. But I prefer to be a gentleman more than an earl. I think it is far more important."

Alexandrina felt something give way in her chest at that, and bit back a sigh of relief.

Adam still frowned and she looked at him, waiting for whatever was perturbing him to be expressed. He shook his head, exhaling heavily. "I don't remember where an earl is in the peerage. I am sorry."

"What for?" Taft inquired with a tilt of his head. "I was not going to ask you, and neither was your mother."

"Grandmother would be so upset," he admitted with a dejected sigh. "I'm supposed to know all about the peerages before I turn six, or there will be no presents."

One of Alexandrina's hands shot to her mouth, and she swallowed hard.

Of all the things to instruct him on, the peerage was the one she would cling to? And to threaten him with such punishment for not memorizing something so inconsequential to a boy his age . . .

Taft scooted forward on the coach seat, looking at Adam firmly, extending a hand to rest on Alexandria's knee. "That is no longer a requirement, Adam. You live with us now, here at Battensay. Birthdays are celebrated with presents, no matter what you have or have not memorized, and there will be cake, too. Assuming you like cake, of course. Perhaps you do not, so there will be no need for cake."

"I like cake!" Adam chimed in eagerly.

"Then we will have cake," Taft told him, offering a fond smile. "And I will tell you a secret. Are you ready?"

Adam nodded with great enthusiasm, his eyes wide.

"It does not matter where an earl is in the peerage," Taft whispered loudly. "Nor a baron. No matter what anybody says, it does not make us any better than any other person. It only means we have a lot of responsibility. Do you know what that means?"

Adam gave another nod, then shook his head instead.

Taft chuckled, his thumb brushing against Alexandrina's knee in a soothing, comfortable motion that settled her creditably. "That's all right. We'll teach you someday. But you don't need to worry about it now. You're not a grown-up yet. You're a baron, I'm an earl, and your mother is a bird."

It was said so simply, so confidently, that both Adam and Alexandrina almost missed it.

Adam burst into childish giggles that warmed Alexandrina's heart. "She is not a bird!"

"Certainly not!" she cried, rapping Taft's hand on her knee, before placing her hand upon his in a staying manner.

Taft met her eyes, still smiling impishly.

"Thank you," she mouthed with her own smile.

He winked and slid his thumb out from beneath her fingers to brush against her hand a little. He returned his attention to Adam. "She *is* a bird. A swan, I should think. An elegant, golden swan. You see how she holds her head up?"

The ridiculous conversation on her apparently aviary nature and being continued until they pulled through the arches of Battensay and into the courtyard, something she had not been able to see upon their first arrival. It was a tidy square of space, seemingly rather centrally located as far as she could tell, and an unobtrusive, but rather fine set of stairs and a door were now before them through the open carriage door.

"Adam, you first," Taft called, gesturing for him to come out and holding a hand to him.

Adam took it without hesitation, then hopped down, looking up at the walls about him. "Are all of these rooms yours, my lord?"

Taft chuckled and reached his hand back for Alexandrina. "You may call me Taft, Adam. And what in the world would I need so many rooms for? One room for spoons, one for shoes, one for cravats, and one for soap? Can you imagine a room just for pears?"

Adam giggled at the idea.

Alexandrina shook her head as she took Taft's hand, stepping out of the coach and looking up at him in amazement. "How are you doing that?"

"Doing what?" he asked as he closed the carriage door.

She gestured to her son, who was now intently studying the fountain and statue in the courtyard. "He's chattering away, and you've made him laugh. He's been travelling with us for two days, and he hasn't . . . I haven't . . ."

Taft took her arm gently. "Give him time, Alix. I was once a lonely boy without friends or family myself, so I thought I might be able to draw him out a little when the opportunity presented itself. I wasn't certain he would find me in the least amusing, so you can imagine my relief."

"Yes, finally someone to laugh at your attempts," Alexandrina said with a quick smile. "Relief, indeed."

He made a face at her but squeezed her arm in a way that made her fingers catch fire. "I want to teach him to play again. Will you let me?"

She could have sagged against him with a dreamy sigh for even suggesting it. "Yes," she whispered. "Please, do. I fear . . . I don't think I would be the one to teach him that. Other things, yes, but . . ." She shook her head, swallowing a surprising lump of emotion. "Not that."

"Hmm," Taft mused as they started towards the house. "Perhaps I ought to teach you as well." He cleared his throat before she could reply. "Come along, Adam! Time to explore Battensay!"

Adam turned at once from the fountain and joined them as they moved up the stairs towards the door, open now with a smiling butler with dark hair waiting for them.

"Welcome home, my lord," the butler greeted, bowing to him.

"Thank you, Gilbert. Alexandrina, this is Gilbert, esteemed butler of Battensay. And this little chap is her son, Adam, Lord Lawson."

Gilbert bowed to Alexandrina, then also to Adam, giving him a smile. "A pleasure, sir. Would you prefer the staff address you as

Lord Lawson or as Master Adam?"

Alexandrina almost shook her head in wonder, looking down at Adam.

He looked up at her and Taft in confusion. "Which one should it be?"

Taft shrugged and looked at her.

Alexandrina smiled down at her son. "Whichever will make you happier, Adam. Neither is wrong."

He frowned in thought, his lips twisting, then looked up at the butler again. "I would like to be Master Adam, if you please. I am not grown up yet."

The impulse to laugh rose in her throat, and Alexandrina turned her face towards Taft's arm to hide it.

"Perhaps not, Master Adam," Gilbert said as he straightened. "But you are certainly very mature for your age." He gave Alexandrina a warm smile and nodded once. "Welcome to Battensay, ma'am. If you'll follow me, I'll introduce you to Mrs. Clayton, the housekeeper. I am sure we can save the rest for another time, you must be tired from your journey."

They moved into the house after him, and Alexandrina leaned closer to Taft. "Where in the world did you find him?"

"I didn't," he admitted with a laugh. "He was here when I was born. My parents were gone so much, he became more of an uncle than a butler. Hardly the way of things, but you would never be able to get me to remove him. He could commit murder and I would hide the body."

"I'll hand you the shovel," she replied. "He's extraordinary."

Taft nudged her a little, grinning like a boy. "Welcome home, Lady Harwood."

She nudged him back, shaking her head. "You're ridiculous."

"You have no idea," he said with another laugh. He quirked his brows, then dashed on ahead of her, nodding at an approaching woman with gray curls peeking out from beneath her cap.

"Greetings, Mrs. Clayton. Hope you're well."

"Tolerably, sir, thank you," she answered without batting an eye as he passed her and tapped Adam on the shoulder.

"Come on, let's pick out a room for you," Taft suggested to Adam, nudging his head for the stairs and beginning to jog up them. "Last one up is a billy goat!"

Adam stared after him in confusion, then started to climb the stairs himself almost hesitantly, before increasing his speed as he moved out of sight.

Alexandrina blinked, then looked at the housekeeper watching her with wry amusement. "Is he always like that when he is here?"

"Oh, yes," Mrs. Clayton replied, nodding fervently as she exchanged a look with a chuckling Gilbert. "A child at heart, that one, and sometimes in spirit, too. Good heart, though, and excellent company."

"Yes, I'm beginning to notice." Alexandrina exhaled and began to remove her gloves.

"Lady Harwood, this is Mrs. Clayton, the housekeeper," Gilbert said, rather unnecessarily at this point. "She knows everything that goes on here at Battensay, and I generally come to her with my own questions."

"Oh, stop that," Mrs. Clayton scolded, gesturing as though she would rap him on the hand. "You will give her ladyship such an impression of me."

Alexandrina smiled at her. "Believe me, Mrs. Clayton, I am learning all too well that first impressions are not always correct. Now, would you be so good as to show me to my rooms? I should like to change and freshen up, and then, if you are not too busy, I would enjoy sharing a spot of tea with you."

CHAPTER 11

It was entirely possible that Adam would be a more difficult case for Taft to work on than his mother was, which he would never have guessed in a million years.

The boy was certainly more prone to play and fun than his mother, but he could not seem to let go of the reserve and decorum his grandmother had instilled in him.

Manners were all well and good, but a boy in the countryside deserved to romp and play and get into all manner of scrapes. Adam continued to ask about his lessons rather than to explore, no matter how Taft tried to convince him.

Alexandrina was not interested in arranging for tutors yet, given there was still an entire life with them at Battensay to adjust to, but if the routine of Stonehall was what he was used to, perhaps they ought to consider implementing something of a schedule for him. He would have chafed at such a thing at Adam's age, but he'd had an absent upbringing, not a restrictive one.

Going out to the village of Godfrey for the day had been his suggestion for them all at breakfast, as a way to help them get acquainted with the area as well as some of the villagers, and he had great hopes that Adam would be as fascinated by the place as Taft had been. After all, there was an ancient oak tree perfect for climbing, ruins of a long-demolished abbey to explore, and if one was fortunate enough to see it, a rather thriving market day that any active child would consider a feast for the eyes, if not also for the stomach.

If Adam was not completely enamored by the village and begging to sneak off to it in the days following, Taft would forfeit desserts for an entire year.

Which he had no intention of doing.

The only question he truly had, then, was what his wife would make of it.

He could see the concern in her eyes whenever Adam said something rather unchildlike, when he would look at something childish with disdain, when he sat in silence rather than engage in conversation or activity. It was clear the boy had been stifled in the months when his mother had been removed from his life, by the idea of a child his grandmother had wanted him to be.

To rid a child of his youth in such a way while she had indulged a son in housing his mistresses under the same roof as his wife?

Utter madness. It was fortunate they had been able to retrieve Adam when they had, hopefully before it was too late to remind him of the childhood to be had.

Taft looked at the boy now as he rode with his mother on a horse. The day was fine, so they had opted to ride rather than take the carriage, and Alexandrina had proven herself to be an excellent rider. He should have anticipated that, as she seemed to excel in everything she set her mind to. She managed beautifully with the staff at Battensay, had settled into a comfortable routine from day to day, and had already begun to make plans for redecorating a few of the rooms. He had no doubt that she would take an interest in other aspects of the estate, just as he'd offered in the past, but her focus now was Adam.

He could not blame her for that.

He was rather focused on Adam as well.

They had gone fishing yesterday, as much as was possible, and Adam had studied Taft's actions and manner the entire time. He'd made no move to take up the small rod Taft had brought for him, preferring to watch Taft and witness his success, or lack thereof. He had made minimal commentary on the process, but his eyes, so like his mother's, did not miss a single motion.

If there was a next time that Taft took his stepson out to fish at the lake, and Adam chose to be an active participant, he had no doubt that Adam would have far more success than Taft would.

Alexandrina caught him looking at them now, her expression turning quizzical.

Taft grinned in an attempt to recover himself from the awkwardness of being caught gawking. "I think you will both enjoy Godfrey very much. It is not the most popular market town in Berkshire, nor the most populated, but it is surprisingly well stocked with everything you could wish, and the people are marvelous. I've not found anyone nearly so agreeable in Reading or Wokingham, though I've heard one must meet the locals in Windsor and Slough."

"The locals at Windsor?" Alexandrina laughed a little. "Do you mean His Majesty? The Queen, perhaps?"

Taft chuckled and shrugged. "As I said, I cannot speak for myself. Godfrey is my favorite. I used to run the four miles from Battensay on the fine days in summer and spend hours spying on the different shops and stalls. Mr. Jones, the blacksmith, used to make me odd things from the scraps of his metal. I've a whole collection of them somewhere in Battensay."

Adam gave him a bewildered look. "What about your nanny, Taft? Was she not with you?"

Taft tried not to smile at the boy calling him by his given

name. It had been the bulk of Taft's emphasis for him since arriving at Battensay, and some days were better than others. "I did not have a nanny, Adam. I had a few tutors, but they were not about much in the summers. And there were no other boys my age in the area."

"That sounds lonely," Alexandrina murmured, resting her chin on Adam's head, which made Taft wonder if she was thinking of her son as well. His lack of companions, lack of loving adults before they got him, lack of freedom in his days . . .

Taft had been able to run free and do as he pleased, but Adam's life had been quite the reverse.

Not anymore, though. They would help him.

And hopefully, so would Godfrey.

"I had friends at Eton," Taft assured his wife quickly. "It was only the summers at Battensay that were so without company." He looked at Adam with a fond smile. "You've a good many years before we even think about school for you, so perhaps we might find some fine young lads in the neighborhood for you to be friends with, hmm?"

Adam did not look remotely convinced. "Grandmother said it was not good to waste one's time with those beneath our station. I don't know what that means, but she was quite certain about it."

Taft barely avoided looking at Alexandria at that comment, knowing how dismayed she would feel about it. She would feel such guilt about the influence of his grandmother's teachings and opinions, about his adherence to them through no fault of his own, about not being there to combat or offset such things. She would blame herself for this, and he could not let her.

"I don't think it is wise to waste time in anything," Taft mused aloud, bringing his horse closer to them. "Much better to be gainfully employed in one's activities, even in leisure. But station has little to do with that. Good company can be found anywhere, as can bad. We're not better than anybody else because of our station. It's a person's manners, actions, and nature that render them a certain quality."

"You mean . . . being a good person?" Adam asked with a serious expression he most certainly inherited from his mother.

"Just so," Taft replied, giving the boy a quick nod. "That does not require a high station, does it?"

Adam obediently shook his head.

"Can you think of a good person who is not of your same station?" Alexandrina pressed, glancing down at him.

"Mrs. Evans at Stonehall," Adam said at once. "She used to bring me honey cakes if Grandmother got particularly cross with me."

Alexandrina bit down on her lip hard, looking at Taft with almost pleading. "Taft? Can you think of one?"

He gave her a soft, sad smile, catching the hoarse note of emotion in her voice. "Mr. Craig, the butcher in Godfrey. At the end of each day, he gives the scraps of that day to the poor families in the area so they can have meat. I think he intentionally puts some aside, but he insists otherwise."

"That is *very* nice!" Adam exclaimed in shock, his eyes round.

Taft nearly laughed but smiled instead. "I think so." He raised his eyes to Alexandrina. "Alix? Your turn."

Alexandrina nodded to herself, swallowing. "Erm . . . Mr. Gilbert."

Adam looked up at her. "Our butler?"

It was difficult for Taft not to feel a tug in the center of his chest at hearing Adam using the word *our* to reference Battensay. He'd yet to have that opportunity, and now . . .

Well, now he was even more determined that his stepson consider the place home. And consider Taft a stepfather, and not just a man who lived in the same house.

He wanted to be the boy's father, as much as he was able. Without knowing how Adam felt about the late Lord Lawson, or what he had been told, however, it would be difficult for Taft to move too far in that direction.

Alexandrina might be able to give him insight, but it also might be best to continue his attempts to teach the boy to play.

If not teach his mother as well.

"Yes," Alexandrina was saying, apparently immune to the effect of Adam's word choice, "our butler. He was so warm to you and me when we arrived at Battensay, do you remember? And he was very good to Taft when he was a boy. Not just a butler, but a friend."

Adam's attention returned to Taft. "You were friends with your butler?"

Taft laughed once. "I still am. I love receiving his letters when I am in London. He tells me all about life at home and makes sure I don't forget them."

"I want to be friends with Gilbert, too!" Adam cried suddenly, beaming brightly. "Do you think he'll let me?"

"I think he would like that very much," Taft assured him. "After all, I am far too old to slide the bannisters now, and he will need someone else to do that."

Alexandrina's sweet smile suddenly turned to a scowl. "Taft."

He winced and leaned closer to Adam. "I'll teach you all about that when your mother isn't around."

Adam snickered a little and nodded.

It was the most promising sign of impishness Taft had seen from him yet.

Hope was not lost.

They reached the edge of Godfrey then, and Taft grinned at the sight of it. He hadn't been to Godfrey for the pleasure of it in some time, usually coming in for business or to prepare things for a gathering at Battensay. He'd forgotten how the sounds of the shopkeepers going about their business caught his attention, twisting his head back and forth across the street like a church bell. How the smells of the bakery ovens and the blacksmith's forges could combine with that of horse and damp rock into something somehow pleasant. How the neat, tidy appearance of whitewashed upper stories over sturdy brick bases of stores along Main Street made him smile with a strange inner pleasure.

It was one of his favorite places in the world, and he seemed to forget that each time he went away.

There was no market today, which he had anticipated, but there were still plenty of things to do and to see, plenty of people to greet. And there were certainly plenty of people greeting Taft now as he rode in, giving curious looks to the woman and child riding along beside him.

"Are you always so popular?" Alexandrina inquired softly when the seventh person called out to him in welcome.

Taft cast her his classic Society grin. "Always, my dear. Wherever I go."

Her normal expression of utter derision was all the reply he received.

He'd almost forgotten how things traditionally were between them, and it was rather delightful to be reminded.

"Well, where should we go first?" he asked his wife and stepson. "I've no business here today, so we are entirely at your leisure."

"Are we really?" Alexandrina looked around them with wide eyes. "I had not thought . . ." She frowned a little, twisting her lips.

"What?" he pressed, losing a little of his playful manner. "What had you not thought?"

She met his eyes without much expression to them. "I had not thought about my own interests in Godfrey. I presumed we were riding in on an errand you must do, and Adam and I would simply see what we could on the way."

"I am sorry I was not more clear," Taft apologized, pulling

his horse to a stop before swiftly dismounting. "We can leave the horses here at the mews. Then we might walk and explore as much or as little as we like."

Alexandrina nodded, gathering the reins in one hand as Taft came over, reaching up for Adam.

Adam went without hesitation, his eyes as round as anything as he glanced around them. It would not take a person of great observation to guess that the lad had never seen a town or a village and had been confined entirely to Stonehall's walls and boundaries.

Knowing the attitudes and tastes of the dowager Lady Lawson, Taft could not say he was surprised by that. The woman likely never went anywhere without ensuring she was the lowest person of station present. No one beneath her could possibly enter her presence.

That would include all common neighbors, businessmen, and animals belonging thereunto.

"There is so much to see," Adam breathed as his small feet touched the ground, one hand gripping the edge of Taft's jacket in a hint of anxiety.

Taft smiled down at him. "Indeed, there is. And we will see it all by and by." He reached up for Alexandrina, who had already begun dismounting herself, so he simply steadied her as she made her way to the ground.

She flicked a fleeting smile of thanks at him as she brushed at her skirts, one hand still gripping the reins of her horse tightly. "Right, then. The mews, you said?"

He bit back another grin at her brusqueness, which he considered to be a sure sign of her own nerves or defenses. She was a funny thing, his wife, torn between her sincerity and her dignity at any given time. He did not mind, but it was an interesting paradox that he did not feel ought to be. One could be both sincere in emotion and dignified in bearing, but for Alexandrina, it was not so.

He'd have to work on that with her.

"I've never seen a mews outside of London," Alexandrina commented as they handed the horses off to the stable hands working there. "But I've never spent much time in a country town. Is that common?"

"I have no idea," Taft replied easily. "I only know how they do things in Godfrey, and in Godfrey, we have a mews. It proves rather convenient for the market days, and, considering the ever-growing number of houses and neighborhoods springing up at the edges, it seems to serve the town well. And it is even more useful for me when I entertain at Battensay, for I always know where I might hire additional workers for the stables." He grinned at the older man presently currying a rather fine Cleveland Bay. "All right, there, Timmons?"

"Right as rain, my lord!" he called back with a wave. "Entertainin' at the big house?"

Taft glanced at Alexandrina and Adam, grinning. "Not yet. This is my wife and her son. Alix, Adam, this is Mr. Timmons, who knows everything there is to know about horses, and refuses to leave Godfrey and come work for me."

Timmons chuckled and stepped away from the horse, sweeping his hat off and bowing to them both. "Begging yer pardon, milady. Master. I'd have greeted ye proper had I known."

"A pleasure to meet you, Mr. Timmons," Alexandrina said with a smile and a nod. "And what keeps you here in Godfrey rather than taking up a position with Lord Harwood?"

"Bein' me own master, ma'am. No offense to his lordship—it would be a right pleasure to work for him—but I've taken a liking to answering only to myself."

Taft nodded in understanding. "I cannot argue with that, nor have I yet. But the offer stands, as you well know."

"I do, sir, and I'll not forget it." Timmons eyed Adam, who

stared at the Cleveland Bay with more intensity than he had the whole of Godfrey on his arrival. "Would you like to come see the horse, young master?"

Adam looked up at his mother at once. "May I?"

"Of course, if Mr. Timmons does not mind." Alexandrina gestured for him to go along, her smile soft.

The boy scampered over to the stable master and the horse, gaping up at the animal. "What do you call the horse, sir?"

Taft bit his lip on a laugh at hearing Timmons addressed as a sir, but the politeness was certainly commendable. And if he was any judge, this would be the place Adam would dash off to, if he took it into his mind to do as Taft had done and vanish to Godfrey on a whim.

"Chestnut is his name," Timmons told him, evidently tickled by Adam's manners. "He's just arrived after a journey from Plymouth with his master. So we give him something good to eat and then give him a good, honest rubdown. Like so." He began currying again, brushing the animal with long, even strokes.

The horse exhaled and shook himself against the action, his coat rippling beneath the attentions.

"He likes that!" Adam said with a laugh, turning to look back at Taft and Alexandrina.

Taft leaned closer to his wife. "Did you know he loved horses?"

Alexandrina shook her head, fingertips at her mouth, barely hiding the smile there. "No. I did not know he loved anything at all. This is the most alive I've seen him since he's been with us."

"Remind me to get him a horse for his birthday," Taft murmured, grinning as Adam took a turn with the curry comb.

"He does not need one. He will only be six."

Taft nodded his head towards Adam. "Look at that smile and tell me again he does not need one."

Alexandrina hesitated, then sighed in resignation. "Yes, all right. Will you teach him to ride?"

"As soon as you like. I'll introduce him to Mr. Lyle at our stables and give him full permission to go there as he pleases. Lyle has four sons; he knows how to manage children under the setting." He gave her a sidelong look. "Would you mind if he does chores there? If I know Adam, and I think I'm starting to, he'll want to know everything."

"As long as he stays out of trouble and danger, I don't mind at all." Alexandrina shook her head again, laughing very softly. "That's my little boy. I was worried he was gone for good. I would not love him less for it, but I'm so grateful he still exists in there."

Taft slipped an arm around her and pulled her in for a quick kiss to her head, which meant very little, considering the bonnet he wound up kissing instead of her hair, but the thought was there. And she did not shove him off, so perhaps he might continue such familiarities when there was no obstruction to her hair.

Why he wanted to engage in familiarity with his wife was a little less clear, but he would go with the impulse.

Impulses rarely led him astray. Anymore.

After a few more minutes of Adam chatting away with Timmons, and even with Chestnut himself, Taft cleared his throat. "Adam, we must go, or the baker will have no cake to spare."

Adam turned to him with wide eyes. "We are getting cake?"

"We are?" Alexandrina asked in a low voice beside him.

"If it will get us moving, we'll get four," Taft muttered. He nodded to Adam. "Only if there are any left!"

Adam looked up at Mr. Timmons, who laughed. "Best go off, then, young master. One should never pass up the chance at cake."

As though he had been instructed, Adam nodded and darted over to them, taking his mother's hand without prompting.

That alone was worth some cake.

Taft nodded at Mr. Timmons, who tipped his cap at the group with a smile before returning to his work. They turned away from the mews and back out to Main Street, moving in the direction of the bakery.

It seemed that a few minutes with the horse had unlocked Adam's tongue, for every three steps or so brought about a question about this sight or that person, this scent or that observation, and it was all Taft could do to answer each in turn. Alexandrina had fewer questions, but she looked around them with just as much interest as her son. Her attention was more drawn to the bookshop, the confectionery, and the perfumer, the latter of which almost startled Taft, though he did his best not to show it.

He would be remembering that one and paying far more attention to her choice of scent from day to day. He was not above purchasing gifts if it would gain him favor in the eyes of his wife, and the closer he could get to her tastes, the more favor he was likely to receive.

Knowing how likely he was to irk her about something or other, it would be in his best interest to have such knowledge on hand to make up for his ways.

They finally reached the bakery, and as he'd hoped, Adam was enchanted with the place. One would think the boy had not eaten in months with how he bobbed from place to place, rocking on his heels and toes as he took in every aspect.

"Does our cook not take offense when you bring home wares baked by other hands?" Alexandrina asked as Mr. Hobbs, the baker, prepared their order.

Taft shook his head. "No, I think she rather likes that I don't plague her with my whims constantly. Besides, even she comes to get a rye loaf from Hobbs here, isn't that right, Mr. Hobbs?"

Hobbs laughed his deep belly laugh. "I'll ne'er admit to anyone what Mrs. Wilhite does or does not procure from my shop, milord. I know good an' well how that would go down with the town gossip." He turned with the box of cake, handing it to

Alexandrina with a smile. "For you, milady, I have also included a sample of this week's special tarts. Don't let his lordship have any, they are not for him."

Alexandrina grinned rather impishly. "I thank you, Mr. Hobbs. One must be very clear with his lordship on such matters."

"Don't I know it, ma'am." He looked over at Adam, currently prodding a massive bag of grain in the corner. "And would you like a soft honey roll for your morning, young master? Fresh from the oven, and I must have someone tell me if they are good enough to sell."

"Yes, please!" Adam cheered as he ran over to them. He reached up for the proffered roll and promptly took a bite, his eyes widening as he chewed.

Hobbs chuckled. "Good, then?"

"Yes, sir!" Adam told him around the bite. "The best roll I've ever had!"

They all laughed at that, Hobbs nodding his thanks. "Then I shall send a dozen or so up to Mrs. Wilhite at Battensay for you later, young master. Many thanks for your help."

"I'll help whenever you like," Adam chirped, taking another bite.

"Heaven help us," Alexandrina said, putting a hand on his shoulder and squeezing a little.

Hobbs smiled at her. "He's a pleasant lad, milady. Most impressive."

Alexandrina's cheeks colored slightly. "Thank you, Mr. Hobbs."

"And when might we expect your house party, my lord?" Hobbs asked Taft, turning only slightly more serious. "It is about that time, yes?"

Oh, devil take it. He'd almost forgotten about his summer house party, and there would be more comment about its absence than any scandal he might or might not have been involved in.

"Yes," Taft said slowly, more concerned about the reaction from the woman behind him than anything else in the recent days. "Soon. I'll send a notice out to all, as per usual. Her ladyship and I were just considering dates."

"Were we?" Alexandrina murmured for him alone. "How curious."

This was going to be deuced awkward.

"Good day, Hobbs," Taft said quickly, tapping his hat and taking his wife's arm to steer her from the store. "Thank you for your kindness."

Hobbs waved at them, winked at Adam, and went back to his work, likely laughing at Taft's impending doom.

Out in the open air once more, Taft released Alexandrina's arm, starting to whistle in the hopes she would not pursue the subject.

"The house party," she said flatly, dashing those hopes at once. "Still intent on continuing the tradition, I take it? Even now?"

"It *is* a long-standing tradition," he replied with a quick nod. "Very popular. It's been the making of many matches and the improvement of many reputations."

Alexandrina scoffed softly. "How fortunate for you. When is it?"

Taft winced. "I never tell more than a fortnight in advance. It varies from year to year, and only a select group are invited. They come if they can and refuse if they must."

"Refuse," Alexandrina repeated. "At their reputation's peril?"

"Usually. One would never dare refuse." He grimaced and pinched at the bridge of his nose. "I rather liked the recklessness of it all and acting on a whim."

"Of course, you did," his wife quipped, her strides becoming more clipped in their swiftness. "You enjoy flouting your incomprehensible popularity and controlling what you can, knowing how people leap when you ask them to."

He frowned at the jab. "That's hardly fair."

She turned on her heel and faced him, causing him to rear back in surprise. "Nor is asking me to play hostess to the madness when we have just arrived, and with my son in tow as well. I take it there is no cancelling it this year?"

Exhaling slowly, Taft shook his head. "Not unless you wish for more gossip and rumor. If we are to maintain that we are nothing remarkable or scandalous in a couple, it must go on, as it always has done. I can limit the numbers. You can have final approval of the guest list. We don't have to invite anyone that you do not like."

"Then it will be a party of one," she snapped.

He tilted his head at her. "Two, I should think."

Her brows knitted together in a dark glare. "Would you?"

He held up his hands in surrender, then gestured to Adam, who was playing a sort of skipping game with the wooden planks covering a shallow hole in the ground. "Adam and yourself."

She looked at her son, then sighed, her shoulders drooping. "Yes. Yes, I'd have him there." She turned to face Taft, looking less murderous now. "Would any of your guests have children they could bring? As much as I dislike people in general, he needs to associate with other children."

Taft considered that, his first instinct being to reply that no one would want children at his house party, but his second being much wiser and restraining the first. "I think I know a few. We would need to get creative with the schedule, but there is certainly room for that. There's even a second nursery, so why not?"

"I will plan the activities for the children and families," Alexandrina told him, turning and beginning to walk once more. "Those who wish to engage in activities separately will have alternatives you can provide. It will be more work for Mrs. Wilhite, not to mention Gilbert and Mrs. Clayton, but . . ."

"They are all up to the task," Taft assured her quickly. "Some years, the party has been quite large and rather extensive."

She gave him another dark look. "Why does that not surprise me?" She shook her head, rolling her eyes, and sputtered an irritated exhale. "I hate gossip and scandal. Why can we not just quietly mind our own business?"

"Not all gossip is bad," Taft ventured, though it would have undoubtedly been better not to. "What if it is being said that we are marvelously happy and living better than anyone's expectations?"

"Then we would have to live up to that for appearances," she retorted without humor or energy. "Appearances and lies, just as in everything else."

He took her arm gently, pulling her to a stop and giving her a thorough look. "Alix, I am not suggesting we pretend anything, nor would I ever suggest that we lie. Yes, our marriage occurred due to one, but that cannot be helped now. Have I lied or been false to you from the moment that agreement was arranged?"

Her fair eyes searched his, then she shook her head. "No. You might plague me, but you have never been false."

"Thank you. And I would not ask you to pretend you adore me, for heaven's sake." He tried for a smile, hoping to provoke one of her own. "No one is that skilled an actress."

"So long as you recognize that," she muttered, not quite smiling, but hardly frowning either.

"Oh, believe me, I am well aware that I am a nuisance." He patted her arms and moved past her. "Adam! Pull that plank off there. I want to show you something."

Adam did so, looking at Taft curiously.

Taft pulled another off, widening the gap between planks and revealing the puddle that had filled the hole. "Think I can skip the planks without touching the puddle?"

"Oh, good heavens," he heard Alexandrina grumble behind

him.

"No," Adam insisted, beginning to smile. "I don't think so."

Taft quirked his brows. "Watch." He moved to the edge of the planks, stepping on the first with one foot and balancing carefully. Then he hopped to the next cleanly, followed by the next, and the last without a wobble. "Ha!" He turned from the other side and gave his stepson a triumphant smile. "What do you say to that?"

Adam gaped in delight. "You did not even stumble!"

"Nor would I!" Taft crowed. "Your turn." He glanced over at Alexandrina, who was shaking her head.

A woman was approaching, eying Taft and Adam with a curious smile.

Alexandrina saw her and smiled herself, though hers was pitying. "His lordship is not well," she said by way of explanation.

The woman nodded in understanding and continued on her way.

Taft barked a laugh and watched as Adam skillfully managed the planks, alternating his feet rather than use the same as Taft had done. "Well done," he praised, clapping the boy on the shoulder. "We'd best be off home now, or your mother will kill me."

Adam snickered and nodded, moving in the direction of the mews as though he had done so a thousand times.

Alexandrina shook her head at Taft as she approached. "Are you all of seven years old?"

"Hardly. I was not that coordinated at seven."

"You looked ridiculous."

He grinned down at her, entirely unashamed. "My dear Alix, that was precisely the point."

Her expression told him she was not remotely convinced, but he would accept that.

After all, Rome was not built in a day, and nor were his wife's defenses to be breached in one.

Time would be his ally. Time and exposure. And life, if she managed not to kill him.

CHAPTER 12

Killing her husband was beginning to sound like a very good idea to Alexandrina. She had been a widow once before, and she was not so far removed from it that she would mind it again. Mourning would be no sacrifice, as she never wanted to go anywhere as it was, and black suited her coloring well enough. She'd need to see how he'd settled the will and inheritance first, as the surprise in Stephen's had been rather unpleasant, but Taft was not Stephen, so it might be easy enough.

After the house party, of course.

There would be no need for a further scandal when they were still trying to smooth over the first one.

She should not have been surprised, she supposed. Marrying Taft would include marrying the life he led, and he lived a life of social engagement and events. It would only follow that that life would also extend beyond the borders of London.

It would have been nicer if she did not have to deal with it so soon, but their marriage had not exactly come about by convenience in timing, nor in selection. Why should it lead to any kind of convenience in life?

They'd already sent out the invitations to the select few that they agreed on as far as guests went, and a few that Alexandrina did not agree on, but Taft assured her were critical to the success of the event. Whether that success was related to his own popularity or that of abating the gossip and scandal of their marriage, she did not know and he did not say.

It was entirely possible that they were one and the same.

She didn't like it, but that was the truth of it. She had married a very popular, very influential man. The darling of Almack's. The center of any given space.

And she was . . . Well, she was nobody's darling. The corner of any given space, if not completely separate from that space. And she was not popular, had no influence, and would have had difficulty in getting anyone apart from her extended relations to attend any party or event she was hosting.

Even then, a few would have sent their regrets.

You could be less unlikable.

Taft's comment from just after their time in the gardens came back to her now, clenching her throat and stomach in one. She had been likable once. Not popular, but at least pleasant and friendly. She'd had the hopes and dreams of every other girl in Society for herself and participated in all of the trimmings and trappings just as much as the rest.

That girl had vanished some years ago, and Alexandrina as she was now had no desire whatsoever to do anything remotely social or engaging. She wanted to live her quiet life without interference from others, and without the opinions of anyone else.

More than that, she was actually quite nervous.

She did not want to be unlikable, she only wanted to be free of artifice. And in being so, she had lost any sort of restraint in her speech or moderation in her opinions. Which had made her unlikable.

She did not want to be known as the pleasant Earl of

Harwood's unlikable countess.

She did not want to be a commentary when his name was discussed.

She did not want to be the reason his popularity waxed or waned.

The more she thought on it, the more nervous she became. The more her chest tightened. The more her palms sweat. The more she wanted to cry.

She wouldn't, but she wanted to.

She would be stronger than her fear. She would.

"Whatever you are trying to convince yourself of, I am sorry."

Alexandrina turned in her chair, blinking at the sight of her husband leaning against the doorway of the drawing room. "What? Why are you sorry?"

Taft smiled crookedly, though there was a softness to it that caught at something in her chest. "Because it's probably my fault. I know you well enough by now to know that you rarely, if ever, have to convince yourself of anything on your own accord. I mean, you married me because I said something ill-advised in my attempts to be heroic." He grimaced in some apology, somehow managing to smile while doing so.

She smiled back, just a little. "That is true."

"So will you tell me what I have done now that requires such concentration and conviction?" he pressed, looking perfectly at ease in the casual pose, somehow emphasizing his athletic frame and his pristine attire at once, the respected country earl as well as Society's pet.

Everything and nothing in one bewildering man. And yet, even the nothing was intriguing.

Nothing in the world confounded her more than him.

"Alix," Taft said softly when she didn't immediately respond.

She swallowed, meeting his eyes. "It's the house party," she told him in a small voice.

His brow furrowed with concern. "It is that unpleasant of a prospect for you?"

The question wasn't a demanding one—he actually asked it with unusual sensitivity and understanding—but she managed to flinch as though he had mocked her with it.

Just as Stephen had always done with his demands.

"Damn . . ."

Alexandrina forced herself to face him again, her cheeks flaming in mortification.

His eyes were wide, and his posture was no longer casual. He was at complete attention, fingers rubbing against each other at his sides. He seemed completely at odds and uncertain, but there was no mistaking his horror.

"What?" she whispered, wishing she could shout it at him like the tower of calm and strength so many took her for.

He shook his head and started into the room. "I am trying my best not to take you into my arms and soothe whatever hell that blackguard put you through. No one should flinch like that when their husband asks a simple question. Alix . . . You do know that I would never strike you, don't you? Or belittle you? Or . . . whatever made you do that . . ."

Alexandrina released a very slow breath. "I don't know anything anymore," she managed, swallowing hard. "People say all sorts of things and do differently. But I believe you are a better man than he ever was. I do not fear for my son with you, and I do not have to protect myself so vehemently against you. Will that suffice?"

"No," Taft told her, his voice dipping even lower. He closed the distance between them and took her hand, looking down at her fingers. "But it will have to do until you are capable of believing more."

"And you are content with that?" she demanded, more bite entering her tone than she had meant.

He did not rise to the unintentional baiting, and simply nodded. "How can I not be? You require it, therefore I am content to wait. I know you don't mean to slight me with your doubts, and I firmly believe you will come to like me a little with time."

She couldn't help the giggle that escaped then, and he grinned briefly at hearing it.

"Take the time you need, Alix," he insisted. "I am not going anywhere, and neither is my respect."

Alexandrina curled her fingers around his hand, gripping a little. "Thank you, Taft."

He nodded again, his smile slight and crooked once more. "Will you tell me why you dread the house party so much?"

"I do not like Society," she said without venom. "It is really as simple as that. I do not enjoy associating with those in Society, and I do not enjoy partaking in their events."

That seemed to confuse him. "At all?"

She would have laughed had it been in any way amusing. "Why should I partake in Society? People as a whole aren't worth associating with if all they do is gossip, spread lies, and judge a situation they know nothing about."

He released her hand long enough to pull a chair over and face her. "That has been your experience?"

"Not entirely, no," she admitted with a light shrug. "That is simply all I have known since the day I married Stephen. From him, from his associates, and then, after his death, from everyone else. Suspicion and rumor, condescension and superiority, as though I am the reason my husband is dead. As though I was the one to betray the vows of our marriage when it was, to these same people, perfectly acceptable that he did. Repeatedly."

She scoffed to herself, shaking her head as the bitter taste of the memories came back to her. "I can tell you precisely what was whispered behind fans at balls, describe with exactness every disparaging look a stranger has bestowed on me, and can even relate what has been said about my son from the day of his birth. Good Christian people who claim to follow the sermons preached every Sunday but have no charity in their hearts for me. As if I have committed the greater sin than any of my husband's simply by existing in their world."

She met Taft's eyes squarely, feeling the fire of indignation in her chest. "Why should I want to be part of them? What could they possibly offer me beyond the agonies I have already known at their hands? Nothing could be better than the bliss of the ignorance I have given myself where they are concerned."

Taft looked as though he had been struck across the head with a broom, his mouth working absently as he reached out for her hand again. "Alix, I had no idea."

Alexandrina took pity on his ignorance and placed her hand in his, squeezing tightly. "Why would you? You are the adored of all. No flaws at all despite being so very flawed."

His brow furrowed as he gave her a slight nod. "Thank you, I think . . ."

"We're all flawed, Taft," she told him, softening the entire exchange by managing a smile herself. "That is what people and Society tend to forget. No one is perfect. But some of us are doing the best we can."

He nodded, covering their hands with his other one and rubbing gently. "You have risen above it, you know. You really have."

Now she snorted indelicately. "Avoidance is not rising. It is a retreat for the sake of self-preservation."

"Retreat is not a crime."

"Nor is it especially brave."

"I don't care," he retorted, seeming a little frustrated, even playfully, that she would not accept his intended compliment.

She gave him a disparaging look. "You've never done it."

"You don't know that."

Nothing else he could have said would have surprised her more. She gaped at him openly, all sensation in her body seeming to still apart from the feeling of her hand encased in his. And even that was having trouble discerning hot from cold.

"Tell me," she pleaded softly, wondering if it were at all possible for them to be alike in some way.

Taft hummed a half laugh, now absently rubbing her hand between his. "My parents were just as involved in Society as I am now. Perhaps more so, I'll never be quite certain. They loved me, and were wonderful people, but I could never compete with the draw of London, or any good house party. I think I must have been lonely at times, been forced to come up with creative means of entertaining myself, and the like. I don't recall very much."

There was a note in his voice that he tried to hide, but Alexandrina caught it. A sad, wistful edge that spoke of something deeper, a forgotten ache that belonged to a solitary boy left alone in a great house.

It was something she prayed she might spare Adam from recollecting in his adulthood.

"I learned very quickly," Taft went on, sharing a smile that did not quite reach his eyes, "that the best way to connect with them would be to become like them. That did not mean much while I was young, when I was left with the staff at Battensay, and it did not mean a great deal more when I was at Eton, though I had observed my father closely enough to know how to gather a great many friends."

"I can imagine," Alexandrina murmured, reluctantly smiling at the image of a young Taft collecting his first followers.

"It was astonishing how interested my parents became in what I did when I had gained that popularity." He shook his head, chuckling at the memory. "And when that continued on to

Cambridge, they would boast to their friends about me. Prepared the foundation for my entrance to Society, I suppose. I went to London more than Battensay, at their request, so that I might attend their parties. And such was their pleasure in it, and in my joining them, that I enjoyed it as well. It became an addiction, in a way. Being in that environment, garnering such attention and respect, cultivating such a reputation. It was heady, indeed."

It was an enlightening speech he was giving, and certainly heartfelt, but where exactly he found the retreat she had expressed had yet to be made clear. She would give him a chance, however, just as he had done for her.

Taft had trailed off, now staring off at nothing. What, exactly, had sent him there, she could not say.

A single word he had uttered caught her attention in retrospect. "Was?" she prodded.

His eyes raised to hers. "Was. Is, in the moment. Was, in the quiet afterwards. It also did not take me long to realize that what I lacked in all of this was substance. My parents had found this pleasure in Society together, after building a life and living however they did before I arrived, but I had reached for it to connect with them. Not for my own enjoyment. And despite everything, even my fond memories of events with them, connection is what I lacked after all. I retreat, Alix, into the Society pet because it is what I have trained myself to do. To be. That was how I could avoid being the lonely child roaming the halls of Battensay and wondering when the next letter from his parents would come, knowing good and well they themselves would not come until a birthday, Christmas, or Battensay party."

And there it was. The truth of Taft Debenham, Earl of Harwood. The heart of him. He remembered more from his lonely childhood than he had admitted, and his entire character and being opened up before Alexandrina like a blossom in the hedgerow. His desire for connection, his embracing of company, his skill at navigating events and the guests therein, his understanding of the ebbs and flows of the Societal tide . . . and yet also being the man who could skip planks with Adam, could give Alexandrina her moment of triumph she hadn't known she'd needed, could view a butler as an uncle and a stable master as a friend.

There was a kinship between herself and her husband that she had not seen, could not have known. She had hidden from Society to save herself pain, and he had thrust himself into Society for the selfsame reason.

What a tragic pair they could have been.

"Was that why you started the summer house parties here?" she asked him, fighting the wave of emotion rising within her, still determined to appear unmoved where she could with him.

He nodded, his expression almost as raw as his confession. "It had been their tradition to host a party at their whim here. I simply arranged for it to be in the summer when I inherited. I have all of these people who are anxious to be invited, would pay me a fortune, have offered me their eligible daughters to come . . . and I have no idea if any of them would still claim friendship if I lost everything I had. Larkin Roth would, and your family would, but beyond that . . ."

"I would."

She hadn't meant to say anything at all, but neither could she wish the words back. It was a true statement, after all, though she would not necessarily have said before this conversation that she was actually friends with her husband. Partners, in a way, and allies, certainly, but friends?

Until this moment, she had not known she could place him in that category.

But she could. And she would.

He searched her eyes for a long moment. "If I did not know how you value honesty, I would say I doubt that."

"Thank you for respecting my integrity enough not to."

Alexandrina smiled, feeling lighter now than she had in some time. "Taft, you have a gift with people. Something I will never have and will always envy. They are drawn to you, not just because of your title or your money, but because of your nature. Your openness. And yes, even your charm."

"You think I'm charming?" he asked with a teasing grin, his playfulness returning to his eyes.

"A doorknob would find you charming," she retorted. "That does not mean you are not also a source of great annoyance."

He chuckled softly. "Fair enough."

Alexandrina wet her lips, facing him a little more fully. "Taft . . . there is a reason why you are as popular as you are. Perhaps you do retreat into that figure out of habit, but it is not all pretend. What I saw as a superficial character at best goes far deeper than that, and holds more sincerity than a great many people I have encountered. The more I get to know you, the less grating that man in the past becomes. You truly care about the experience others have, whether at your own gathering or anyone else's. Why else would you ruffle your own appearance and stride into a garden to save a spiteful cat from rumors?"

"I don't recall a cat in the garden," he murmured, his thumb finding a tender, almost ticklish spot on the side of her hand that seemed connected to the pit of her stomach. It caught her breath, and he paused, lingering there and pressing a little, clenching her stomach. "Just you."

Her breath rushed out of her in a not-quite-silent gust, and the impulse to kiss him rose in her mind. She swallowed, fighting it back even as her face seemed to burst into flame. "I am not likable," she whispered, wondering how she had let herself be led into this moment, these sensations, this utter listlessness that was somehow also an intense, tingling awareness of every part of her body and mind.

Taft rumbled a very soft laugh that she felt deep in her chest.

"Not true. You are incredibly likable. All one has to do is put forth the effort, and liking you is all the more rewarding for it."

Oh, heavens, would he not kiss her now? She was completely at sea, and a heated sea at that.

He knew it, too. His smile altered, becoming full of fire and awe, barely there and yet encompassing all. His eyes were dark, almost lacking in any color, scorching the depths of her in a way she had never experienced before. Nothing had ever felt like this, and no power had pulled her so temptingly.

A new tension lit the hand he held, drawing her closer, and she went, following the pressure without any inkling of resistance. Her heart pounded in her ears and through her lungs, each breath seeming tight as it attempted to escape from her. Her knees brushed his, screeching fire to each toe in a rippling turn.

"Alix," Taft breathed, almost as a question, almost as a sigh, inquiring and pleading and declaring in one hushed word.

Yes, she echoed without words as her nose brushed his, her eyes fluttering at the contact. *Yes, please!*

"Erm, pardon me, my lord, my lady," Gilbert's voice interrupted with a faint throat clearing. "The groundskeeper's additional staff have arrived, and Mr. Myers wishes to confer with you both before they get to work. With the guests arriving tomorrow, I thought it best . . ."

"Yes, quite right," Taft said on a rough groan, running his mouth along the bridge of Alexandrina's nose and brushing her brow quickly. "Dammit." He pulled back abruptly, shaking his head rather like a dog doused with water, something guttural ripping from his throat as he did so.

Alexandrina felt an echo of the same irritation, reluctance, and determination to regain sanity run down the length of her spine in a cold shiver. She removed her hand from his, shaking it a little to try and rid the imprint of his hold from it. She swallowed twice and pushed to her feet, lifting her chin in the most dignified way she could.

"Right," she said briskly, the lingering tremors of a most peculiar interlude ricocheting down the back of her legs. "Grounds. Taft?"

"Ready when you are, my lady. We must have smooth grounds for the hunt."

She flicked a look at him in some annoyance, mostly pretended. "The hunt? Surely, you mean we must have a bowling green."

"Games, Alix?" He snorted softly, shaking his head. "Children's entertainment."

"Then it is a good thing I intend it *for* the children's entertainment, you maddening donkey."

"Hee-haw, my lady, and may your evening toast be charcoal."

She hid a smile as they proceeded out to meet the groundskeeper and his staff, the easy bickering with her husband as comfortable now as the feeling of home. Now that she knew what simmered beneath his surface, and her own, there was a new edge to everything.

An edge upon which she would lightly begin to tread.

CHAPTER 13

A good party must include three crucial elements. One, a grand setting wherein merriment and entertainment can take place. Secondly, guests to fill such a place, and ones who will appreciate the effort of the host appropriately. And third, amusements to fill the time of the guests in the setting to prevent boredom, monotony, and independence of thought.

One would never wish for a guest to have a better idea than what the host had planned.

Taft had yet to suffer from such a travesty, but this could very well be the year that it happened. Not due to his lack of planning or an alteration in his extensive creativity, but simply because his mind had other things to occupy itself.

His wife.

He had been flaming from head to toe for three days, completely confounded and scraping the sides of the proverbial barrel for some semblance of whoever he usually was for these sorts of affairs. Thankfully, his guests had not seemed to be aware of the shift in his state, nor had any comments been made about his wit being in any way delayed.

But gads, he felt like an ox in a sink pit if she was within ten feet of him.

Across the room, he was safe enough, though his attention wandered to her more often than not. If she was on his arm, he could manage politeness, but not much further. They'd had a ball the first night, and had danced together, but it had been a country dance, so there had not been much time for dwelling on the turn of her throat or the touch of her hands, though he'd had difficulty sleeping as he recalled the perfect fit of her gown, the fortunate placement of jewels in her hair, and the exact curve of her smile when he'd said something perfectly amusing over dinner.

He had always known his wife was attractive, but in the days since marrying her, she had grown more and more beautiful, nearing the point of being unable to look upon her without fear and trembling. Appreciation, naturally, but there was a sense of impending doom, as though she might strike him down and damn him to some ghastly eternal end without her.

It was a dreadful state to be in, and he had never been more uncomfortable in his life.

Which was why he had taken Larkin Roth aside this morning before the activities were well under way and made sure there was plenty of port in the study for them both.

"It is not like you to panic," Larkin mused from the seat he had taken up near the window while Taft paced before the shelves of books. "I'm rather enjoying this."

"I am *not* panicking," Taft snapped, barely glancing at him.

"Pacing usually means panicking," Larkin said with a smile. "Or analyzing. As you rarely do either, this is a delight. If you're simply going to wear a path in the rug, I'll help myself to the port."

Taft nodded and resumed his pacing, twisting his lips as he considered the words he could use to describe anything he was feeling or experiencing. He still had distinct memories of Larkin being driven mad by Sophia in their early days, but their mutual attraction had been painfully obvious to Taft, and likely to anyone else with eyes. Their blindness and resistance had seemed ridiculous to him, their sparring an amusing form of courtship.

Now he was a married man whose wife was constantly in his thoughts and his bantering with her was starting to mean more than several sincere conversations he'd had over the course of his life. He was wildly attracted to her, and there was no possibility of mistaking that, but there were still so many unanswered questions, so many walls she had that, while not constantly built up, seemed to appear at a moment's notice. Every step forward brought at least one and a half steps of retreat, though the steps forward seemed to bring them closer and closer together.

It was that closeness that drove him to this distraction. A whisper of possibilities that constantly lured him into the unknown. A promise he had never made yet dearly wished to.

Alexandrina was now his most particular siren, and he was without defenses against her.

"Interesting conversation you're having with yourself?" Larkin inquired mildly, laughter in his voice. "One of you is putting up a fair argument, I can tell."

Taft stopped in his tracks and glared at his friend. "You have no compassion."

"For you? Of course not, I am quite certain you have earned it." Larkin propped his feet up on the nearby ottoman, crossing his ankles and nursing a glass of port. "Care to share? Or did you just need a witness to your complete self-mastery?"

"I can't think," Taft muttered, rubbing a hand through his hair.

"This is not surprising, I've long doubted you ever could."

Taft ignored the lying impudence. "Alexandrina," he said by way of explanation.

Larkin's eyes widened. "Oh . . ." he said slowly. "Yes, I see. Reached that point, have you?"

There was nothing to do but nod. "I have kissed her once. One time, and that was for show back in London. No doubt you heard about it."

"Saw the end of it, as it happens," Larkin replied, his tone no longer amused.

"I can't think of anything else," Taft ground out, his hands becoming fists at his sides. "Every bleeding second. At this rate, it will be a damned miracle if I don't pluck her up and kiss her senseless in the middle of luncheon because she smiles at me."

Larkin barked a wry laugh. "That would make for some interesting gossip, if the pair of you are angling to return to the prime topic of conversations."

Taft groaned at the very idea and turned away. "No, that is *not* what I want. What we want. Something else needs to happen, something more shocking so that we fade into the background. Alix doesn't want the attention, and I don't want that for her."

"Very considerate of you, but until this house party is over and nothing shocking happens, you cannot expect to fade in any way, let alone into the background." Larkin slid his feet from the ottoman, setting them firmly on the floor. "If you are wishing to be unremarkable and ordinary as far as couples go, you have to be the most boring version of yourself that you have ever been. She will need to be a touch more lively than her usual public persona, but hardly warm. Perhaps gracious is the word she would need."

"Makes sense," Taft murmured with a nod, coming to the chair opposite Larkin and sitting. "Not quite colorless, but avoiding vibrancy." He ran his hands over his face, thinking quickly. "But at the same time, we cannot have it be said that this party is in any way lacking. Have you heard anything yet?"

Larkin gave him a bemused look. "You think your other guests are going to confide in me about their feelings? Taft, you had to handle everything at the house party we held at Rosennor because Sophia and I were clueless."

"What do you mean 'were'?" Taft grumbled. "You still are clueless."

"And you are asking me for advice."

"Not really, simply confiding."

"At any rate," Larkin went on, rolling his eyes, "most of the chatter I have heard relating to you and your wife at all seems to be more about Jenkins."

That was not what Taft had expected, and his thoughts came to a screeching halt. "Jenkins?" he repeated in shock. "Why?"

Larkin grimaced and glanced out of the window. "I hadn't meant to mention it. I don't think it signifies."

"If he is being talked about in relation to me or my wife," Taft told him firmly, "it damn well does signify. What is he doing?"

"Complaining, mostly." Larking exhaled roughly, looking back at Taft. "Sophia and I returned to Rosennor when you left London, so I have not seen or heard any of this myself, you understand."

Taft gave his friend a look, gesturing impatiently. "I promise not to hold you in any way responsible for the gossip you now relate, all right?"

His friend simply waved a hand as though to mimic him. "Jenkins is tired of hearing about his part in the garden, tired of the blot against his character, and further tired of hearing how he was challenged to a duel and did nothing about it. He insists that none of it is true, that he would never treat a woman the way he is being accused of, and that he cannot recall anything of the sort. But the gossip continues."

"Well, he *did* attempt to take advantage of Alix," Taft muttered darkly. "Thankfully, she has a steadiness of mind and strength of character that is unmatched, freed herself, and took the situation neatly in hand. I don't care about the duel, unless he continues to make noise about my wife. It was simply intended to aid the story I spun."

"I know that, and you know that," Larkin said, "but it does nothing for him. And with you not being in London to add to the story or make amends, he can continue to be outraged without being silenced. If people continue to spurn him, he could make trouble."

Taft nodded, feeling rather sour about the whole thing. "We tried to stay long enough to arrange matters for Alix and Adam, and to prove it was not a whim, so that we might leave without comment. She thought, and I did as well, that being in London much longer would put strain on us both. We wanted to get her son and get to Battensay, and I cannot apologize for it."

Larkin gave him a knowing look. "I am not criticizing you, for pity's sake. In fact, I think Adam is a lad well worth any effort you had to exert. He's terribly good with Adrian, and I think Sophia might try to make a match with him and any future daughter we have."

The very idea was enough to make Taft laugh and raise his spirits creditably. "She'll have to be as pretty as her mother, but I'll mention it to Alix."

"Speaking of your wife," Larkin said, smiling a little more, "she seems different. Less preoccupied with her own thoughts, less distant from those around her, a trifle more color in her eyes . . . I would not call her warm or lively, but she is certainly more amiable than one has seen her in the past. It's rather perfect for the mistress of Battensay."

"Yes, she is taking the role on rather well," Taft agreed, recalling the sweet demeanor his wife had borne this morning, going so far as to greet each guest in the breakfast room and ask after their comfort and welfare. It might seem a simple thing, what any proper hostess of such a party should do, but it was entirely out of character for Alexandrina, and therefore, it was extraordinary.

She was extraordinary. Despite her anxieties and reserve, her apprehension about Society and its inhabitants, their opinions of her, and how she had fared in the past, she was engaging with them without his prodding, and doing so without appearing strained. He would not go so far as to suggest that she might be enjoying the party, nor her role in it, but she was taking it on all the same. She was not an actress, his wife, and there would be no pretending at anything. If she took on an action or a course, she fully intended something by it and was sincere in doing so.

Which was another thing that distracted him to no end.

They had come exceptionally close to kissing the other day, and it had been destined to be quite the kiss. He could have tasted it, and still felt something of its excitement and desperation on the edge of his tongue when he recalled it. And he could recall it. Every blistering second.

The swirling depths of the exquisite blue and green of her eyes, never quite one or the other, the auburn tinge to her hair that only appeared in certain light, the near perfect porcelain of her complexion, the glow of sunrise in her cheeks . . . She was everything of the beauty in nature at once, and something he had never quite seen before at the same time. And to have such a beauty leaning towards him, her full lips parting on unsteady breath, her rare tenderness on full display without guard or resistance . . .

He had never wanted anything more in his entire life than to kiss her then. To breathe new life that only she could provide. To remind himself of the wonder of her lips, trace each part of them in a way he had not dared to before, to erase the memory of their first kiss, or that of any other man, from her mind and mouth so that only that kiss, his lips, his touch remained. Such desire had consumed him, caught him in its tide, and even now, he felt incomplete and unresolved because of the interruption of such a moment.

A moment that could only have come about because Alexandrina meant it. She would not have pretended such a thing, not after her first marriage, and not with her honesty of character. She had meant it.

And heavens, he did as well.

He was at sea, and still his siren called to him.

What was he to do?

"Are you going to say anything else while you've got me trapped in here, or might I return to your excellent house party and find my wife and son?" Larkin queried with a distinctly teasing air. "I believe your wife has an extraordinary picnic planned for the families today. Were you going to join her and Adam in this, or entertain the unmarried guests instead?"

Taft gave him a bewildered look. "Of course, I will go with them. Why wouldn't I? I never miss anything that happens at the Battensay house parties."

Larkin raised a brow. "Because half of your guests will not be attending, as I understand it. I suppose they could, but I know of at least four who have no interest in being around children, despite the fact that there are ten rather entertaining children presently in the house. Have you planned an alternative for them?"

"No," Taft retorted defensively, until he recollected that he had, in fact, meant to do so. Alexandrina had suggested such a thing for the same of all involved, and Taft had simply presumed that all of the guests would wish to participate equally. After all, who did not enjoy a picnic held on a stunning estate whose grounds had just been trimmed and tidied, let alone in close proximity to an orchard?

That was it, they could go into the orchard. There was no fruit ready to pick from the trees, but it was entirely possible the strawberry beds might . . .

Oh, dash it, there was nothing else for them to do. They were all due to go into Godfrey tomorrow, but perhaps he would offer them the chance today?

Why should there be an option? They were having a picnic,

and that was that. He would arrange for additional lawn games to be brought out, for certain, and humbly eat his words before his wife's triumphant expression.

For there would certainly be one.

"I think we should both excuse ourselves from this room and find our wives," Taft told his friend as he rose from his chair. "Though I suspect yours will be more enjoyable. I've amends to make."

"What makes you think I do not?" Larkin asked, standing as well and heading for the door. "My wife is only just outside of the window of sickness in being with child, but she is no less irritable. It is entirely possible that I am wearing my cravat in a completely horrid fashion that she will object to."

Taft made a show of examining Larkin's rather simple, albeit neat cravat. "Not horrid. Boring, but not horrid."

Larkin nodded without retaliation. "I will take boring, thank you. After all, I would never want to be confused with you."

"You would need to be attractive to even come close," Taft assured him with a pat on the back.

"Sophia finds me attractive."

"I've been meaning to talk to you about the quality of her eyesight . . ."

They chuckled together, sharing rather boyish grins before parting as Larkin went up the stairs towards his wife and Taft moved on to the other parts of the house in search of his.

There was some sort of irony in that, though Taft was not going to pause long enough to dwell on it.

Two friends who had never really spoken of marriage, nor declared any intentions of doing so, now quite literally revolving around wives.

Larkin was in a love match, there was no question.

Taft was . . .

Well, it was complicated.

Finding Alexandrina proved quite difficult, after his fifth room without success. He had seen several guests, all of whom had smiled and greeted him as though they were feeling rather marvelous, and while he might have found that to be enough to deter him from a task once, it was not so now. He wanted to find his wife and he was not going to stop until he did.

Curious thing, that.

To his surprise, he found his wife and his stepson out on the lawn setting up the bowling green. Though the picnic and lawn games were some time away, they were lining up the games and balls as though the games were imminent.

Were either of them tempted to practice such a thing, or was his wife simply being overly prepared for the impending activity?

"I think that one needs to move a little to the right," Taft called from the terrace, leaning on the nearest balustrade.

Alexandrina looked up at once, scowling at him, though a corner of her mouth ticked in a way that made his stomach flip.

Adam, however, picked up the nearest pin and moved it to the right. He looked up at Taft. "Is that right, Taft?"

He nodded, opting not to inform his stepson about the joke he had missed. "Perfect, Adam. Why are you setting up the nine pins already?"

"I've never done it," Adam told him without shame. "Mama said she would teach me so I can play after the picnic."

Taft glanced at Alexandrina, who smiled at her son and then looked at Taft almost shyly. "Did she, now?" Taft mused, more for her than for the boy. "Does Mama play nine pins?"

Alexandrina propped her hands on her hips, which did rather marvelous things to emphasize her figure. "Mama has done, I'll have you know, and a basic knowledge is all that is required in this."

"Has she, indeed?" Taft nodded in approval. "Were you any good?"

She narrowed her eyes at him. "I was better at archery, my lord, but I did well enough."

The image of his wife shooting at a target was one he could not relinquish, nor confine to his imagination alone.

"I was thinking of inviting all the guests to participate in the games," Taft told his wife quickly, straightening and drumming his fingers along the railing. "It wouldn't be difficult to bring out the proper things for Battledore and Shuttlecock, or for bowls, or pall mall . . . perhaps some targets . . ." He trailed off, grinning at her in expectation.

She did not react. "If you like," Alexandrina replied, as calm as she had been, her hands moving from her hips, unfortunately. "And provided no one will be snide about it."

Taft barked a laugh. "You think our guests will be snide?"

Alexandrina's look told him everything, and he held up his hands in surrender.

"What would the targets be for?" Adam asked, interrupting what could have been an interesting conversation.

"Archery," Taft told him, moving along the railing to the stairs and coming down to them. "Firing arrows at a target and trying to get as close to the center as possible. Mama has just said she was better at archery than nine pins. What do you think?"

Adam thought about that, then shrugged. "I don't know. I have never seen her do either one.

He and Adam looked at Alexandrina with some expectation.

She returned their looks in turn. "What?"

"I would pay a great deal of money to see Mama shoot arrows, personally," Taft said to the boy, folding his arms while he surveyed the attractive personage of his wife in an attempt to dare her into doing something playful.

"She still has to teach me nine pins," Adam insisted firmly. "She promised, and Mama always keeps her promises."

Taft glanced down at his stepson with a smile. "As she

should. So you think she ought to teach nine pins and then shoot archery later?"

Adam nodded. "Then we will know which one she is better at, because we have seen them both."

It was the most perfect response Taft could have hoped for, and he gestured to his stepson as he gave his wife a triumphant look.

Alexandrina shook her head at them both. "This is ridiculous. I was only trying to teach Adam nine pins so he might play today."

"Which we have established you will do," Taft said easily, knowing how it would provoke her.

"And surely, as hostess, I must ensure everyone else is enjoying themselves, rather than taking enjoyment myself." Alexandrina looked at him for confirmation.

He refused to give it and shook his head very slowly. "No, Alix. The Battensay house party is all about enjoyment, and you would do well to participate. I'll do it, too. Archery, I mean. Let's both do it. Surely, you wish to best me."

She exhaled loudly in exasperation. "Taft, I am your wife, not your playmate."

Taft gave her a slow smile. "In an ideal world, you would be both."

Her cheeks colored, her throat worked, and she folded her arms tightly. "What would be next?" she demanded. "Leap frog? Blind man's bluff? Are you going to challenge me to a foot race when it's done?"

"If it suits me," he shot back, finding her outrage rather entertaining. "You can say no."

"You aren't letting me say no now!" She growled under her breath. "I am already stretched to the limits of my comfort, and now you want me to play like one of the children without actually involving any children?"

"We'd never let the children do archery," Taft told her,

snorting softly. "I am actually an adult, despite what you think."

Alexandrina quirked a brow. "Are you, indeed?"

"Please, Mama. I want to see you shoot arrows." Adam's sweet voice broke into their conversation, asking for his mother to do something as simple as play.

Coming from him, that was more significant than anything else could have been. Adam barely played himself, and yet . . .

"All right," Alexandrina finally replied, her expression soft as she looked at her son. "For you, I will do it."

Adam beamed up at her, then up at Taft as well.

It was impossible not to feel lifted by such an expression.

Taft looked at his wife, ready to apologize for his actions, only to find her staring at him, wearing the most determined expression he had ever seen in his entire life. "Alix?"

"I will beat you soundly, my lord," she told him with utter seriousness. "I hope you are prepared for the embarrassment."

"I can think of worse things than being bested by my wife," he answered with a quick smile. "I will rally."

"I do hope so." She nodded once and turned to Adam, smiling once more. "Would you like to start, darling? Taft needs to learn this as well; he doesn't know the game."

There was nothing to do but laugh at the neatly fired barb, no doubt a preface to the arrows that would come later.

CHAPTER 14

If Alexandrina wore a pocket watch, she would have been constantly checking it throughout the entire picnic. She had no specific time wherein the activities were supposed to begin, but she would feel better about the impending challenge her husband had laid down for her if she had a clock to look at, and something besides her pulse to mark the passage of time. She could have examined shadows, she supposed, and noted how they changed with the shift in the sun's position, but they had decided to have the picnic in an open patch of the lawn, so the only shadows were those of the guests.

Looking at the shadows of everyone around her might look peculiar, and she was doing her utmost to not look peculiar.

Sophia Roth had assured her before the picnic began that she was doing well, but Alexandrina had no confidence in her hosting abilities. She knew Sophia would understand that, given the party at Rosennor a few years ago, but Sophia was at least a warm and engaging person.

Alexandrina could not claim the same.

Her husband might have managed to find her likable at

times, after working at it, but no one else was going to work at it. And he could simply be trying to make the marriage more enjoyable.

Taft was that sort of person. Not insincere, but focused on making the best of something, even if no one else could.

Why he had been so determined to have her participate in the activities with their guests, she could not say. He knew she was not the sort to do that, and he would not let her graciously bow out by claiming to be the hostess. What else would he insist on, her starring in a theatrical?

At least archery was something she enjoyed. It had been a few years since she had practiced, but before she had Adam, she'd done so fairly regularly. And before her marriage, it was something she had rather enjoyed.

Not usually with others, though. As with her other accomplishments, she preferred to keep such things to herself. It was too easy to receive criticism and judgment if she performed, and she'd had enough of that for a lifetime.

She could only hope that Taft wouldn't bring many others over to the archery targets. If he could encourage others to play Battledore and Shuttlecock or one of the other games he had suggested, she might have this competition against him privately. It could be a continued part of the bantering they were so keen on engaging in, something to continue the delicious tension they had recently found, something . . .

Something they could do together. They were friends, after all, and spending time with him without others around was beginning to sound like a marvelous idea. She did not have the courage to say such a thing, but the impulse arose whenever she saw him.

Among other impulses.

Kissing him being chief among them.

She was constantly biting down on tingling lips when he

appeared, and there was something about his hair that made her fingers clench. It came as a surprise, then, that she was actually finding relief in the house party, in a way. The more distraction she had, the less she could dwell on tingling lips and clenching fingers, let alone her husband's broad shoulders, tempting hair, and particularly irresistible crooked smile.

And the distance between them because of the guests and duties allowed her a chance to breathe and gather whatever defenses remained against him.

There were only a few at this point, but this morning's spat had given her fuel to put up more, if needed.

There was no telling with Taft.

"I confess, my lord, I am pleased to see you looking so hale at this house party," Mrs. Gable said from a nearby blanket.

Alexandrina frowned at the comment and glanced at Taft where he sat, just on the other side of Adam.

His brow furrowed as he chewed a bite of bread with jam and butter. "So am I, Mrs. Gable," he replied after a swallow. "But why should you not?"

She seemed surprised by the return question. "Why, as we passed through Godfrey, we had heard that you were not well. One of the ladies assured us that her sister had heard from Lady Harwood herself that you were not well."

Taft looked at Alexandrina in confusion. "Have you been to Godfrey in the last few days?"

"No, not since we were all there together." She paused, thinking back, and then, when realization dawned, smiled rather widely, laughing once. "Oh . . . Oh, that."

"What?" Taft demanded, looking mildly concerned. "Did you tell someone I had the plague or something?"

Alexandrina gave him a bewildered look, still grinning. "You were with me the entire time, Taft. Don't you recall?"

He shook his head. "I've been a trifle occupied. What

happened?"

"You were skipping planks with Adam," Alexandrina reminded him, the humor of the situation growing by the moment. "And I said you looked ridiculous."

"And I said that was the point," he recalled, still not realizing what had happened.

Alexandrina nodded, still smiling and trying not to burst out laughing. "That was not all I said. I did speak to a woman there, and I said . . ." She gestured for him to finish, if his memory had finally caught up.

A startled laugh erupted from him, and he brought a fist to his mouth to stifle further laughter. When he'd recovered enough, he managed, "And you said I was not well."

"Precisely," Alexandrina quipped, nodding once. She smiled kindly at Mrs. Gable, who had been watching the exchange with some confusion. "His lordship is very well, and he has been well since our arrival at Battensay. It was a simple misunderstanding. Your concern, and that of our neighbors, is very considerate."

Mrs. Gable managed a smile, looking a trifle uncomfortable. "I feel rather silly now. As if you would continue to host the house party if his lordship were unwell." She shook her head, sighing to herself. "I must fetch more lemonade. Excuse me." She rose and moved to the table of beverages set up nearby.

Alexandrina watched her go, then looked at Taft with some concern. "I was trying to be sympathetic. Have I offended her?"

Taft shook his head. "Situational, Alix. Gossip being proved false to an innocent party. Nothing to concern yourself with, I promise. A bit of embarrassment, that is all."

"More gossip, more scandal." Alexandrina shook her head with a groan.

"Rumors of my not being well hardly constitutes a scandal," Taft told her softly, scoffing a little. "Not all gossip is an evil. Just a natural tendency of people to talk, and details getting skewed in the process."

As though that were innocent enough. Honestly, could he not see the problem there? Their guest was embarrassed because of the misunderstanding, and Alexandrina's pointing that out had only made it worse, though she had tried to do so gently.

She did not know Mrs. Gable well, but if she were of a sensitive nature, that could be a rather lingering embarrassment.

"Alix," Taft murmured in an almost musical voice.

She shook her head. "I thought it was funny to have the misunderstanding, but Mrs. Gable genuinely was pleased you were well. I shouldn't have said a word."

"If the gossip and misunderstanding is harmless, then it will not hurt to leave it alone," Taft agreed. "But you did not do anything wrong. I don't want you to fear what people say anymore. It doesn't matter."

"Tell that to Mrs. Gable," Alexandrina suggested.

He turned to look over at the table of drinks, then nudged his head towards it. "You tell her. See?"

Alexandrina looked, and Mrs. Gable was chatting away rather comfortably with another guest now, no flushed face or hint of embarrassment in sight. She even looked over at her and Taft, smiling with genuine warmth, her brief moment of mortification apparently forgotten in those few moments she had been away.

Alexandrina had never seen anyone recover from embarrassment so quickly or so completely, and unless Mrs. Gable was an incredible actress, she truly was unruffled by the thing now.

Taft made a soft hum of a laugh, drawing her attention back to him. "What?" she asked, smiling in response to his own crooked grin.

"You," he told her. "You, who hate Society and those who make it up, are really quite caring and considerate. What a heart you possess, Alix Debenham, Countess of Harwood."

Her face heated, and she looked down at the plate before her. "Don't tell," she muttered. "I have a reputation."

"Yes, and I wonder how much longer that will remain." He cleared his throat and turned to talk to someone else, leaving her alone with her thoughts.

She very much wanted to best him in the archery competition, if for no other reason than to feel less under his captivating influence and more in control of her feelings.

He was beginning to see into her heart, and that was rather terrifying. What if he did not like what he saw?

Hiding was so much safer than exposure, even from someone she was coming to regard as much as her husband. And she was coming to regard him highly.

Incredibly so.

He barely resembled the man who had so grated upon her nerves and offended her tastes, though that man had not gone anywhere. He was still in the person of Taft Debenham, Earl of Harwood, but she understood him now. She saw more than that now.

He was so much more than that now.

And heaven help her, she desperately wanted him to like her.

She had not felt any such desires about anyone since the earliest days of her marriage to Stephen, before she had become disillusioned to all matters of the heart. Even now, she did not want to feel this. Did not want her heart to flutter when he entered a room. Did not want to wish for his smile.

Did not want to hurt anymore, even if there was also delight in it.

"Mama, is it time for archery and nine pins yet?" Adam asked brightly from beside her, looking so childlike compared to the young shadow of a gentleman he had been of late.

It was the most beautiful sight she had ever seen.

Alexandrina reached out to run a thumb over his cheek

fondly. "I think it might be, dearest. What do you say, Taft? Have our guests eaten enough to move on into our activities?"

"I think so, Alix," he replied, turning back to her and grinning at Adam. "Are you comfortable enough in your practice this morning to play with the other children?"

"I think so, Taft," Adam quipped, cheekily echoing Taft's own words.

Taft laughed and patted him on the back. "Excellent. Then yes, let us move on." He turned to the guests. "Shall we have some games? Parker, weren't you planning on ruling the roost with your skills at pall mall? And Miss Rawlins, I have seen you at Battledore and Shuttlecock before. Surely you would not deprive us of the pleasure of witnessing such skill?"

And with that easy stroke, the guests were cheerfully off to their activities, encouraged by Taft's warmth and flattery, needing no one to guide or direct.

It was astonishing how efficiently Taft managed such a thing, how well he understood the way to arrange things, where Alexandrina had thought to oversee and give supervision.

But Taft had known better, and everyone was presently occupied.

Apart from her and Taft.

Alexandrina looked around, marveling that all had been taken care of in such a blink, and Taft walked over to her, hands clasped behind his back. "How did you do that?"

"Do what?" he asked, his brow creasing slightly.

She gestured around to the general gathering. "This. Everyone about a task without instruction, without advisement, and without much curiosity for anybody else's actions. Everything is properly organized and delegated. Even the children's nine pins game is supervised, and Mr. Roth seems delighted to be doing so."

"He's dreadful at lawn games of any kind, so he *is* delighted by it," Taft said with a laugh. "That one was quite simple."

Alexandrina took her time to take in each activity, unable to do much more than smile at the sight of them all, then smiled more curiously when a new realization struck her. "There is no one left to participate in archery apart from us." She looked at Taft with some appreciation, if a little speculation. "Was that also you?"

Her husband grinned the most delicious grin known to a woman's eyes. "It might have been. The challenge was my doing, but I know you. I didn't think we required an audience. No one needs to know the Harwoods battle with each other for pride, do they?"

"If they know either of us half as well as they think," Alexandrina said softly, reaching out a hand for Taft to hold, crooking her fingers a little, "they would not be surprised in the least that we do so. No doubt, they think it all we do."

Taft took her hand, catching her breath by lacing his fingers through hers at once. "Isn't it, though?"

If her ribs caught flight, she would not have been surprised, the way they tickled and burst into sparks within her. And if his fingers continued to rub against hers like that . . .

"Still think you can best me in this?" Taft inquired with a chuckle as they moved towards the targets. "I am quite a decent shot."

Alexandrina swallowed hard, willing the fire in her chest to abate. "With guns, perhaps, but arrows are quite different. Far more precise, if you will, and it takes far more patience and skill."

Taft coughed in surprise. "Are you implying I have neither?"

"I merely imply that guns are clumsy things," Alexandrina told him with a light sigh, smiling as she began to feel more like herself, more in control, and less uneasy. "And no one marks the pheasant for a target."

"You are competitive, Alexandrina Debenham," Taft said with a laugh, fingers brushing against hers more pointedly. "Marvelously so. I am not sure I have ever found you so attractive."

Alexandrina almost choked at the words, and what they did to the pit of her stomach. "Attractive? You've never said—"

"You needed the exact words, Alix?" he interrupted in a low voice, almost rasping in a new intensity, his grip on her hand clenching. "You couldn't tell every time I looked at you and couldn't believe my eyes? When I fumbled for words and struggled for breath? When I smiled like a lunatic and took your hand because I had to touch you?"

"Taft . . ."

He brought her hand to his lips, the contact burning a path from her hand down to one particular toe. "Even on the day we married, I thought you were the most beautiful creature God had ever made, and it's only grown in intensity every day since."

Was there ever a more impossible time to breathe than this? Alexandrina bit her lip and looked away, wishing her heart was not clattering against her chest in a way that pulsed into every single joint in her body. Every ounce of sanity in her mind screamed to pull away, to flee from the danger in this intensity, to hide before old wounds reopened.

But no power on Earth or in heaven could have taken her hand from his at this moment, nor could her fingers lessen their grip.

She could not let go. And she would not.

She ought to say something. Anything, really. A thank you or some compliment about his handsomeness or pleasant countenance, or how he stole into her mind and imagination at the most inconvenient times and distracted her from every action she ever hoped to take from day to day. She could have told him any number of things that might give him as much pleasure as she was presently feeling, beneath all the uncertainties and agonies that buzzed about upon her surface.

But no words would come. Not a single word of praise,

though her heart was bursting with feelings of him and for him. She could only clasp his hand as though it were the only thing to keep her alive and pray it would mean enough.

"What a grip, my lady," Taft murmured, as though her thoughts had been spoken aloud. "One might begin to think you've grown rather fond of me."

"Might one?" she tried to quip through a clogged, rather tight voice. "How curious."

"Of course, we know better."

"Do we, indeed?"

"Mm-hmm. You are trying to crush my hand so that I might have more trouble in the upcoming archery." He tutted in playful disapproval, his thumb dipping into her hand right where he knew it would affect her most. "Will your competitive determination know no bounds?"

Alexandrina tried not to laugh, oddly loving the discrepancy between her husband's words and what he was doing to her hand. "No, it will not," she said as calmly as possible, working to be as unaffected as possible. "I told you I would win, and I will."

"But with cheating, my dear. I would never have thought." His fingers gripped against hers for one intense press before relaxing into an easier hold.

"It is a pleasure to surprise you on occasion, my lord." Alexandrina inhaled deeply, then exhaled a sound of delighted anticipation. "Just as I intend to shortly with our competition. Please do keep your chin up—our guests will not like a spoilsport."

Taft's laughter was infectious, and Alexandrina could not help but be caught up in it, laughing merrily and wondering if she had somehow sprouted wings in the last few minutes. She felt as though she might be able to fly from the ground at this moment, soar into the clouds, if not full above them.

That was something she had never felt with Stephen. Not even once. She had always remained squarely on the ground.

The targets were set neatly side by side, and the bows and quivers full of arrows beside them, ready and waiting for their hosts and the contest before them. Alexandrina released Taft's hand at last, moving to the nearest target and taking up a shooting glove. She slipped it on, flexing her fingers until it was comfortable, then picked up the arrows and bow there. Walking over to her indicated position, she turned and grinned at Taft, who was only a few paces behind.

"Would you like to go first?" Alexandrina asked him, gesturing towards the targets.

"Of course not," he scoffed loudly. "Ladies first is not simple politeness. You go first, and then I will see what exactly I must do to even the score."

Alexandrina shrugged and turned to the side, facing her target. "Very well, then. It makes no difference to me." She cocked the arrow in place, then raised the bow, pulling back slowly.

"My, what form you have."

"I am well aware," she replied dismissively, taking the arrow back to its full tension.

"If only I were an artist. My heavens, you'd be my muse just like this."

"Shut up, Taft."

"O, for a muse of fire . . ."

Alexandrina sighed, somehow combining irritation with satisfaction and amusement, then released the arrow from her hold.

It landed a scant few ticks off center, just on the edge of the ring.

"Damnation."

Alexandrina laughed and lowered her arms, turning to her husband with a bright smile. "Your turn."

Taft stared at the target without any hint of humor, almost aghast at the sight. "That's unbelievable. If I were not seeing it, had not watched you loose the arrow myself, I absolutely would not believe it." His eyes moved to her, and he looked utterly adorable in his confusion. "Alix, I had no idea . . ."

"Would it be better to remind you that I told you so now or when I've trounced you soundly?" Alexandrina asked with a giggle.

He smiled at her rather slowly, looking deliciously playful and boyish. "My word, Alix. All this time, I thought you did not know how to play."

She bit her lip, quirking her brows. "I've always known, I simply forgot. And I have you to thank for the reminder."

He chuckled and looked her up and down in proud assessment before squinting. "Does this mean you'll let me start three points ahead?"

"Not in the least," she insisted firmly. She nudged her head towards the target. "Get on with it."

CHAPTER 15

Godfrey was always more delightfully itself when they had the house party guests with them, and this year was no exception. Of course, part of that was due to Alexandrina being so impossibly adorable and keeping Taft on his toes, for some reason he could not possibly understand, but he was enjoying every moment. At this very moment, she was walking along the main street with Adam holding one hand and one of the girls from the house party holding the other, both children giggling easily.

It was the most beautiful sight he had ever seen.

He was saying that phrase quite a lot these days, but he meant it each and every time. How could he possibly know that he would be seeing something more beautiful days or sometimes hours later? It was a bewildering flurry of newness that all fell into the category of astonishment, and he began to grow dizzy with it.

Pleasantly so, but dizzy all the same.

She had soundly beaten him in their archery match the other day and had only crowed over him enough to make him rather proud of her lack of inhibitions. She had reminded him of it yesterday when he'd started to make a wry comment, and it had silenced him creditably.

His wife had always been outspoken, if not critical, but she had never been quite so perfectly cavalier. Not in truth, of course, but wholly in regard to their archery contest. And a little bit towards any future activities they might compete in.

Alexandrina was showing a certain confidence and spirit he had never quite witnessed in her, and it was just between the two of them, which he rather liked. It made him smile without fail, seemed to dare him rather temptingly, prodded him to push her just a little further to see what she would do. One of these days, she was almost certainly going to strike him for his impudence, if not irreverence, where she was concerned.

But she had not struck him yet.

He found that almost as compelling as her appearance. Was she merely tolerating his more ridiculous behavior, as she might have done a child? Or was it possible that he was, in fact, amusing her in truth?

He'd always been amusing to people, it was simply part of the nature he had cultivated, but he had never cared all that much about its success or reach. Suddenly, however, he desperately wanted to be amusing to his wife. He wanted to be entertaining to his wife. He wanted to be attractive to her, comforting to her, exciting to her, and understanding to her. He wanted to be *everything* to her.

And that was a rather harrowing state to exist in.

"Gawking after your wife? That's an interesting pastime."

Taft glanced at Larkin with a slight scowl. "When you've got a wife as lovely as mine, it is difficult not to gawk at any given moment. And for this particular moment, I find her utterly charming and the sweetest version of herself I have ever seen."

"Do you?" Larkin replied, looking a little surprised. "Huh." He turned to look at Alexandrina and the children, his brows knitting together. "I don't see why. She is a mother, after all, and you've seen her be so since coming to Battensay. Why is another child in hand to make such a difference?"

"She's laughing, Larkin," Taft murmured, his friend's almost stiff tone not fooling him. He was being led on, and there was no secret there. And yet he went. "Laughing, and near to skipping. You've seen my wife, you've known how she's been—now tell me that isn't some miracle."

Larkin folded his arms, his mouth twisting. "Now that you mention it, yes, she is rather brighter in countenance and being than I've ever known her. I thought that must be having Adam returned to her or the influence of Battensay, but now I wonder."

"Wonder what?" Taft demanded, glancing at his suddenly smug friend.

He did not respond.

Typical.

Taft glowered and cleared his throat. "Larkin. What do you wonder?"

"Hmm?" Larkin turned to him in apparent surprise. "I beg your pardon?"

Now the man was just being rude, and there was no cause for it at all.

Just because Taft had done the same thing to Larkin a few years ago did not mean that it had to be reciprocated. That simply showed an astonishing lack of good nature.

But a decent sense of fair play, he supposed.

"Never mind," Taft muttered with a shake of his head. "I don't want to know what you've wondered."

"But I rather want to know what you wonder," Lakin said in a particularly wry tone.

Taft laughed once. "Yes, I wager you do. A pity you will not gain any insight into that."

"Because you are having trouble thinking it through?"

"Because I don't have to tell you everything."

"Ah, my mistake. Silly me, I thought you trapped me in the study to whine the other day." He shook his head slowly, folding his arms. "Must have misheard you. The entire time."

"It is not my fault that you misunderstood me," Taft told him. "You've always struggled with comprehension of the more intricate details of life and such."

"Have I? Pity no one has said." Larkin slid him a bemused smile. "How did the archery go? You never told me."

Taft had to laugh at the memory. "I have never failed so spectacularly in my entire life."

"Sure about that? I am quite accustomed to your failures."

"Alix has a calm and accuracy that I've never witnessed in anyone bearing a bow and arrow." Taft shook his head, grinning more to himself than for his friend's benefit. "She outshot me every single time, without question and with great emphasis. It was an utter mastery of the thing, Larkin. Not entirely perfect, but damn near close. I could have been firing straight into the air for all the chance I had of actually competing against her."

Larkin barked a laugh, throwing his head back and letting the laughter roll freely. "Oh, gads, I would have loved to see that. Please tell me she crowed over you in her triumph."

"She did," Taft replied. "Rather delicately, compared to what I might have done in her place, but she does seem to enjoy reminding me of it."

"So I should hope. I always knew your wife was an exceptional woman."

"You did not."

"Of course, I did. I just didn't tell you."

There was no possible way that was true, and Taft returned his attention, most delightfully, to the person of his wife. She glanced over at him now, smiling about something or other one of the children had said.

Once, her smile might have hardened or faded when she

looked upon him, if she smiled at all.

But now . . .

Her smile grew, just a little. Just enough.

Just perfectly.

He exhaled some delighted, satisfied sound at being such a recipient, only to hear rather impolite snickering beside him.

"What?"

Larkin continued to laugh like a child. "You are in so deeply and so completely, and yet so blindly that you do not even realize how helplessly you flail about."

Taft brushed his hand dismissively in Larkin's general direction, something sharp and tight growing in his chest. "Go away, I'm missing the chance to observe my wife without anyone judging me."

"The fact that all you want to do is stare at your wife should smack you in the face with its obviousness, but it certainly won't stop you from judgment," Larkin told him, this time with disapproval. "All I'm feeling right now is judgment."

"Pardon me, my lord, I was hoping you would come into Godfrey with the rest of your party."

Taft turned with a carefully polite expression to the approaching man in a thick leather apron. "Carter, how very good to see you. How are you?"

The blacksmith nodded, smiling in his slight, rough way. "Very well, my lord. Business is good, and I've no complaints. But my lord . . ." He paused, reaching into his pockets and pulling out a small bottle of a rather thick, custard-like liquid, handing it out to him. "My lord, I was ever so sorry to hear about your rash. My wife swears by this salve."

His what? He had nothing of the sort, and that was something rather specific to be accused of. There was no way this was some misconstrued interpretation of his wife's words from the other day, unless someone had let their imagination run away with them.

Which, he supposed, was entirely possible.

Taft took the bottle, frowning a little. "Thank you, Carter. Erm . . . how did you hear about my . . . rash?"

"My girls made a delivery to the kitchens last night, sir, with some of the market fare," Carter told him. "They overheard a conversation between your wife and the cook, and given my wife's fancying herself an apothecary, and being right more often than not, they told us of it. I hope you do not mind."

"Not at all," Taft assured him, taking his arm and nodding. "Please, thank your wife for me. I am sure this will do just the trick."

Carter nodded and turned away, heading back for his forge.

"What sort of rash do you have that your wife needed to speak to the cook about it?" Larkin asked very quietly, his tone more curious than skeptical.

"An imaginary one," Taft said, laughing once and putting the bottle in the pocket of his jacket. "But one I am rather intrigued to hear about."

Larkin chortled and started to walk, Taft falling into step beside him. "I am not a medical man, and nor are you, so how in the world could rashes of any kind be an intriguing topic?"

Taft grinned at him. "I don't have one, you see."

"Yes, I presumed that when you used the word imaginary."

Taft ignored him. "It means my wife is intentionally spreading a rumor."

"That's not very nice, is it?" Larkin looked over at Alexandrina now, standing in front of the confectioner's shop with Adam and the girl, another two children joining them. "Why would she do that? If I recall, she despises rumors and gossip."

"She does," Taft affirmed. He nodded to himself, feeling as though his smile might spread somehow further and crack his face in two. "But she is beginning to learn that not everything people say is an evil, nor something we must control. We spoke of this the other day, just before archery, and it seems that my assuring her of the thing was taken as a challenge. I think I've underestimated her."

Larkin gave him a sardonic look. "In what way?"

Taft shook his head, marveling at his wife. "She is rather devious, despite her appearance of reserve, disapproval, and aloofness. Despite everything I or anyone else have ever thought, she truly is the most entertaining woman I have ever met."

"How fortunate, then, that you have married her."

"Quite." Taft patted the bottle in his pocket, narrowing his eyes.

Larkin caught it, and grinned. "You're plotting revenge."

"I might be."

"And?"

Taft flicked his gaze to his friend and started walking faster, moving down the street and beckoning Larkin to follow. "Come on, we need to get ahead of her and the children. I think I know their route, and there isn't much time."

They moved forward with as much haste as could politely be expected, Taft regularly marking Alexandrina's position and progress as they did so. His guests were forgotten, all of them used to the simple, almost quaint manner of Godfrey's people and her businesses, and hardly needing his direction.

Which was rather fortunate, as he had rather crucial business to attend to that his hosting duties would almost certainly have gotten in the way of.

"Where, exactly, are we heading?" Larkin asked as they moved beyond the confectionary, the bakery, the haberdasher, and the cobbler. "At this rate, you'll be taking your revenge in Slough."

"Slough is in the opposite direction, you tufted bull calf," Taft told the fool, not at all diminished by the mockery. "And if you would pay attention, Larkin, you would know that we are approaching the print-seller shop. Mr. Owens prides himself on his window display, which means the children will want to look, and Alix, being sweet and indulgent in the most maternal sort of way, will pause with them so they might properly admire the thing. Which will mean that they will be delayed for a time, which means . . ."

"All right, all right," Larkin blustered, holding up a hand. "I don't know your plan, so I won't question the process of it. What do you need me to do?"

Taft merely gave him a cocky smile. "Agree with everything I say and don't tell Alix."

Larkin appeared only mildly suspicious. "Is whatever we're doing going to offend her, get me in trouble, or make her cry?"

"None of the above, I swear," Taft reassured him. "It will not be worse than the word going around that the Earl of Harwood has a rash. Less embarrassing, in fact, and more in fun."

"For you or for her?"

"Ideally, both." Taft quirked his brows a bit and headed towards a group of locals he recognized. "Good day, all. How are you faring this fine afternoon?"

They answered in varying degrees of the same noncommittal warmth, greeting him much the same.

"Did I hear, my lord, that you've married since you were last at Battensay?" one of the older ladies said, giving him a bright smile.

It was the most perfect beginning of a conversation Taft could have hoped for, under the circumstances. He could not have written a better one himself.

And he had prepared several in his mind to help himself out, just in case.

"I have, madam," Taft told her, nodding in fond acknowledgement. "And we are very happy, as you might imagine. She's just there, you see. Coming away from the confectionary shop with the children. The beauty in the green."

The group looked where he indicated, and he heard soft, murmuring comments, if not compliments, while they did. Such a thing made him puff up with pride, wishing more people saw Alexandrina for the angel of attractiveness he did, and could appreciate her for more than what she presented to the world.

This group, however, only knew her from sight, and they seemed to find the view pretty enough.

"Lady Harwood is so enjoying life at Battensay," Taft told them all rather fondly. "And Godfrey as well. It is, however, a trifle awkward for her."

"Awkward?" a younger lady squawked. "How could anyone find Godfrey and Battensay awkward, my lord?"

It was a valid question, just as Taft had hoped it would be.

"My lady only speaks Italian," Taft explained, with a sympathetic click of his tongue. "She's trying with English, but it is a troublesome language to one who has never really known it. I've told her that everyone will be patient and understanding, but she is so afraid of being a laughingstock and embarrassing me. Which is utter nonsense, isn't it?"

They all agreed that it was, and suddenly, the game was on.

CHAPTER 16

Battensay was never quite so large as in the middle of the night.

Alexandrina had occasional times where she couldn't sleep, and walking the Battensay halls in the darkness allowed her some time to think and find clarity. More than that, Battensay was large enough that walking it at night tired her out enough to sleep rather deeply.

And she was truly beginning to think of the place as home.

The party was going well, if the comments she was overhearing were any indication, and if the smiles her guests wore should tell her anything. She was finding herself minding the entire event and the hosting duties less and less, and finding the task easier and easier to manage. It was a trifle arduous even now, but not a burden. She longed for a rest in her days and more time to enjoy with Adam rather than with entertaining guests, but she was not filled with dread when she awoke in the mornings.

Taft helped with that. His smile each morning gave her strength and encouragement, and her connection to him was growing ever stronger. The gentle brushing of his fingers over hers when he passed her, the caress of his eyes when they looked on her, the heat of delight that sparked in her stomach when he walked in the room . . . He was the sunshine in her day, regardless of what the sky did beyond the windows.

Walking at night helped to stifle all of that, as she only ever did so alone. Without Taft's influence upon her, everything was far less cumbersome to consider. Far less confusing. Far less terrifying.

Far more comforting.

Not that Taft was not comforting, for he truly was. He was always taking her hands and looking after her, and she was truly grateful for it. The problem was that, in doing so, he was also dreadfully distracting, which only turned the act of comfort into an act of madness.

For her, anyway.

Walking darkened halls removed all of that and stripped her of the walls she had so meticulously constructed over the years, which were growing heavier with every attempt to thrust them up.

She didn't want to bear with them anymore, but the practice was habit by now, and habit was a troublesome thing indeed.

Taft was getting so expert at finding holes in those walls, the cracks she had yet to discover, or somehow tearing them down fully and completely.

Somehow, he could see that there was something behind the walls, and not just the exterior she had constructed. Did not believe the facade. Would not accept it.

And his determination to push beyond her defenses was as endearing as it was maddening.

She was losing the battle to resist him, and she was losing it fast.

She shook her head now as she neared the nursery, which always seemed to be her destination when her mind wandered on these walks. After so many months away from her boy, seeing him safely asleep in his bed was one of the most satisfying and joyful things she had ever known. There was no contentment like it anywhere.

There were other children staying in the first nursery with him, only two or three around his same age, while the others took up the second nursery, and it seemed to be doing Adam good to be spending time with other children. He was not quite up to taking charge in any of their games and activities, nor was he particularly opinionated about what they did, but he participated in them.

It was so much progress, she could hardly believe it, but oh, how she hoped to.

She pried open the door to the nursery as quietly and carefully as she was able, slipping into the room and moving towards the beds, the moonlight streaming through the gap in the partially closed drapes lighting her way and giving the entire room a gentle hue of blue she rather liked.

It made her boy seem so much younger than he was, and she longed for those days.

Smiling to herself in a hint of anticipation, she came to his tidy little bed, only to find it empty, the bedclothes rumpled, and the pillow indented.

But no Adam.

Alexandrina's heart came crashing through her stomach, and through at least three floors of the house, her eyes darting here and there along the bed just in case she was missing him somehow.

But the more she looked, the clearer his absence became.

She covered her mouth with a hand to keep from calling out or making any sort of noise that might disrupt the other sleeping children and whirled from the room. Tearing down the hall, she headed for Taft's rooms, her wrap falling to the ground behind her as she did so. She could not imagine where Adam had gone in the middle of the night, if he had wandered off unintentionally or gone in search of something, if somehow one of the Lawsons had managed to . . .

No. No, she could not allow her mind to take her to such dark places, particularly when it was not possible. The Lawsons would never be admitted to Battensay, and she would not credit them with the courage to break into the house and take Adam back. They'd been more concerned about the money for Stonehall than they had about Adam himself, and Taft had seen to the legalities of Adam's guardianship with such thoroughness that it would serve no one for them to try and get him back. All things considered, they would receive far more benefit by leaving Adam where he was, and she had no doubt they would do that.

Which did not solve the problem of Adam's present whereabouts, but she did not need to fear kidnapping.

It was a small comfort at this moment.

Battensay was an immense house, but if Adam had attempted to find something on the grounds, or, heaven forbid, make his way to Godfrey . . . He had been so fascinated by the horses in the village, he might have gone to the stables to see the horses of the estate. But without Mr. Lyle there to help and keep him safe, the place could be more dangerous than anything else.

Images of a mass of terrified, trampling horses sprang to her mind and she whimpered softly in distress.

Biting down on her lip, she hurried to the door to Taft's rooms, knocking insistently. There were no guests in the surrounding rooms, so she had no fear of disturbing them with the sound, but if she were to scream or dissolve into tears . . .

The door opened just as her chest began to seize up, her fingers tingling as they gripped the doorframe.

"Alix?" Taft looked her over with some concern, his linen shirt loose and tucked into trousers. "What's wrong? Are you all right?"

She hiccupped a dry sob. "Adam isn't in his bed. I was taking a walk, and I went to check on him, and . . ."

Taft smiled, stepping back a little and gesturing for her to come in as he opened the door further. She took a few steps in, noting how light his sitting room was for the middle of the night. His fire was built up, and sitting before the fire in his nightshirt, now looking towards her with a bright smile, was Adam.

She sagged in relief, and Taft caught her, one hand rubbing her upper arm gently. "Oh, heavens . . ."

"He had a bad dream," Taft murmured in a low voice. "I heard him crying out as I came up to bed and brought him in here. It cannot have been more than an hour."

Alexandrina nodded, swallowing hard. "Why didn't you wake me?" she whispered.

His hand rubbed against her arm again, this time more slowly and in an almost absent pattern. "Why should I have? He was well enough, and you deserved some rest. Besides, he is my stepson now. I ought to be of use to him."

"Mama!" Adam called, holding up the bread with cheese in his hand. "Taft made toast! Without the cook!"

Still feeling the remnants of her anxiety, Alexandrina leaned her head back, resting it against Taft's shoulder. "Really, darling? Will wonders never cease?"

"We went down to the kitchens," Adam told her as he took another big bite. "Taft knows where *everything* is down there. Have you been to explore the kitchens?"

"No," Alexandrina murmured, emotion of an entirely different kind beginning to rise. "No, I have not yet."

Tears began to form in her eyes, the enthusiasm of her son the most beautiful sight she had ever seen. He was a child again, rather than the somber image of one she had fetched from Stonehall. Exploring the kitchens of Battensay at night with his stepfather after he'd had a bad dream . . . That was a memory he just might keep for the rest of his life, and while he might not recall the details of his trained reserve and somber months of solitude, he would likely remember being brought to light and fun when he was brought to Battensay.

When he had met Taft.

"I'll take you to explore the kitchens whenever you like," Taft murmured, his mouth near enough to her ear that she shivered with a delicious blend of hot and cold. "It can be quite the adventure."

"Everything is an adventure with you." She hummed a laugh and straightened, moving away from him and heading for her son. She pulled a chair from the corner over and placed it before the fire next to him. "I am sorry you've had a bad dream, darling. It has been quite some time since I've been with you for one. What was the dream tonight?"

Adam looked up at her, then over at Taft. Alexandrina followed his look, giving Taft a curious glance.

Taft shook his head. "I cannot share that information, I'm afraid."

"Really?" She raised a brow and returned her attention to her son. "Won't you tell me, Adam?"

He mirrored his stepfather and shook his head slowly. "Some things stay between men, Mama."

She had to smile at that, even against her will. "Do they, indeed?"

He nodded very soberly, then held up his toast and cheese. "Would you like a bite of toast?"

Alexandrina nodded, bringing the toasted bread to her mouth and taking a small bite. "Mm," she said, handing it back to her son. "That is very good." She slid her glance to her husband before going back to Adam. "Are you *certain* that Taft made it?"

"I beg your pardon!" Taft coughed in indignation, laughter running beneath it.

Adam giggled and cupped his toast in hand as though it was precious. "He did, Mama! I saw him do it! And he taught me, too!"

"He did, did he?" She flicked a dubious look to Taft.

He came over at once and sat beside Adam on the floor without any hesitation. "And what did I tell you before I taught you, Adam?"

"That I should never do this by myself and only with you or Mama," Adam recited with the precision of a perfect student. He looked at Alexandrina with somber eyes. "He made me promise, Mama, and I did."

Alexandrina ran a hand over his hair and smoothed her thumb over his cheek, unable to remove the smile from her face or alter its breadth. "I am so glad that you did. And that Taft had you promise. It is very important."

"That's what he said, too." Adam took a big bite of his toast, looking back into the fire. "Are there other things you can put on toast, Taft? Or is it only for cheese?"

Taft looked at Alexandrina with amusement, then focused on Adam and began a rather in-depth conversation about the various toppings one might apply on toasted bread when it was being done in a sitting room rather than in the kitchens. Adam had some surprisingly creative ideas for options, and Taft vowed to try a few of them at another time.

It was, without a doubt, one of the strangest conversations she'd ever heard, but it kept her smiling and laughing, which was nothing short of miraculous.

This little family of hers was unlike anything she had expected, and she was growing more and more grateful that it was.

What if she had entered into a marriage of convenience that was as formal and distant as she had expected? Would that man have fought for her son as tirelessly as Taft? Would she have been as happy and content in that home? Would she have continued on in her reserved ways, safely protected behind walls of stone that would never come down? Would she have ever laughed or had reason to smile beyond politeness?

What kind of a life would that have been for her?

She would not claim she was in a picture of perfection now, or that she was wholly comfortable, but there was light and ease and amusement. There was safety and calm, adventure and fun. There was consolation and respectability and annoyance, and heaven help her, there was attraction.

There was a great deal of attraction.

She took the chance to consider Taft more openly than she might have done, as he sat beside Adam on the floor, working away at toasting another piece of bread with cheese. It was clear he had started to prepare for bed at some point, being without weskit or cravat, his hair mussed, and the buttons of his shirt entirely undone. He looked younger than he was, and in a way, far more real to her than any done-up version of himself. He was stripped of any artifice or façade, any pomp that might have been attributed to him, and in its place was a natural, relaxed, easy version of himself.

All of that combined with the utter disarray of him was impossible to not appreciate.

How had she never noticed the magnificence of his throat, particularly where it joined with his chest and the glimpse of muscle she could catch in the deep vee of his shirt? And his hair positively begged to be toyed with, to have fingers run through it, to feel . . .

He looked at her then, just as her cheeks began to flame with all sorts of images she ought not to consider in his presence. As though he knew, he smiled in a deeply unsettling, deeply charming way.

She swallowed, and she watched as his eyes followed the motion, which only made her feel more overheated. Rather like she were being toasted over a flame rather than the bread.

Taft glanced at the toast, pulling it out and setting it aside. "Would Mama like some of this? I'll split it with you."

"Oh, why not?" she murmured, straightening in her chair and reaching around her for her wrap, only to recall that she had dropped it in the corridor.

Pity. She could have used it as a sort of armor.

Whether it would be protecting her from her husband or protecting him from her feelings, she couldn't tell.

Perhaps it did not matter

Taft split the toast and handed her half, catching the faint shiver. "Cold?"

She nodded, feeling the answer easier than admitting anything else. "I dropped my wrap in my haste to find Adam."

"Well, I'll go get it for you." He set his toast down on the table and moved around her, patting her shoulder.

"You don't have to, Taft," she insisted, turning in her chair as he headed for the door. "I can move closer to the fire."

He gave her a quick smile. "Of course, you can. But you can also have your wrap. I won't be a minute." He left the room, and Alexandrina had to swallow again.

If she did not know better, she would begin to wonder if this was what having a husband would always be like. But not all husbands were so attentive, nor were they so appealing.

Just this one.

"Eat your toast before it gets cold, Mama," Adam insisted, pointing his finger at her bread. "It won't taste nearly as good then."

"Yes, you're quite right," Alexandrina replied at once, turning back and picking up her bread, grinning at her son.

She continued to watch him as she ate, wondering what his dream had been and how he had sounded before Taft fetched him. What had pained her boy so much that he had been awakened by it? Had he dreamed this way often before they'd brought him here? Had anyone consoled him when it did happen? Or had he been left to comfort himself somehow and had to succumb to the fear and darkness around him?

It made her ache to consider such a thing, to know she had been prevented from offering her son that comfort and peace he so deserved. No child should have to be left to their fears, or to find no help at hand in their hour of need.

If she could manage to avoid sleeping on the floor beside his bed for the next few weeks, it would be a triumph worthy of praise.

"Here we are."

Taft's arms brushed hers as he draped her wrap around her, tucking it against her as though she were a child. His hands rested at her arms when he was done. "Better?"

Touched, Alexandrina reached up and took his hand with her free one. "Much. Come, sit down."

He nodded, coming around her again and, when she did not release his hand, situating himself on the floor at her feet. He gave her a curious look, rearranging their hands to a more natural grip. "What's wrong?"

She shook her head. "Nothing, really. I am still not quite easy about Adam's nightmare, nor my missing it, but at least you were there."

Taft rubbed his thumb over her hand, tilting his head a little. "Did this happen often before? When you were with him at Stonehall?"

"Not terribly often," she admitted, eying Adam as he scooted closer to the fire, staring at the flames and the wood in fascination. "But enough. Perhaps one a month, sometimes as close together as a fortnight, but not usually. My room was beside his there, so I was able to go in and calm him. Sing him a song or two, brush his hair back, that sort of thing. He was so much younger then, so perhaps none of that would work anymore. I . . ."

Sudden tears clogged her throat, stopped up her words, and she looked down at the hand Taft held, willing their connection to give her strength.

His hold tightened perceptibly, but he said nothing.

She exhaled very slowly. "I can protect him from all else in life, but I cannot protect him from this. It kills me to admit it. I don't know if they helped him at all while I was away. I don't know how often he had them, or if he cried himself to sleep. I don't know any of that. But when I have been with him, he has never not needed me for one before."

"Alix," Taft murmured very softly, turning to her more fully and going up to his knees so they might be more on a level. He put his free hand on her cheek, the heat of it coursing through her chilled frame more efficiently than any fire she could have hoped for.

He waited until she looked up at him, then searched her eyes, brushing her cheek a little. "It wasn't that he did not need you. He will always need you. You are his mother, and he knows you adore him. He even told me that his mama usually helps him with his bad dreams, and he had tried singing your songs to himself, but it did not help tonight. I think he had been remembering you when his dreams became too much at Stonehall. You *were* with him, even then."

Her tears began to well up, flooding her eyes and making her view of Taft shimmer tremulously. "Really?"

"Really." He smiled as she blinked the tears back, not a one of them falling to her cheek. "Tonight, he simply needed someone. I was there, is all. If you would prefer it, I'll see to it that you are always summoned, should this continue. But why should you shoulder the burden alone?"

"I always have done," she whispered, shrugging in his hold. "It is all I know."

Taft leaned closer, both hands going to her face, his eyes dark and intense. "You are not alone now, Alix. You never will be again."

"I know," she breathed, her fingers finding their way to his hair after all. She brushed her fingers into the deep golden depths, almost bronze in the dim light of night, noting how his eyes widened and darkened with each passing stroke. "You're here. Aren't you?"

It wasn't a question, but a realization. An affirmation. A confession, perhaps, and so much more.

Neither of them was alone anymore.

Taft's eyes fell to her mouth as he nodded, stealing her breath with the shift. All at once, her lips parted, a sigh of hope and permission and pleading racing out, and it was all the sound he needed. He leaned in, his fingers cradling her face tenderly, and her lips tingled in anticipation.

They had touched in only the smallest degree when Adam yawned audibly. "I think I can go to sleep now."

Taft groaned, his fingertips gripping ever so slightly against her face as he pulled back. "Right. Think so?"

The words sounded light, but his voice certainly was not so. There was a deep, unsteady roughness to it that clawed at Alexandrina's stomach, and she clamped down on her lips hard to keep herself from reacting audibly.

"Yes. I think the toast worked."

Alexandrina laughed and dropped her hands from Taft, settling them into her lap as she looked at her son, now rubbing his eyes. "The toast, hmm?"

Taft chuckled himself, pushing to his feet. "It always worked for me. That and warm milk with cinnamon."

Adam's eyes widened and he gasped, even in his sleepiness. "We didn't try that! Can we?"

Alexandrina gave Taft a scolding look. "Not tonight, sweetheart. Should you have another bad dream in the future, or trouble sleeping, perhaps Taft can teach you that one then."

"Most assuredly," Taft replied with a cheeky grin at her, though the dark heat had yet to fully leave his eyes. "I promise.

Come on, my young chap. Let's get you back to bed."

The three of them walked from Taft's rooms down the corridor together, no question of one of the adults staying behind. They would walk back as a family, and it was perfectly natural to do so.

Perfectly natural. There was something unspeakably moving in that, and Alexandrina would not forget it.

Adam was quick to return to his bed, nearly half asleep already as he pulled the bedcovers up, yawning again. "Good night, Mama. Good night, Taft."

Alexandrina stooped and pressed a kiss to Adam's brow, brushing his hair back just as she'd done when he was a baby. "Good night, my darling."

She stepped aside and smiled as Taft took the chance to ruffle Adam's hair. "Good night, Adam."

The pair of them left the nursery then, Taft shutting the door quietly behind them. Alexandrina folded her wrap around her, suddenly fully aware that she and her husband were alone in their nightclothes in the middle of the night.

After already almost kissing.

Unless a blizzard came through the halls at that moment, something needed to happen between them before the night was out, or she would not be able to sleep tonight. And she doubted any amount of toast or warm milk with cinnamon would help her there.

Taft nudged his head down the corridor towards their rooms, starting to walk without saying a word.

Alexandrina fell into step beside him, heart thundering worse than any storm she had ever experienced.

Someone needed to say something, and if he wouldn't . . .

"You are so good with him," she praised softly. "He adores you."

"And I him," he rumbled, laughing a little. "A boy after my

own heart, truly. And I think he is losing that hollow look from Stonehall rather well. Another week, perhaps, and it will be gone entirely."

"I hope so." She swallowed around a tense lump in her throat, her fingers itching for something, anything, to happen. "I never expected to see you sitting on the floor making toast in the middle of the night."

"I aim to surprise you however I can," he quipped. "I know what it is like to wake in the night without comfort and with no sleep to be found. Mrs. Evans was very kind about it and taught me both toast and warm milk, and how to make it myself when I was old enough."

Alexandrina looked up at him, smiling a little. "How in the world have you turned out to be the sort of man you are with an upbringing like that?"

He stopped and turned to her, his own smile curving in a way that was only matched by the curling of her toes. "And what sort of man is that?"

Oh, he was too clever, and her neck began a slow path of burning towards her ears. "Wonderful," she managed, fixing her eyes at the vee of his shirt rather than his face. "Caring. Intuitive. Irksome. Playful. Kind."

"Alix . . ." Taft interrupted in a rasping voice she felt to her core. "It might kill me not to kiss you now. Kiss you and mean it. Please . . . please tell me I may."

Her heart soared into the vicinity of her eyes, and she breathlessly laughed once. "You did not ask the first time," she reminded him in a whisper.

He shook his head and reached for her hair, long and streaming about her shoulders. "That was for the scandal. This would be for us." He toyed with the ends of her hair, curling it around his fingers as his chest grew unsteady with his breathing. "Alix . . ."

A confidence and certainty unlike anything she had ever known took over and she placed her hands on his chest, slowly sliding them up towards his neck, loving the feel of the tremor beneath her touch. "What if I were to kiss you, Taft? Would that kill you?"

"Yes," he clipped with a firm nod. "And I could only hope to die such a glorious death."

"Well, then," she breathed, rising on her toes as she latched her fingers behind his neck and pulled him to her. "I wish you a good death."

Their lips fused with an insistence she had not expected, her own energies pouring into the kiss beyond what she had ever felt capable of giving. His hold on her was more cradling than clenching, but there was no denying the power in it. Again and again, his mouth passed over hers, and hers molded to his, each new contact as exhilarating as the last, spinning her into a frenzy that cried for more. And made her give more.

She arched into him, his hold pulling her to the tops of her toes as he slowly, deliciously devoured her with kiss after kiss, every moment of breathless anticipation worth it for this incandescence. She sighed against his mouth, the action bringing her closer still, and she felt, and tasted, a rumble of approval from him, the sound lighting up a great many things within her.

Her fingers clutched at his hair, dragged through it, became her anchor as well as her weapon. She slid one hand to his jaw, brushing against the stubble there and creating the most extraordinary new angle for their kiss. She gripped at it, fusing his mouth to hers with a newfound need that confounded her, but felt so incomparably right that she had to give in.

Had to have more.

Taft moved his mouth to her cheek, his breath hot and rampant. "I'm at my wit's end, love," he whispered, the words causing a flurry of sensation on her heated skin. "If you don't go to bed now, I won't be able to let you."

She nodded against him, everything a haze about her as she nuzzled against his mouth and his chin, letting herself be lowered to the ground before she comprehended what he had said.

Oh . . .

She nodded again, this time with more clarity, and rested her head against the power of his chest while her breathing galloped on ahead of her.

He wrapped his arms around her tightly but kept his hands safely from her body. "Not the thing I expected, death," he mused on a wry laugh.

Alexandrina snickered. "No? I think I might have died as well, though my heart is quite clearly assuring me I live and breathe."

"Second life, I reckon. Wonder if it's any different." He kissed the top of her head in a perfunctory way, then exhaled slowly. "What a shock this is, Alix. Did you expect it?"

She shook her head. "No, I most certainly did not." She pulled back a little and looked up at him, smiling. "But it would have made the garden incident so much more interesting."

Taft snorted a laugh and touched his brow to hers. "You'd have killed me for trying that."

"Would you have wanted to?" she shot back, giggling to herself.

He was silent for a moment. "I've always thought you were beautiful," he whispered. "I just didn't know what to do about it. Everything about you was uncertain for me, and that was different."

"I'm not sorry for it," she told him. "I wanted to be different."

"I'm delighted now that you were. None of this would have happened if you'd been like everyone else." He lifted his head and kissed her brow tenderly. "Go to bed, sweet Alix. I'll see you in the morning."

She stepped back, out of his arms, and gave him a bemused look. "But will you kiss me tomorrow?"

"Oh, I bloody well hope so," he said without hesitation.

Alexandrina grinned at him, nodding in thought. "And while you're in an accommodating mood, would you care to tell me why the good people of Godfrey were trying to speak Italian to me today?"

He snickered like a child. "I thought it adequate payback for word being spread that I have a rash."

"A what?"

He sobered just a little, starting to look wary. "A rash. Carter's daughters told him you told the cook I have a rash."

"I said that you *were* rash," she told him, still grinning in delight. "Why would I make something up?"

His eyes narrowed. "You're teasing me, aren't you? Trying to make me apologize, right?"

She only shrugged. "I'll leave that to you to decide. Good night, Taft." She turned and started to walk back to her rooms, biting down on her lip hard to keep from laughing,

"This is a joke, right, Alix? Alix?"

"Good night, Taft!"

CHAPTER 17

There was nothing like a ball for entertaining one's guests and seeing them suitably occupied for an entire evening. It was always the highlight of his Battensay parties, and the fact that they only had three or four while they were there was a source of great consternation for the regular guests. Normally, Taft would agree with them.

Tonight, however, he wished the whole party would end after this particular ball and leave him and his wife in peace.

Or, rather, in solitude.

He had been all anxiety and consternation throughout the day, and he blamed his wife for that.

After their almost unworldly exchange in the corridors last night, he had barely seen her for more than three minutes today, and that had not been enough time for a flirtatious smile, let alone a kiss or a few words of carefully hidden compliments.

She'd certainly looked stunning, far more today than in any day past, and her smile had seemed easier to come by for all those around her. Less forced and less strained, all told, and both her eyes and her color had been bright. He did not flatter himself that he was the cause of any of it, though he would dare enough to hope it was.

The blasted woman kept looking at him when she could, too, and each time something rather sharp lanced the back of his left knee and clogged the base of his throat.

Three full minutes of sharpness and speechlessness was quite enough to be getting on with, particularly when he was well aware that it would have been more had they not had the hunt today for the gentlemen.

A good ride and a brisk day's breezes had done a great deal to soothe him, even with Larkin poking fun at him the entire time. His friend had no sympathy whatsoever for a man so wildly tossed about, and insisted it was the way things ought to be until either he or Alexandrina found a more solid footing for them.

He was hinting an inordinate amount about whatever footing he suspected that to be, but refused to come right out and say it.

Taft had shown his displeasure by outshooting his friend in the hunt five to one.

Larkin claimed he was no great hunter, but Taft refused to listen to that

Now they were at the beginning of the ball, and Taft only wanted to see his wife. Being the second one of the party, there was no need for them to open the event with their own dancing, so he supposed it did not matter when she presented herself to the ballroom.

All that was waiting for her here was a desperately anxious husband who only wanted to hold her hand. Or cart her off to a closet or alcove and kiss her until he could not remember his own name.

Whichever would suit best.

"Waiting for your wife, Taft?" Sophia Roth inquired gently from his right side, her face laced with laughter.

He smiled at her sheepishly. "Is it so obvious?"

She lifted a shoulder in a light shrug. "Not particularly, but you would normally be dancing by now, and yet here you stand. Your public smile is in place, of course, but your eyes keep moving to the door."

"Must you be so observant, Soph?" he asked with a laugh. "How can a man get away with anything?"

"My husband asks me that on a fairly regular basis, I fear," Sophia admitted on a sigh. "I cannot help it, I simply notice things."

"Thank God you do," Taft insisted. "We would all be lost if you did not."

Her look became more speculative at that. "Then might I tell you something else I have noticed?"

Taft winced at the question. "I will most likely regret this but go on."

Sophia nodded. "I think your wife might be in love with you. And more than that, I am heartily convinced that you are in love with her."

Taft's heart gave an unsteady beat and a half as he stared at his friend's wife, who was also his friend, he supposed, and found himself nodding before he meant to. "I think you are right about the latter, but I cannot speak to the former."

"What?" Sophia squawked, clearing her throat afterwards to minimize the impact of her screeching. "I am so sorry, I don't know what came over me."

"Surprise, I should think." Taft said lightly. "Or outright shock. I doubt you expected me to answer like that."

"Hardly." She coughed rather delicately, snapping open her fan and waving it in a steady pattern. "But at least I have won the bet with Larkin. He told me not to come over here and said you would adamantly deny it if I did."

Taft chuckled easily. "What were the stakes of the wager?"

"Use of a comfortable chair in the orangery," she replied with a quick smile. "You know how he hates the furniture in there, and I have yet to give in. If he won, I had to have a more comfortable arrangement in there. But as I have won, I need not worry."

"Happy to help." Taft shook his head in disbelief, the bizarre nature of the Roths' living arrangements still nothing like he had ever heard before. Larkin would own one room, but Sophia the furniture within it, or vice versa, and until their son inherited both parts of the will outright, there was nothing they could do about it. And, if their antics were to be believed, they had found their own amusement in the thing.

He could not imagine such a scenario playing out well at Battensay, particularly now that Alexandrina had learned so very skillfully how to compete and manipulate where he was concerned. He would have found himself somehow out of house and home in no time at all simply because she would have found a cleverer avenue to the arrangement than he would have.

She was infinitely more intelligent than he was, there was no doubt, and just as quick. Heaven help him if they had daughters, for they would undoubtedly be just like her.

Daughters . . .

The idea made him smile. He would love to have a son, of course, if for no other reason than to keep the title and the estate in his direct line, but he would not object in any way to daughters. Loads of them. A houseful of girls to make his life merry and hellish in one. Sons would be wonderful for Adam, so perhaps there ought to be a few of those.

As though he could pick and choose. But he most certainly wanted children now. As many as Alexandrina would consent to. A large family with madness aplenty, so none of the children need ever feel lonely or without friends.

Then the world could discuss the Harwoods for far better reasons than his lordship's weskit or her ladyship's reserve.

A mass of children would be a far better reason, and he

looked forward to the prospect.

If, that was, his wife felt the same way.

That was an almighty if.

"So you're in love with her," Sophia prodded, breaking into his vision of a chaotic nursery.

Taft nodded, swallowing at the acknowledgement. "Indeed."

"Truly?"

"I would not lie about this."

"Of course, I did not mean . . ." Sophia put a hand on his arm, squeezing fondly. "I am so happy for you, Taft. You deserve such happiness."

"The happiness would be complete if she loved me in return," he told her, even as his throat clenched in fear. "I cannot hope that far yet. Dream it, perhaps, but hope . . ."

"She does," Sophia insisted. "I know it."

Taft turned to her, his smile turning a little sad. "Did she say so? Tell you herself? Use the very words?"

Sophia frowned. "Well, no. But you must admit that she is very reserved with regards to true emotions. Her words, perhaps not, but her feelings . . . Love is such a tender, vulnerable one, and I cannot think she would confide that to anyone but you."

"Exactly," he replied, turning back to survey the dancing, though none of it had any interest for him. "If she would even confide that to me. My wife is a tower of strength, even against herself. If she comes to love me, it could be several years before she manages to admit it. I can wait as long as it takes. It will not stop my loving her, nor my devotion to her. I've told her from the start that I will not press her on anything, and I mean to keep to that."

The woman beside him sighed again, this time patting his arm gently. "You are a good man, Taft Debenham. I know many people say it, but the truth of it goes deeper than anyone knows."

He smiled and picked up her hand, kissing her glove fondly. "Thank you, Soph. Are you dancing tonight?"

"I think I may this one, if you'll take me," she suggested, nodding towards the floor. "It is not so vigorous as to make Larkin upset."

"A pity, that," Taft teased. "I do so love making your husband upset."

Sophia whacked him hard on the arm, making him laugh, and for the next few minutes, his thoughts were distracted from seeking out his wife. It was probably for the best, given his earth-shattering revelation.

Although the earth had not shattered from it. Nor had it moved in any particular direction. The ground had stayed firmly beneath his feet, and all of his internal organs had remained in place. Apart from his heart beating out of time, nothing extraordinary had come over him with it.

Because he'd already known that. Hadn't admitted it, of course, hadn't put it in those particular words, but he had known. It made sense that he loved her. It was so obvious that he loved her. It was the least bewildering thing he had ever heard in his entire life.

Nothing had ever been so perfect as his loving her.

So it could not be a surprise, really.

Now, if she were to love him . . .

Well, hell would have to freeze and heaven ignite, the earth spin into madness, and all logic and sense he'd ever accumulated in his life dissolve into nothingness.

He would not object to that.

Not in the least.

Sophia did not seem to mind that he was not particularly attentive a partner, though her soft laughter told him she knew all too well that his thoughts were more agreeably engaged. He might not be actively seeking his wife at the moment, but he was certainly dwelling upon her.

Who could blame him for that?

The dance with Sophia did not last much longer, which was fortunate, as the more he danced with her, the more he wished to dance with Alexandrina. Not that Sophia was a terrible dancer or that the dance with her was pure drudgery. On the contrary, she was quite graceful and made for an enjoyable partner.

Which was why he wanted to dance with his wife.

He led Sophia back to the edges of the ballroom, making sure to see to her care, given her condition, and then, once he was satisfied and she waved him off, he went to find his wife.

Enough was enough. Surely she was in the room by now. Surely she was gracing everyone here with her presence, and the only person who was not partaking of the blessings of such was him.

Considering no one wanted her in this room more than him, there was a great irony in that.

Taft smiled as he passed other guests and neighbors, who had been invited to the ball as per his usual arrangements, which meant the room was fuller now than it might have been on another night. It was clear he was cursing himself in all of this, and he would be the one to get in his own way. No doubt he had passed his wife twenty times or so in the evening and she would be in a raging fury when he finally noticed, which he would absolutely deserve.

He might actually get struck, after all of this time. He was undoubtedly past due.

He would accept it if he could only set eyes on Alexandrina.

As though the heavens were on his side, there was a sudden parting in the guests to his left, and a vision in a rich plum gown stood there, brown and auburn hair plaited, coiled, and pinned into the most exquisite bouquet of art he had ever seen on a female head. Her eyes fell on him, and the breathtaking blue-green hue of them arrested him into complete immobility. Her mouth curved in a smile he had never seen her wear, something shy and tender, hopeful and expectant.

He'd have marched over to her and hauled her into his arms had there not been an entire ballroom of guests around them. And if he could feel his legs.

His eyes raked over her from head to toe, taking in every aspect of her appearance, from the embroidered netting forming the stunning front panel of floral and vines to the three lines of ribbon forming her hem. From the whispers of sleeves to the intricacies of her bodice. From the exact curls at her temples to the jeweled pins in her hair.

Pins he envied and would very much love to pluck out and cast to the floor.

There was no question he adored her. There was no question he found her beautiful and desirable and majestic. But there was also no question that beneath that beauty and desire, beneath the appearances and impressions, was a heart that beat as powerfully as anything he had ever known, that reached for his in a way he could not believe. A heart that he desperately wanted to be able to hold in his keeping.

Everything about Alexandrina was perfection in his eyes. From her defenses to her vulnerability, from her beauty to her wit, from her love for her son to her intolerance for idiots. Everything was just as he would wish it, and he wanted nothing else.

He wanted no one else.

Just her.

Alexandrina took pity on him and started towards him, her smile turning slightly wry. "You haven't said a thing, my lord. For a man of your natural sociability, that is a great concern."

"My apologies," he murmured, unable to look anywhere but at her. "I find words singularly lacking."

"Do you?" She hummed a soft laugh, her cheeks taking on a trifle more color. "Those words did well enough."

"Paltry," he assured her, the temptation to kiss her bordering on the unholy. "Barely worth the breath to carry them."

Alexandrina's smile deepened. "That is a compliment in and of itself, my lord. You are quite a feast for the eyes yourself."

Taft felt a growl rise in his throat. He took Alexandrina's gloved hand and raised it very slowly to his lips. "If you have any desire to remain in this ballroom without a second scandal, Lady Harwood, I would cease your praises at this moment." He kissed her hand, gripping her fingers hard so she might know just how much he meant his words *and* his actions.

She shivered very slightly. "But there is so much more to say."

"Alix," he ground out. "Now."

She clamped down on her lips hard, a soft giggle escaping. "Very well, my lord. Would it perturb your propriety to dance with your wife? I presently do not have a partner, and it would seem a convenient time . . ."

"Yes." He took the hand he still held and pulled her behind him as he turned to the floor, moving through the guests with as much determination as one might trample leaves in autumn.

He would have counted any fallen bodies in his path with the same dismissiveness. There was nothing else to his life or this night or this moment but his wife, and the feeling of her hand in his. He had no idea what the present dance was, nor did he care. Anything that would allow him to look at her for an extended period of time, hold her hand without shocking anyone, and ignore everyone else who was supposed to be under his present stewardship as host.

Taft eyed the gathering patterns, his mind working slower than normal as he attempted to determine their course. Groups of four couples were forming squares, and he nodded quickly, moving to the nearest one. A quadrille, then. Perfect. He would have preferred a waltz purely for the proximity and intensity of it, but a quadrille would do. The sets were long, and the exchanging of partners was limited.

Most of the time.

If he'd thought of this earlier, had a trifle more sense before he'd set eyes on his wife, he would have bribed the dance caller to keep the partner exchanges at a minimum. He would do his task creditably, as far as dancing was concerned, but the less time he spent with other ladies in his square, the better.

The less time his wife spent with the other gentlemen in the square, the better.

When had he become this possessive boor of a man rather than the composed and collected gentleman he had long been praised for?

Simple, he answered himself. When he had fallen in love with his wife.

Surely he was not to be blamed for that.

"A quadrille," Alexandrina murmured beside him. "Pity it is not a waltz, but at least it is not a reel."

He could have groaned at the agony of their similar thoughts. "I would dance a jig with you if there were nothing else available to me," he told her from the corner of his mouth. "Nothing would be too exerting or too long. Everything, however, would be too short. Everything."

"Are you trying to make me burst into flames?" she hissed with what seemed to be true irritation, which, oddly enough, settled his own madness a little.

So he was not alone in this. Brilliant.

"If I can, yes," he replied without much concern. "Why should I be the only one dying?"

"You said you would kiss me today."

"You ought to have been available today."

"You could have sought me out."

"Don't push it. I am not above dragging you from this room and having my way with you in the corridor."

"Sounds intriguing. What precisely would that entail?"

Oh, devil take it, he was never going to live through this first set, let alone any of the others. Why had he ever provoked her into sharpening her own wit at his expense? In this present state, even banter was deuced exhilarating, and there was no woman on earth who could banter like his Alexandrina.

The music needed to start, and it needed to start now.

Blessedly, it did so, and he was able to move rather than stand beside his wife and make only-just-polite conversation.

Taft crossed to the woman opposite him, extending his right hand, breathing a breath of Alexandrina-free air while he could, though he found himself already craving it, despite the return of relative sanity. He turned and reached out with his left, finding Alexandrina there, as the pattern allowed. The moment his hand touched hers, his ribs began to ache, and their brief exchange of hands and clashing eyes was wildly short before they were side by side again.

"I hate quadrilles," Taft muttered, nodding once before he moved again to cross the square to repeat the pattern.

When Alexandrina took his hand again, she hummed a soft note. "There are worse things."

They turned to face each other, Taft straightening as they did so, taking in a careful breath in an attempt to maintain his sanity. They mirrored each other in motions, eyes locked in a wordless battle wherein the stakes were high, and the victory would be sweet. Although who would win and who would lose, as well as what exactly losing would entail, was rather murky.

They took each other's hands, turning in a circle, Alexandrina's grip on his hands impossibly clenching and pulling all feeling from anywhere else in his body. He only knew the feeling of her hold on him, the very length and breadth of his fingers as they held hers, each crease in his palm, every callus scraping against the fabric of his glove.

And just as intimately, he knew her hand. Encased in fabric, certainly, but a mere matter of material could not lessen the familiarity of her delicate fingers, the strength she possessed, the slightest shift where his ring sat on her finger.

It gave him a deeply primal sense of satisfaction to feel the simple band beneath her glove, to know that this woman before him was, in fact, bound to him. Custom did not dictate that he also wear a ring as a symbol of such, but her ring bound him just as surely. He was hers, God help him, and for far beyond time than 'till death do they part.

Even death would not break this hold she had on him.

Suddenly, a quadrille was the worst possible dance he could have shared with her, the drudgery of the length and multiple sets enough to kill a man who only wanted to hold his wife.

Alexandrina smiled at him further still as they parted hands, moving with the lady opposite in their next pattern. The subsequent motions of the dance were lost on Taft, even as he participated in them, absently moving this way and that. He could only be acutely aware of the location of his wife at any given time, any length of distance between them too much to bear.

He finally understood what the poets and romantics meant when they described love as madness.

There was no other word for it.

At last, it was time for the side couples to engage in the patterns, leaving Taft to stand beside Alexandrina and patiently wait.

He reached out his hand and hooked a few fingers into hers, not gripping so much as holding. Connecting. Embracing.

He heard Alexandrina hum softly beside him. "Next time, I must have a waltz with you, my lord. I think it would be quite engaging."

"You'll never waltz with anybody but me ever again, my lady," Taft murmured, curling his fingers more securely against hers. "I insist they are all mine."

She looked over at him, her smile rather telling, sending his heart careening into each of his lungs in turn.

"Lord Harwood!"

The music in the room came to a stop, as did the dance, all heads turning towards the doors.

Taft frowned at the interruption, at the firm tone of the call, at the volume of it. Who would bellow at him during a ball rather than seek him out?

"What is it?" Alexandrina hissed, her voice hitching as both hands seized his.

"I don't know," he replied. "Come with me."

They moved through the crowd to the ballroom entrance, and Taft stopped in his tracks when he saw the man standing there, looking almost murderous. "Jenkins?"

Alexandrina gasped softly behind him.

Mr. Jenkins barely spared a glance for her, keeping his gaze on Taft. "You challenged me to a duel, Harwood. I will not let my reputation continue to be tarnished by that. I insist we follow through. I accept your challenge, sir. Let us duel at dawn."

CHAPTER 18

Alexandrina was going to die, and nothing was going to convince her otherwise. A sleepless night spent pacing her rooms and the distinct feeling that her heart had somehow left her chest only convinced her that it was true.

Her husband was dueling at this very moment. Over her.

It was the stupidest thing she could ever imagine, two men shooting at each other over offenses given. Mr. Jenkins would not listen to reason when she and Taft had gone to speak with him in the study, away from the guests in the ballroom. He would not accept Taft's insistence that it was not necessary, that all had been set to rights since Taft had married Alexandrina, nor would he accept that he really had made an attempt to take advantage of Alexandrina being trapped in that rosebush.

He would not listen, and Taft could not refuse him if they wished for his reputation to remain intact. Apparently, such things were worse than engaging in a duel at all, given the legal haziness of the thing.

Idiocy in its purest form. Who had made these rules anyway? No one of sense, she was sure, and no woman with a husband she cared for.

A husband she adored.

A husband she loved.

Oh, heavens, she loved him! She'd loved him for ages and simply never let herself use the words, or even think them. She'd never considered why he had grown so attractive in recent days, despite having seen him at occasional intervals over the years without any disturbance to her frame of mind. Why the touch of his hand was enough to soothe her darkest worries. Why his kiss was the answer to every question, despite not knowing at least half of those questions herself. Why she wanted to be with him at every minute of every day, if such a thing were possible.

Why she was dying now, thinking of him walking to the fields determined by the seconds in this duel. She had no idea who Jenkins had chosen, nor did she care, but Larkin Roth would be with Taft, and she had begged him last evening to do everything he could to stop the duel entirely. To keep Taft safe. To bring him home to her.

To Taft, she had not said a word. Could not. She had held his hand as long as she could, treasured the feeling of his lips on hers in the one gentle kiss she'd had yesterday, followed by the sweet impression of his mouth at her brow as he'd held her. No words had been spoken. No grand farewells. No "if only" or "I wish" or "if the worst should happen," no lingering looks or sighs, no apologies or final messages of hope or confession. He had simply held her a while, then suggested she go to bed before kissing her hand in the most heartbreaking manner she could have imagined, and she had cried tears into her pillow for at least an hour after.

She could not stop this duel. She had asked him before she had retired. She could not race out on a horse, even if she knew the location of the thing, and demand that this insanity end, given there was no resolution for Jenkins. She had married Taft to save her reputation so she would not have to marry Jenkins, and while it saved her reputation to do so, the effects had not reflected well on him. Nor should they have, considering what he had tried, but the stain was something he could not bear, so the duel had to commence.

She could have raged at Taft for suggesting such a thing, even in his act, but how was she to know that it would be taken up in earnest? How could Taft have known? It was all supposed to be part of the act, not something given with genuine effrontery. Yet now her husband was standing on a dew-dampened, fog-shrouded field, waiting to meet a pistol head on.

It was all too real from something that had started off as an act.

Real consequences, just as her marriage had been.

How could one side of the consequences bring her such joy and fulfillment when the other was the means of ruining her life?

She cursed herself now as she sat in her rooms, staring out of the window in her sitting room, the fire low and without any warmth. Why had she not raced down the stairs when she had heard Taft leave, thrown herself in his arms, begged him not to go, or at the very least, told him that she loved him? He should not go to his potential death without knowing how she felt, but she could not give that up when he might not come home. She could not let those walls vanish entirely for him, offer the very last piece of herself that he did not already possess, succumb to the temptation to lay her heart bare for him to do as he wished

She should have done it. She should have been brave enough to be vulnerable. She should have said something. Anything. Asked him to come home, wished him well, given him one more kiss to express what her words refused to convey.

But no. She had been cowardly and remained in her rooms. Retreated into herself and thrown up those same stupid walls she had built in her time with Stephen. She had no need of protection from Taft. She needed to bring him within her walls, not leave him standing outside of them.

If he came home, she would be different. If he returned to her, there would be no more walls. If there was a future for them, she would do her utmost to lose herself in him, blend the two of them together until beginnings and ends meant nothing.

The depth of her feelings for Taft was agonizing, and the loss of him would do more to destroy her than anything she had ever endured with Stephen. She had wanted to protect herself from such intensity, but she could not resist falling in love with Taft any more than she could have kept herself from drawing breath.

It was inevitable, and she would not regret it. Could not. She felt more alive than she had in her entire life, more resembling the woman she had always wanted to be, more aware of life and existence and more willing to treasure both.

Taft had brought her to life, and she had not even known she had been dead, so to speak.

She did not want to continue living in this life if he were not there to do so with her.

Death had brought her freedom from her first husband. It would bring her imprisonment with Taft.

Her cheeks tingled now in the chill of her rooms, almost startling her from the clouds of her thoughts. She rubbed at one, only to find that tears had been there, silently releasing her fears and regrets and aching without her even realizing it. Taft had never wiped her tears, she realized as she stared at the remnants of them on her thumb. She had always been so careful, so composed, so in control that any tears had stayed contained in his presence.

Walls even in her tears.

How could he love a woman who could not let herself cry in earnest before him? Assuming he could ever love her at all, of course. She could not see how, even if she yearned for him to.

Being loved by Taft would be the epitome of all the hopes and dreams she had ever had for herself or her life. She would never need anything else.

Please, she prayed, though she had not done so in earnest since she was a child. *Please, let him come home.*

She could not do anything if he did not come home.

She would not even have a piece of him to carry forward if he died. They had never been intimate, so there could be no child. She ached now for a baby bearing his features and manner, his eyes or his hair, anything remotely resembling him so he would not remain only in her memories.

Empty arms had never seemed so poignant.

Alexandrina glanced slowly at the clock on her mantle, acknowledging its time. Almost two hours now since she had heard him go. It should all be over now, for better or for worse. Her husband could be dead or wounded now, or Jenkins could be and her husband in danger from the law. Whatever would follow from this duel would begin now, and she would have to deal with it shortly.

But how could she even rise from this chair and face it? It would take strength she did not have. It would take her husband appearing in her room and taking her hands, pulling her to her feet, and holding her against his chest.

Short of that . . .

The sound of horse hooves on the gravel outside made her heart stop. Was it one horse? Two? Could she hear her husband's voice or his footfall?

She couldn't wait here to find out. She needed to see, needed to know.

She surged to her feet, fatigue and exhaustion forgotten as she raced to her door, flinging it open and barreling down the corridor. Her breath raced faster than her feet, hitching on every inhale and rasping on every exhale. Thoughts of silence were gone, and any disturbance their guests experienced by her flight insignificant.

The fate of her husband was at hand, and there was nothing to be calm about in that.

Her feet scampered frantically down the stairs, miraculously avoiding any tripping or stumbles in the process. She'd have slid the railing to get there all the faster if she thought she could manage it safely. Even then, she was tempted. She latched onto the balustrade at the end, swinging herself around it to continue her flight towards the entrance of Battensay.

The door opened ahead of her, and she skidded to a halt, afraid to cross the last several yards of corridor to meet it.

What if . . .?

A tall man in a dark greatcoat entered, linen shirt loosely tucked into dark breeches, slightly dirty boots encasing his perfect calves. His dark golden hair was slightly damp and windswept, a morning's scruff evident on his chin and jaw even from her present position. Another man entered behind him, catching sight of Alexandrina and tapping the first to indicate her.

Dark eyes suddenly turned to her, and though she had known it was him, none of it was real until that moment.

Taft was alive, and he was here.

A shuddering, gasping sob crashed against her ribs before escaping her, and her legs gave way with the sound, sending her collapsing to the floor as tears began to flow freely. She covered her face, curling into herself as wave after wave of relief coursed over and through her, consumed everything within her. Sobs shook her frame, rippled across her arms and into the depths of her skirts, where her legs quivered weakly.

Clipped steps sounded faintly in her ears, and strong arms came around her, pulling her against a warm chest and securing themselves around her.

"Oh, love," Taft murmured as he tucked her head beneath his chin. "It's all right, I'm here."

She gripped his shirt in hand, burying her face against him as she continued to sob, unable to catch her breath, unable to speak, unable to think anything beyond the feeling of him.

"It's all right," he told her, one hand rubbing softly over her unbound hair. "Everything's all right."

"You're alive," Alexandrina managed to force out, the words barely intelligible. "You're here. You're . . ." She shook her head, fisting her hold on his shirt to bring him somehow closer.

Taft groaned and pressed his mouth to her hair. "Oh, Alix, don't cry so. I cannot bear it."

"I must cry, Taft." She hiccupped as hot tears continued to run freely from her eyes. "I am long past due. Just hold me. Please, please, just hold me."

His arms tightened around her further still. "Believe me, Alix. I am not going anywhere."

Her tears refused to slow, refused to stop, refused to abate as she clung to him, wished she could bury herself in him, in all that he was, and never be freed.

Taft's hand continued to run over her hair slowly, smoothly, occasionally tangling gently in the dark tresses. "Is this because of the duel?" he asked in a low, tender voice. "Because it frightened you?"

"No," she told him with a choked sniffle, raising herself to take his face in her hands. "It's because I love you."

His eyes widened, his hand stilling in her hair. "You what?"

Alexandrina leaned in and brushed her lips over his, the kiss more of a caress than anything else. "I love you."

He kissed her then, with more insistence, his fingers gripping more tightly into her hair, the pain of it only serving to remind her more that he was here, that she loved him, that there was a future of some sort, and that she could continue to love him in life, not just in death.

He moaned softly against her mouth, breaking off and dusting light, grazing kisses across her face. "You love me," he repeated, his breath almost scratching her skin. "Thank God. But how? Why? Because I defended your honor?"

"No," she sighed, leaning into him and sliding her fingers into his hair with one hand and gripping his neck with the other. "Because you stand by me when no one else does. Because you make me smile when I want to do anything else. Because nothing feels more like home than being with you."

He tilted her face back towards him and kissed her slowly, deeply, and quite thoroughly. "My sweet Alix . . ."

"I've loved you for ages, Taft," she admitted, the words almost tumbling from her lips. "I didn't know it until I thought I would lose you, and then . . ." A weak sob choked her words, and she shook her head. "I was so afraid I would never be able to tell you."

"Well, this is fortuitous."

The rumbling bemusement of his words forced her to pull back just enough to meet his eyes. "Is it?"

"Quite," he said with a nod. "You see . . . I have found myself madly in love with you, though it has been some time since I've known it."

Alexandrina grinned, brushing his hair back. "Liar."

"No, it's true," he insisted. "I've loved you from the very moment you demonstrated your exceptional skill in archery. Been quite a thorn in my side, that has."

"You seem recovered enough."

"One gets used to the idea. Becomes quite tickled by it, actually."

"Does one? How bizarre."

He chuckled softly, wiping tears from her cheeks, kissing her brow, then her lips. "I love you, my darling. I never knew . . . never imagined we could have this."

Alexandrina sighed and hugged herself to Taft, resting her cheek against his chest and loving the feeling of his arms so perfectly and completely encircling her. "You called me love very early on in our marriage. Do you recall? On our way to retrieve Adam, when you took the time to comfort and encourage me. You called me love."

"I remember," he rumbled, his fingers tracing absent patterns along her back, pressing his mouth to the top of her head.

"You knew it then," she murmured, softly kissing the skin at the vee of his shirt. "You might not have known you did, but you knew."

"I don't believe you were far behind me, if that was true," he confessed, clumping her hair in hand in a sort of massage she quite enjoyed. "For a woman who rarely smiled in the whole course of the time I knew you before, you certainly smiled a great deal at me after."

Alexandrina hid a smile against his chest. "I did not realize I was smiling."

Taft laughed once, very softly. "I know. That was why it meant so much. Why it moved me so. I wanted to keep you smiling. To bring such happiness to your life that smiling was the most natural thing in the world."

"You refused to let me keep you at arm's length. You immediately turned from a man who could barely stand me to a man who ensured I could stand. As though the vows you took meant more than the breath used to express them." She swallowed fresh tears, shaking her head. "I could not resist that. Could not help but to take up the same cause for myself."

"I am ever so relieved you did." He sighed into her hair. "Would you like to know what happened in the duel?"

Alexandrina stilled in his hands, then inched closer. "If I must. Is Jenkins dead?"

She felt Taft shake his head. "No, and nor is he bleeding in any part of his body. Despite his insistence that the duel must take place, he was rather polite once we reached the field. We took our required paces, and I fired before the call, directly into the air above me rather than in any way towards him."

"You did?"

"I could not take the chance of firing at him," Taft told her. "He has no memory of his behavior towards you and is mortified by the idea he that he would have done so. You were not harmed, and I married you to stave off the scandal. What good would drawing his blood do?"

It was a valid point, and one she had wondered often in the last several hours.

"But that would leave you rather exposed to him and his bullet," she pointed out. "You could have died in an instant."

He nodded, his mouth pressing against her hair again. "I could have, I suppose. If he had fired at me."

Alexandrina reared back in surprise, her hands resting on Taft's chest. "He didn't?"

"He did not," Taft confirmed with a shake of his head. "Faced with the prospect of shooting me without provocation, Jenkins balked. Spent his shot in the ground, and that was that. Our seconds were satisfied, and honor has been preserved. Or some such."

It was too simple, too neat an ending for such a complicated and bewildering issue, particularly when it could have ended so much worse for both or either of them.

"And it's over now?" Alexandrina asked as she searched his eyes. "No more trouble."

Taft shook his head once more. "No more trouble. Our guests will attest that there was an acceptance of the challenge, and our seconds will confirm that the duel took place. We will invite Jenkins to our spring London party to prove there are no hard feelings, and that should be all."

"If Jenkins will drink in more moderation and never wander in darkened gardens," Alexandrina muttered darkly. "It could have been so much worse."

"And that will be a battle for someone else to fight, my love," Taft told her firmly. "As far as you and I are concerned, it is over. And so is our scandal."

Alexandrina sighed softly at the idea, sliding her hands to his neck again. "I can hardly believe it. Can we really go on to live a quieter life? One without scrutiny and gossip?"

"For the most part, yes." Taft's hands settled around her waist, tugging her ever so slightly closer to him. "There will always be some with me, and likely a little with you, but nothing scandalous. And in London, it will always be worse than here. But we need not spend a great deal of time in London if we do not wish to."

"I can accept that," Alexandrina told him with a nod. "I can be the Lady Harwood that you need, one that perfectly complements your ways and nature."

Taft leaned in, touching his brow to hers. "You already are the perfect Lady Harwood, Alix. Nothing about you needs to change. I am yours."

He pressed his lips to hers, and she folded her arms about his neck, bringing them almost flush there on the floor of the entry. His arms held her there, wrapped completely around her, his mouth working wonders against hers, catching every sigh and every hum, stealing every ounce of sanity and restraint she had left. She was helpless in his arms, yet somehow also strong. There was a power in this embrace, and she would happily spend the rest of time just here, just like this.

"I love you," she whispered against his lips when he let her breathe a moment.

He grinned, nuzzling against her in a way that made her tingle from head to toe. "I love you, Alix. I'd fight a thousand duels to prove it to you."

Scowling, she lightly smacked the back of his head. "If you

are ever in another duel again, I will fire a pistol at you myself."

He pulled back, raising a brow. "And ruin a romantic declaration?"

Alexandrina shook her head. "There is nothing romantic about risking death at dawn. I found your offering me toast in the middle of the night more romantic."

"Then I will toast a thousand slices of bread every night to prove my love to you," he vowed with a deferential nod. "After which I will probably feel quite ill and have to apologize to Cook for using so much of her bread when you won't eat that much. Waste is quite the crime, you know."

"Good manners even in your love for me," Alexandrina said on an impatient sigh. "You're ridiculous."

"And yet you've just said you love me," he reminded her, drumming his fingers along her sides, his brows rising meaningfully.

She looked upward. "Heaven help me."

Taft brought a hand to her chin and slowly tipped it back down, one finger dusting along her bottom lip when her eyes met his again. "I don't know about you, love, but I do believe it has."

And then he kissed her again, quite thoroughly.

Without getting struck.

EPILOGUE

There was nothing—apart from his wife and child—that Taft Debenham, Earl of Harwood, loved so much as a good party.

Which meant leaving one prematurely was rather painful.

But it could not be helped. Some things were just unacceptable, and would not be tolerated, even for one so good-natured and sociable as him.

Insulting his wife was chief among those reasons.

Mrs. Dylan had forgotten herself, as she tended to do from time to time, and Taft had overheard her ask why the Earl of Harwood insisted on bringing his sour-faced wife to every event he attended, and how it brought down the enjoyment of all.

Being a rather patient, understanding man, when his wife was not attacked by tactless hags who thought themselves so very influential, it had come as quite a surprise to those around them when Taft had turned to the woman rather directly.

"There is nothing sour about my wife, madam, and nothing in which I can find fault, so you can imagine how shocking it is for me to hear that anyone else can. I bring her anywhere I go, if she wishes to go as well, because I cannot imagine any moment of my life without her."

It had been at this moment where he had taken his wife's hand in his and lifted his chin rather proudly.

"If her beauty and her delightful, engaging presence is too much for your pathetically delicate sensibilities," he had declared, "we will remove ourselves from your rather thin air. Lord knows, we have far more pleasant things to do at home."

And with that, he had turned and strode towards the doors of the ballroom, making his sincerest apologies to the host and hostess, both of whom quite understood. Then they had left the house entirely and piled into their carriage to return home to Harwood House.

He shook his head now as he thought on it. London was certainly not what it once had been for him, though whether that was due to his own change or that of the city itself he could not say. But something had changed, and he was not sure he minded.

"Taft."

He blinked and looked across the carriage at his stunning wife. "Yes, my love?"

Alexandrina gave him a flatly exasperated look. "Thank you for what you said to Mrs. Dylan. That was very sweet, if a trifle dramatic."

"I'm a dramatic man, my dear. It could not be helped." He shrugged his shoulders, smiling broadly at her. "What did you think of the ending?"

She rolled her eyes. "Oh, Taft. Why in the world would you give them that impression and what, precisely, did you have in mind?"

He chuckled and folded his hands across his lap. "Honestly? I want to sit in that lovely drawing room you made over without any footwear on either of us, with a roaring fire and a hefty glass of wine. Beyond that, anything goes."

She looked rather dubious, her fair brow furrowing with impressive creases. "That's not what it sounded like."

He sat up as the carriage rolled to a stop before their house, grinning wide. "That's the idea, love. Let them infer what they will, spread entertaining gossip, and the only point actually being made is that no one gets to insult my wife and remain unscathed." He nodded firmly, wanting to make damn certain she was clear about that.

Just as he was.

He climbed out of the carriage and turned to offer her a hand out. Alexandrina's smile was sweet, if a little bemused, as she took it. "I'm oddly touched, Taft. I really mean that."

"Well, feel free to shower me with gratitude, if it suits you," he told her, turning a trifle serious, "but get used to it. I'll discover who my true friends are by and by, and therein will lie our circle. Your own private circle may contain whomever it will, as will mine, but together . . ."

"You know," his wife said, starting into the house and removing her cloak, "that word doesn't make me cringe as much as it once did."

His ears began to burn and his fingers tingle, just as they usually did when she began to talk of them in any particular terms. "Indeed? How peculiar."

She nodded easily, surveying him from the entry table by which she stood. "I may even bestow something rather rare upon you."

"My heart doth quiver in anticipation."

With surprising grace, Alexandrina crossed to him, curving her lips in a smile that flipped his stomach. Grabbing his lapels, she tugged him to her and kissed him slowly, deeply, and without any hesitation whatsoever. She expertly wrung every iota of thought from his mind and lit every fiber of his being with a fire that would not easily be doused.

It was all he could do to cradle her face in his hands.

No sooner had he done so than she pulled back, sending him

reeling into her, needing her hands on his arms to set him to rights.

He took in a slow breath of cool, almost clear air. "Right . . ." he managed through a rough, hoarse voice. "I am amending the plans for the drawing room, if you don't mind."

Alexandrina stepped back to lean upon the entry table, leaving him surprisingly cold without her. "Personally, I thought it sounded rather good, though I would suggest a change in location."

His toes perked up at the suggestion. "My thoughts exactly. And perhaps a few less layers in our attire, given one ought to be comfortable at home."

"Naturally," she replied. "Your cravat, for example, seems most uncomfortable."

"And your gown," he offered, gesturing to the delightful garment, "for all its exquisite detail, must be rather restrictive."

She dimpled a smile at him "Oh, good, you noticed."

He nodded. "I did, as well as the number of combs and pearls in your hair. Must scratch the head in places."

"You know, it does tend to get uncomfortable by the end of the night."

"I am happy to avail myself to their removal, should you wish it."

"That would be lovely. I do much prefer my hair completely loose."

A groan rose up from the base of his kneecaps to his lungs. "So do I."

Alexandrina laughed very softly, the sound doing nothing for his present state of incineration. "You are ridiculous, Taft, but I do love you."

"I love you, too, Alix." Even the words seemed filled with fire, and his mouth was suddenly parched by them.

"I've been keeping a secret from you, my love," Alexandrina admitted with a slight grimace. "I hope you will forgive me."

Taft cleared his throat, wondering at the change in topic. "I am certain that could be arranged. What is it?"

"A baby."

"Ah."

Her chin lowered, and she stared at him quite seriously, then widened her eyes. "Taft."

"What?"

"Did you hear me?"

"Yes . . ."

"What did I say?"

He frowned. "You said . . ." He trailed off, jaw dropping, mouth gaping.

Now she smiled. "There it is."

She was . . . and he was . . . and they were . . .

"A baby?" he managed, the words thin, but carrying all the hope in the world.

She nodded, grinning rather wildly. "Yes. Before winter. Surely you wondered why I was unwell . . ."

He shook his head, still breathless and struggling to comprehend. "I thought . . . I thought . . . Bloody hell, I have no idea what I thought because I am an idiot, but I am so delighted by the news that I'm not sure my idiocy is relevant. Alix!"

He crossed to her side of the entry now, with far less grace than she had managed, and hauled her against him, hugging and kissing her in a frantic pattern between delirious laughter.

Alexandrina took his face in her hands and kissed him softly, which did wonders to settle him. "I am so happy, Taft," she whispered, her thumbs brushing his cheek. "I have wanted this for so long."

"So have I, my love." He wrapped his arms around her, kissing her hair repeatedly, then sighing as he held her to his heart. "I did not know I could love you more than I did five minutes ago, but that was a paltry love compared to this."

"And what about tomorrow?" she asked, curling further into his hold.

Taft chuckled very softly. "I will absolutely love you more than this tomorrow, no question."

"And the day after?"

He glanced down at her, trying for a hot smile despite feeling rather singed himself. "I am happy to discuss the subject of the extent of my loving you at any time, Alix. At great length."

"That should be arranged," she suggested innocently. "Tonight, if possible."

"Before or after the removal of footwear and other cumbersome accessories?" he inquired, running his fingers up and down the center of her back in a way he knew would make her shiver.

On cue, she did so, which brought her even closer to him. "Somewhere in the middle might be best."

He nodded rather thoughtfully, his mind already running rampant with ideas. "I shall endeavor to remember to do so."

"I'll remind you."

"Oh good. I may need a reminder sooner rather than later."

"Naturally. You are particularly forgetful about such things."

He snorted softly. "Am I? I don't think so, I'm rather adept at them."

"No, it's not true," Alexandrina insisted, her hand resting on his chest and sliding firmly upwards, which made *him* shiver. "You get so carried away and forget all sorts of things. Including the discussion of loving me. Quite forgetful."

Taft adjusted his hold on his wife, tearing his glove from his hand with his teeth and cupping her face with his newly bared palm. Her eyes fluttered at the contact, and he ran the very tip of his thumb along her cheek. "Perhaps *you* need a reminder," he rasped, his eyes falling to her lips.

Her lips parted in a dreamy smile that undid him. "Perhaps I do."

Therein followed much reminding, and much loving, and in due course, a healthy, content, rather perfect baby girl.

And her healthy, opinionated, equally perfect younger brother, who followed exactly twenty-three minutes after.

For more in the Supposed Scandal Series:

Her Unsuitable Match
by Sally Britton

A Bride in Black
by Heather Chapman

To Marry is Madness
by Ashtyn Newbold

For more from these authors: The Entangled Inheritance Series

A Provision for Love (Book 1)
by Heather Chapman

His Unexpected Heiress (Book 2)
by Sally Britton

Rivals of Rosennor Hall (Book 3)
by Rebecca Connolly

An Unwelcome Suitor (Book 4)
by Ashtyn Newbold

ABOUT THE AUTHOR

Rebecca Connolly is the author of more than four dozen novels. She calls herself a Midwest girl, having lived in Ohio and Indiana. She's always been a bookworm, and her grandma would send her books almost every month so she would never run out. Book Fairs were her carnival, and libraries are her happy place.

She has been creating stories since childhood, and there are home videos to prove it! She received a master's degree from West Virginia University, spends every spare moment away from her day job absorbed in her writing, and is a hot cocoa addict.

Made in the USA
Middletown, DE
14 July 2023